Elaine Faber

Black Cat
and the
Secret in Dewey's Diary

A tale of history, mystery, riddles, and gold.

Elk Grove Publications

Black Cat and the Secret in Dewey's Diary

Published by Elk Grove Publications

© 2019 by Elaine Faber

ISBN-13: 978-1-940781-25-9

A portion of the proceeds from the sale of this book are donated to support feline rescue projects.

This novel is a work of fiction. Names, characters, places, and incidents either are the product of the author's imagination or are used fictitiously. Any resemblance to actual events, locales, organizations, or persons, living or dead, is entirely coincidental and beyond the intent of either the author or publisher.

Cover photo *Castle*: © Ondrej Prosicky, Shutterstock ID: 243547396: *Cat*: Cat'chy Images, Shutterstock ID: 1186383313; and *Book*: © Elaine Faber

Cover design and book formatting: Julie Williams, juliewilliams.us
Printed in the United States of America

Acknowledgments

Special thanks to friends and family who helped make his novel possible.

Critique groups: Dee Aspin, Ellen Cardwell, Erin Bambery, Susan Wright, Ramona Kelly, Margaret Duarte, Carolyn Radmanovich, Sharon Darrow, Judy Pierce, Norman Miller

Beta Readers: Lois Parrish, Ruth Powers, Ellen Cardwell, and Erin Bambery

Cover design, typographer: Julie Williams

Publisher: Michael Faber—Elk Grove Publications

In remembrance of Boots and Amber. Always in our hearts, they live on in the Black Cat Mysteries as Black Cat and Angel.

The Story Behind the Story

In 1987, my daughter, Londa Faber, and I went to Austria and Germany. While there, we heard an odd tale of folklore that inspired me to write a poem…

The key to the treasure is in Hopfgarten.

Touch the feet of the babe that lies beneath the king,

In the place where the storm clouds…

Are frightened away by the ring.

Over the years, I wrote three fictionalized short stories based on the sights, sounds, scenery, feelings and insights we experienced in Austria. Black Cat and the Secret in Dewey's Diary includes elements of our adventure in a full length cozy mystery novel. The poem became the catalyst for the novel.

Black Cat and The Secret in Dewey's Diary is a dual tale, with half of the story taking place in Fern Lake where Black Cat and Angel face challenges aplenty, and the other half in Austria and Germany as Dorian and Kimberlee follow the clues in a WWII soldier's diary, searching for a treasure in gold coins, missing for over 50 years.

Elaine's Website –http://www.mindcandymysteries.com

Email your questions or comments to Elaine.Faber@ mindcandymysteries.com

Amazon reviews are welcomed and encouraged.

Glossary of Characters
in Order of Their Appearance

Angel: previously called Noe-Noe, Black Cat's soul-mate.

Black Cat: previously called Thumper, now acknowledging his true identity. Hero.

Kimberlee: heroine of our story. Treasure hunter, extraordinaire!

Amanda: Kimberlee's six year old daughter, one of Black Cat's favorite 'persons.'

Mrs. Herman: home from the hospital at last, but just as mean and hateful as ever.

Brett: still writing drivel he calls 'True Crime' novels, but it keeps the family in Kitty Crunchies.

Dorian: Kimberlee's cousin, Fern Lake Police Department's sweetheart.

Sam: Dorian's golden retriever who pretends to tolerate the cats.

Virgil: Dorian's boyfriend and Fern Lake's lead criminal detective.

Jack and Chance: Fern Lake Lodge's manager, and his golden retriever.

Dewey Brooker: author of the WWII diary that started the search for lost gold.

Hans Kreuger: the German lad who met Dewey on the battlefield.

Rajinder: the delicatessen owner who feeds the town's feral cats.

Mr. Ollingham: the attorney doing his best to fix Fern Lake's legal woes.

Grandmother Lassiter: Kimberlee's grandma, even more hateful than Mrs. Herman.

Father Kreuger: Hopfgarten's favorite priest and Hans's cousin.

Joseph: a Hopfgarten resident who has searched for the key for over fifty years.

Chapter One

Why do humans hold grudges? - Black Cat

Gentle breezes fluttered the sails of the boats on Fern Lake, then twisted and twirled toward the shore, across the broad lawn that separated Brett and Kimberlee's quaint Victorian house from the Fern Lake Lodge office. The branches of the giant oak tree trembled.

From time to time, a leaf drifted down and skittered across the grass toward Angel, the sleek golden cat sitting on the sidewalk. She lowered her head. "Why must I close my eyes, Black Cat? You're being silly. What kind of surprise do you have?"

Her black and white tuxedo mate dropped a dead mouse at her feet. "Okay, you can open your eyes now." He danced beside her, his whiskers a-twitch.

"What is…?" She jumped back. "*Hssszzzt!* Get that filthy thing away from me. You know I don't eat dead things. *Yuck!*"

Black Cat's ears drew back. He stepped away. "I…I caught it just for you. I thought you'd like it." Ever since their arrival back in Fern Lake, Angel was unsettled and unhappy in spite of his efforts to show her the sights. Maybe she was homesick for the adopted Nevada City family where they spent the previous months. "You've been so down in the dumps lately, I thought a nice fresh mouse would cheer you up." Black Cat grasped the sodden rodent between his teeth and started around the house. "Nevow mind. Ow take it to Amanda. See'll appwissiate…"

Loud voices floated across the lawn separating their house from the residence attached to the lodge next door. Black Cat dropped the mouse, lifted his head and gazed toward the lodge. "What's going on over there?"

Kimberlee, Black Cat's *person*, stood on the sidewalk at Mrs. Herman's front porch, engaged in a spirited discussion with the cantankerous old woman. "Come on, Angel. Something's wrong. Let's go see." Black Cat dashed toward the ruckus. Though Mrs. Herman had returned from the convalescent hospital after almost two years, the ill will between her and Kimberlee still seemed in full bloom.

Angel raced six steps behind. "I'm coming. Wait for me." She skidded to a stop at the foot of Mrs. Herman's steps.

Mrs. Herman's face scrunched into a scowl as her hands grasped the hand grips on her metal walker. "What do I have to do to get you to leave? You're not welcome here. What do you want?"

A rosy bloom touched Kimberlee's cheeks. A jar of homemade boysenberry jam and a bouquet of roses peeked over the top of the gift basket she carried on her wrist. Her smile wavered. "I cut these roses from my garden. I thought you might like them." She held up the basket. "I could put them in water for you." She stepped onto the bottom step.

Mrs. Herman's nurse appeared at the screen door. "I heard voices. Do you need something, Mrs. Herman?" She smiled at Kimberlee. "Oh! Hello there. How nice. What beautiful roses."

Mrs. Herman glared at the nurse and then turned to Kimberlee. "I don't want her stinking roses or anything else from her. Nurse Burkett? Get this pest off my porch. It's bad enough she lives right next door, now. I can't believe she has the nerve to show her face on my doorstep."

Black Cat lowered his ears. No doubt these two had *history.* From Mrs. Herman's tone, the two years away from Fern Lake in the convalescent home hadn't softened her bitterness toward Kimberlee, however undeserved and misguided. *Why do humans hold grudges?*

Black Cat danced near Kimberlee's feet. *Oh, dear.* This was not going well, at all. The color in her cheeks drained from rosy red to the color of clotted cream. The wicker basket trembled on her wrist. "A lot of good it did to try and be a good neighbor. Like it or not, Brett and I live next door now, so get used to it." She held the basket toward Mrs. Herman's face. "Here. Welcome home."

Mrs. Herman flung her fist at the basket and knocked it from Kimberlee's hand. As it tumbled to the ground, the flowers flew one way and the jam jar smashed onto the concrete step. Berry jam oozed across the step and dripped over the edge. Kimberlee jerked back, but not before the purple jam sloshed across her white shoe.

Mrs. Herman hissed through clenched teeth, "You might live next door now, but maybe not as long as you think. Don't forget…your father died in that house over there. If I'm lucky, the place will burn down with you in it."

Kimberlee's face turned deathly pale. She bit her lip, backed off the porch, and stepped down on Angel's tail.

"*Yow!*" Angel arched her back and licked at the offended appendage.

"Oh!" Kimberlee hopped to the side, her lips trembling. "Is that a threat? So help me God, I'll see you dead before I let you come near my house or harm my family. And, that's a promise."

The nurse frowned and took Mrs. Herman's arm. "There, now. That's quite enough. You better come inside and lie down."

"*Humph!*" Mrs. Herman stumbled back inside her house, dragging her walker. The door slammed behind her. Boysenberry jam dripped from one step to the next where it settled in a puddle amongst the shards of broken glass and scattered flowers.

Kimberlee ran back across the lawn toward her house, tears streaming down her cheeks. She disappeared behind the rose bushes into her yard.

Black Cat turned to Angel. "Well, wasn't that a corker? Mrs. Herman still holds a grudge after all this time. We'd best go home.

I don't think this is a good time to introduce you to our crotchety neighbor."

The fur rippled across Angel's back. "Do you think?" Her bruised tail switched from side to side as she followed Black Cat across the lawn to Kimberlee's little Victorian house near the lake.

Angel and Black Cat lay curled together on the swing on the wisteria-covered front porch. Lulled by its gentle swaying, Black Cat draped his tail around his nose and nuzzled deeper into the flowered cushion, enveloped in the reverie of a sleepy fall morning. *Ah, peace and quiet. Now, I can rest...*

"You know her better than I do," Angel meowed. "Would Kimberlee really kill that old woman if she came over here? I mean, *really?*"

Black Cat's eyes snapped open, his languid musings dissolving. *What?* "Are you serious? Of course not. Kimberlee is the most gentle, loving lady I've ever known." He lifted his head and yawned. "She'd shoo a fly out the door rather than take a swatter to it. How could you even think such a thing?"

Angel lifted her nose. "How should I know what she might do? You know her better than I. You heard what she said."

"Our *persons* say a lot of things. They're besotted by the sound of their own voice. They don't mean half of what they say. Not literally."

"What's their story, anyway? That old woman hates Kimberlee with a purple passion." Angel twisted to lick her offended tail and then settled back onto the cushion. Her head jerked around to follow the flight of a bee buzzing overhead. It landed on a wisteria blossom hanging beside the swing.

Black Cat sighed. "It happened ever so long ago, I can't even imagine why they're still mad. You have to understand, humans aren't like cats. Cats can fight, rip out each other's fur, and the next time they meet, they don't even remember what they fussed about. Rather than let bygones be bygones, humans harbor guilt and anger until their hair turns grey and they get lines around their eyes and mouths. That's the way they are. I can't think of another reasonable explanation. Go to sleep."

Angel pawed at Black Cat's head. "I can't sleep until you tell me why Mrs. Herman has such a hate on. What happened?"

Black Cat sat up and stared at Mrs. Herman's house. "It's really too complicated to explain. Mrs. Herman has done things in the past that hurt people. Several years ago, when Kimberlee first came to the lodge, Mrs. Herman tried to hurt Kimberlee and Amanda, and—"

"Our Amanda? She tried to hurt that sweet child? Oh, that makes me so mad." Angel switched her tail. "I don't like Mrs. Herman."

Black Cat licked his front shoulder. "You didn't know her before, like I did. She was my *person* for a long time before Kimberlee came to Fern Lake. She took good care of me. Something happened when Kimberlee came. It was like a switch flipped in Mrs. Herman's head that made her act crazy and hateful. Then, Mrs. Herman went to the hospital. I guess she's still holding onto hate. She didn't used to have gray hair and wrinkles around her mouth when she was my *person*."

"So, that's why humans get grey hair? Because of hate in their hearts?"

Black Cat blinked. "That's what I've been told. By nature, they're unforgiving. It's one of the things about humans we can't understand. After living around other humans for years, there's always someone they can't…or won't…forgive. Sooner or later, their hair turns grey and they get wrinkles in their faces. It happens to all of them, so it must be true."

"Makes sense. It proves why cats are superior to humans. But, I'm still worried that Kimberlee might—"

"Don't worry. As sure as kittens in the spring, Kimberlee won't hurt Mrs. Herman."

"About that… Don't count on having any kittens next spring. I heard Kimberlee tell Brett she thought it was time to make an appointment to take you to the—"

Black Cat leaped off the swing. "I'm not going to listen to that. *La la la la!*"

Angel's whiskers twitched. "Just sayin'…"

Chapter Two

...a cat needs a name that's peculiar... - T.S. Eliot

eatly stacking the dishes in the dishwasher, Kimberlee reached for the coffee pot. Her hand trembled as she poured two cups and carried them to the living room. Now was a good time to talk to Brett about her run-in with Mrs. Herman.

She handed Brett a cup and sat in the leather recliner beside the fireplace. The crackling fire and soft music from the stereo usually had a calming effect; but, at the moment, her mood was anything but calm. "You should have been there, Brett. You wouldn't believe the dreadful things Mrs. Herman said, even with the nurse standing right there, listening. The old bat as much as threatened to burn down our house, with us in it." Kimberlee sipped her coffee and grimaced. *Too hot. I should have put in more cream.*

Brett set his cup on the coffee table. "I'm sure it was all bluster. She's old and sick. How could she actually do such a thing?" He chuckled. "I can see it now. Here she comes across the lawn pushing her walker with one hand, a can of gas in the other hand, and the cigarette lighter clenched between her teeth."

Kimberlee shook her head. "That's not funny. You shouldn't make light of someone threatening our family. You weren't the one she spoke to that way. What would you have said?"

"I would have laughed in her face and patted her hand. Can you imagine how furious she'd be if she thought you were indulging her temper tantrum? It would serve her right and it might teach her a lesson for being so nasty. I don't mean to tease you, but I don't think you should worry. I doubt she has enough strength to leave her house." Brett stood, pulled back the fireplace screen, poked the embers, and threw another log on the fire.

Kimberlee laid her head against the back of the chair and closed her eyes. "I suppose you're right. She makes me so mad. If I'd have known she would come back from the hospital, I might have thought twice before moving into my parent's house next door to the lodge."

"I'm glad we did. I love it here."

"I do too." Kimberlee turned toward the ringing phone. "I'll get it." She shoved up from the recliner and picked up the receiver. "Hello?"

"Hi. It's me. What's new by the shores of the Gitchi Gummi?"

"Oh, hi, Dorian. I was telling Brett about tangling with Mrs. Herman this morning. He said I shouldn't worry so much. I should let it go."

"I completely understand your frustration. I ran into a couple last week on a domestic conflict call. We had to call in backup because the husband was out of control. Don't let Mrs. Herman get under your skin. She's always been hard to get along with. I'm surprised they discharged her from the hospital with her level of disability and Alzheimer's. Not only does she need a full-time caregiver, me thinks she has a wee screw loose…upstairs."

"Screw loose or not, she'll regret the day she comes snooping around my house. I have a gun and I'm not afraid to use it."

"Now, now. Play nice."

"Just kidding." Kimberlee carried the phone to the kitchen, wiped the top of the stove with a wet sponge and glanced at the clock. "I have to go to The Book Nook this afternoon. Why don't you come and visit me? You remember that nice single guy I told you about who took care of the cats this summer in Nevada City?" She grinned. "He called yesterday afternoon. He might be coming to Fern Lake to visit. I suspect he's looking for a mother for his little girl. I thought of introducing you two. You'd like him."

"Who are you? Yente, the matchmaker? I don't need you adding to my troubles. Besides, Virgil is already quite enough trouble, thank you very much."

Kimberlee sighed. "Forgive me for trying to help my old-maid cousin."

"Well, stop. Look, I'll try to swing by the store later. I have to drop into the precinct for a while and finish up a report. See you later."

Kimberlee hung up the phone. Dorian was always so conscientious about her paperwork. Not nearly so conscientious about picking the fellows she chose to date. She gave the stove a final swipe, glanced around the kitchen, and nodded. "That does it." She pulled a pound of frozen hamburger from the freezer and shoved it into the cold oven to thaw for dinner. "Brett? I'm taking a quick shower and heading to the store for a few hours. I need to unpack a shipment of books and log them into the computer. Do you want me to take Amanda or can she stay with you?"

Brett called from the living room. "I'll watch her. I'm going to fix that front gate this morning. It's been on my *to-do list* too long. I'll take her over to the bait shop for ice cream later. We'll be fine. Take your time."

"Thanks. Dorian's dropping by the store later. I'll be home in time to cook dinner." Kimberlee picked up a couple of plush toys from the floor to carry to Amanda's bedroom. As she passed Black Cat on the sofa, she waggled a stuffed bear in front of his face. "*Boo!* Bear's gonna get ya."

He opened his big gold eyes and jerked his head. Kimberlee stroked his back. What a summer they'd had, grieving and searching for the cats after they were lost on the way home from Texas. *Thank God, John and Cindy gave them a good home in Nevada City. We used to call them Thumper and Noe-Noe, but John called them Black Cat and Angel. Maybe we should keep those names.* Are cats confused when someone changes their names? Wasn't there a poem about cats having three names? She thought back to T.S. Eliot's poem her mom used to read to her as a child.

Kimberlee tossed the toy bear into Amanda's room and continued down the hall. She turned on the shower and recited aloud from memory. "When I tell you, a cat must have three different names. Something, something and still one name left over, and that is the name no human can discover—But, the cat himself knows, and will never confess." Kimberlee grinned. "It went something like that, but that's all I remember. So, it's official," she announced to the back scrubber hanging from the shower head. "According to T.S., a cat can abide having more than one name. So, we'll keep the names Black Cat and Angel, since that's what they got used to all summer in Nevada City."

Kimberlee pushed the conflict with Mrs. Herman from her mind, finished her shower, and tied her dark hair into a pony tail. She kissed Amanda goodbye and headed toward the front door.

Chapter Three

Are we going to be left behind and get lost again? - Angel

Overhearing Kimberlee's plans, Black Cat decided to accompany her to the store. He wondered if Angel would like to come since she hadn't been there yet. Black Cat usually accompanied Kimberlee to the bookstore several days a week. He would climb on the shelves, play hide and seek behind the boxes in the store room, and sniff the flowers on the plants. He always greeted the customers who visited the store to buy a book or coffee and a sweet treat. They loved to stroke his white bib and marvel at his four big white feet with six toes on each foot. Some folks came to the store specifically to visit him. The tourists coming to browse through the books and unique handicrafts were charmed to find a shop cat with his color and polydactyl toes.

Since his return from being lost all summer, the regular shoppers often dropped by to welcome him home with a loving rump pat or a special treat.

Black Cat caught up with Kimberlee at the door and reached his paws up her leg. *Meow! We want to come, too.*

"Do you want to come with me, Thum...*er* ...Black Cat? There won't be any customers to fawn over you. We're closed today, remember?" She ran her hand over his back and up the length of his fluffy tail.

Angel ambled in from the kitchen, water glistening on her white whiskers. *You going somewhere? Can I come?*

Kimberlee picked up Angel and cradled her. "Would you like to go with us, Angel? It should be nice and quiet for your first trip to the store." She shouted down the hall, "I guess I'm taking the cats."

Brett stopped tapping on his computer and called from his office. "Okay. See you later,"

Do I look all right? Angel twisted in Kimberlee's arms, trying to see Black Cat trotting beside Kimberlee. *Where are we going? Maybe I should have groomed my furs first.*

Kimberlee opened the driver's side car door and set Angel on the seat. Black Cat jumped in beside her. *You look lovely, as always. Don't worry. We're going to the bookstore. You'll like it.*

You told me I'd like Mrs. Herman, and I didn't like her at all. She stepped on my tail.

Black Cat leaped over the back of the seat into the SUV storage space. *No, she didn't. Kimberlee stepped on your tail, and you know it was an accident. Don't be such a Princess. Come back here. There's more room, and you don't have to look at the cars passing. It's kind of scary if we aren't in a carrier.*

Kimberlee started the car and drove onto the street. Angel hopped over the seat, put her head down and closed her eyes. *Tell me when we get there. I don't want to look.*

Scaredy-cat. It's only a few blocks. We'll be there before you know it. When we get inside, there is the cutest—

Brakes squealed. *Blam!* The car jerked to a stop, throwing the cats against the back of the front seats.

Oww! What happened? Angel's wails filled the air. *Did we have another accident? Rowww! Are we going to get lost again?*

Black Cat lifted his head and peered out the window. *We didn't crash. Kimberlee tapped the bumper of the car in front. It must have stopped too fast at the light.*

Kimberlee rolled down her window. A man appeared by the side of the car and leaned down. "What's the big idea, lady? What—"

"Harold?" Kimberlee's mouth dropped open. "Is that you? What are you doing here?"

The man peered in her window and scowled. His face looked vaguely familiar, somewhat resembling the stable master they met in Texas earlier that summer. The man beside the car had a clean-shaven face and closely cropped grey hair instead of a beard and a ponytail. He wore a dark suit and a white shirt and tie, instead of the blue jeans and checkered shirt that Harold wore on the ranch. He barely resembled the man from Texas. "I don't know you, lady," he said. "My name isn't Harold. Didn't you see me stop?" He glanced at the cats in the back seat. His cheeks paled and he quickly looked away. "Well, there's no damage, so let's just forget about it and be on our way."

Kimberlee opened her door and stepped out. "I'm sorry. For a minute, I thought you were someone else." She ran her hand over the front of her bumper. "It looks okay, but I think we should at least exchange information." She turned and reached into the car for her purse. "I'm Kimberlee Clarke. I…" The man returned to his car, climbed in and sped away. "Well, for Heaven's sake. Lucky me." Kimberlee slid onto the car seat and slammed the door. "He sure looked like Harold. *Huh!*"

Did you hear what she said? Angel whispered. *Does she mean our Harold, from Grandmother's ranch in Texas? I didn't get a good look at him, but he smelled like Harold.*

Black Cat stood on his hind feet and peered out the front window. The man's car turned right at the corner, toward the lake. *I don't know. There was something about him…He looked so different, it was hard to tell. If it was Harold, what is he doing in Fern Lake?*

Kimberlee continued down the street to The Book Nook and pulled her car to a stop in front. "Okay, end of the line. Everyone out. Come here, Angel. I'll carry you." Kimberlee fished the keys to the store from her purse. She hefted Angel onto her shoulder, unlocked the front door, and stepped inside. The pleasing scent of flowers and the faint hint of old books wafted through the room. She glanced around at the hand-crafted items made by local authors, artists, sculptors, gardeners, and photographers.

Kimberlee set Angel on the floor and circled the store, flipping on lights. "*Brr!* I'll turn on the heater. It'll warm up in a jiffy. Give Angel the grand tour while I see about some coffee."

Black Cat rubbed against Angel's shoulder. "Follow me." He ambled across the shop and stepped through the curtains into the storeroom. "Check this out. It's the cat tree Kimberlee put up for me. That's Amanda's toy box." Black Cat climbed the tree and peered down from the top shelf. "It's a nice place to nap under the heater vent when it's real cold outside."

Angel stood at the door and gazed into the storeroom, her gold eyes wide. "*Wow!*" Boxes, parcels and baskets lined the shelves. She jumped onto the worktable and sniffed at the scissors, packing tape, and address labels. "What's this?" She sniffed at an unopened parcel. "It smells musty. Why would someone mail something musty to a bookstore?"

Black Cat jumped from the cat tree onto the table and sniffed the package. "Let me see. Sometimes Kimberlee gets books from other bookstores or from auction houses. That's probably what it is. Leave it and come with me. You need to see the cat bed Kimberlee made for me in the front window. It's warm and sunny up there. When people walk by, they stop and say how beautiful I am, and—"

Angel snorted. "You're so conceited. Just because you have four white feet and too many toes, doesn't make you *all that.*"

Black Cat lowered his head. "Why are you so mean? I'm just trying to show you around the store. I thought you wanted to see everything. You don't need to be so snotty." He jumped off the table, raced across the store, and curled up in his cat bed in the front window.

Kimberlee turned from her desk. "Where's the fire, Black Cat? Did you show Angel the litter box by the back door? We don't want any accidents, and no scratching on the books. That's the rule." She walked into the storeroom where Angel pawed at the parcel on the worktable. "What have you got there, Angel?"

Kimberlee picked up the package. "Oh, it's probably that book I ordered." She cut the tape on the package with a pair of scissors. "Might as well get it logged in and priced." With the tape cut, the brown wrapping paper fell away and a worn journal lay on the table. Kimberlee picked it up and frowned. "Oh, this isn't what I thought I bought. Good thing it didn't cost much." She thumbed through the book. "I thought this was a book written by a WWII American soldier on the battlefield. This looks more like a personal diary." She tossed it on the table, and turned away.

Angel sniffed the book again. *There's something...* She jerked, jumped off the table, and raced toward the front of the store where Black Cat lay curled on his cushion in the window. "Black Cat, come quick. You need to see this."

"Oh, you're talking to me now? I thought you didn't like pretty boys." He lifted his nose and peered out the window. Across the street, two teenagers rode bicycles up and down mounds of dirt in the vacant lot.

"I didn't say I didn't like you." She pawed at his tail. "But, you need to come and see the book Kimberlee unwrapped. There's something about it..." Angel jumped to the floor and trotted back toward the storeroom. She stopped and looked back. "Are you coming?"

Black Cat stretched, jumped from the window and followed her back to the storeroom. *I won't hurry. Don't want her to think I give a snap when she wants me to do something.*

Kimberlee turned as Black Cat strolled past her desk. "You guys keeping out of trouble? There's Kitty Crunchies in the bowl by the back door if you're hungry."

Back in the storeroom, Angel hopped onto the table and pawed at the book. "Make her look, Black Cat. There's something important inside." She kneaded the table with her front feet.

"Why? What is it?" He sniffed the book. "It smells funny. Musty…"

"I sense something important in the diary. Kimberlee needs to read it. I feel it in my bones. Make her read it."

"How am I supposed to do that? I can't exactly twist her arm." Black Cat sat back on his haunches, his tail switching from side to side over the table edge.

"I know you can do it. You're so clever and handsome and… and…brave." Angel rubbed against the side of Black Cat's face. A purr rumbled in her chest.

"So, now I'm handsome and clever. A minute ago, you called me a conceited pretty boy. What's changed?" *I'll make her squirm. Then I'll forgive her.*

Angel hung her head. "I'm sorry. I…I…don't know what's gotten into me. I miss Cindy and John and the kids. Do you think we'll ever see them again?"

"I heard Kimberlee say John and Cindy might come for a visit. You know the children have good homes. I'm sure they're happy. That's the best we can hope for."

"Be patient with me. Everything is so new and strange. Maybe in time, I'll—"

"What are you two chattering about?" Kimberlee stepped through the curtain. She stroked Angel's back. Angel ponied up onto her hind feet. She gave Kimberlee a fetching *silent meow.* Lifting her feet to Kimberlee's chest, she curled her toes in and out in her fetching way.

"What is it, Angel? Does ums' want some cream? All I have is artificial coffee creamer. I don't think you'd like that." Angel purred and put on her best *little girl lost* performance.

Kimberlee scratched Angel's back. She reached for the journal.

Oh, Black Cat! She's picked it up. Make her read it. Angel quivered with excitement,

Black Cat pawed at the book before Kimberlee could pick it up.

The book fell and plunked onto the floor, open to the title page. Then, as so often in the past, the storeroom faded, and, instead, the scene from a bygone day played out before his eyes...a memory from one of his ancestors. He was in a little bungalow...

A child...a little girl with long blonde braids who resembled Amanda, came through the front door with a lovely young woman. The child held a black and white kitten with white feet and too many toes, and a white bib and tummy.

"Can we keep him, Grandma? Mrs. Wilkey's son, down at the grocery store, brought him home from Oregon where he was visiting his aunt. She doesn't want him and Katherine says it's okay. Can we keep him?"

"I don't know. What will Ling-Ling say about a little intruder in her world? One cat is really all we can afford." Grandma glanced at her granddaughter. "What do you think?"

The young woman nodded. "I think Maddie can handle the responsibility of taking care of a pet. It will be good for her. We might be at war and things are tight, but we're not broke. We can manage one more mouth to feed. Let's give it a try."

Black Cat blinked as the scene faded and he was back in the bookstore. This kitten was one of his ancestors... But, what did it have to do with the diary Kimberlee received? Whatever the connection, the diary had triggered the memory. But, why did Angel think it was so important? What mystery did it hold for Kimberlee? He held his breath as she knelt, and picked up the diary.

Chapter Four

Could it have been Harold, from Grandmother's ranch? - Kimberlee

Running her hand over the front of the diary, Kimberlee's fingertips tingled, almost as if she touched a living thing. She drew in her breath. A stream of light from the window fell across the soiled and spotted leather cover. Could it be from mud, sweat, blood, or all three? She ran her finger over the letters etched into the leather, then flipped it open to the first page: *January 1944—The Journal of Dewey Brooker*

The binding was tight. Some pages were yellowed, dog-eared, and wrinkled. She opened the book to the last page. The last entry read September 1955. Good to know that the soldier survived the war. She turned back to the first page…

January 4, 1944 Mother sent this journal as a Christmas gift. Will try to record experiences. Arrived in England a week ago. Boot camp was tough, but guys say fighting over here is horrendous. The battalion expects to be sent to the front soon. Just because I'm a soldier now, I'm supposed to fight and not be afraid to die, but I am afraid. I want to live. I want to marry Betsy and have a family. Pray God I survive this mess. Pray God I don't let the fellows down when we're under fire. Whose idea was it to send eighteen-year-old boys to war? Isn't that a job for a grown man? Movie tonight.

A chill crept up Kimberlee's neck. She skimmed through the next few pages. Most of the entries were similar, describing the boredom of marching and training on the English base, with little to entertain the men except letters from home and occasional movies. As the weeks progressed through spring, Dewey wrote about training with the medics. *There's gossip of a secret deployment soon that could end the war.* Kimberlee couldn't turn the pages fast enough.

The mood in Dewey's camp was high and expectations of being sent to the 'front' peaked through May. Though having no details, everyone expressed opinions of where and when 'the big one' would take place. Each night before Dewey said his prayers at lights out, he expected to be yanked from his bed and sent into battle before revelry the next morning.

By now, Kimberlee felt as if she knew Dewey personally. He was eighteen years old. He received three letters a week from his high school sweetheart back in Grants Pass, Oregon. His widowed mother worked at a department store, and his younger brother, Jimmy, played on the high school baseball team.

Dewey enjoyed painting and playing the flute. When the war ended, he hoped to work at his uncle's auto dealership in Garnett, Kansas, a town of little more than 3,000 souls. He began to worry whether he would survive, hearing enough horror stories from his companions to fill his days with anxiety and his nights with nightmares. Everyone seemed on edge, jumping from fits of boredom, eager to get back into the fight and beat the Germans, and yet terrified they might not survive the battle they feared on the horizon.

Kimberlee paused at the date June 3, 1944. Her heart raced. She knew enough history to know what horrendous battles and loss of life would occur when the U.S.A. and its allies stormed the beaches of Normandy. Given the date and the location of Dewey's battalion, Kimberlee knew he would be caught up in the month-long battle that claimed 10,000 lives, including many of Dewey's companions.

"I should stop now," she said to the cats curled up on the storeroom table, fast asleep. "I'm not getting anything I planned done this morning." She laid the book down and checked her watch. Almost lunch time and Dorian would be there any minute. "Don't let me disturb your nap, guys, but I need to get to work. This is your fault, Black Cat. If you hadn't knocked that diary on the floor…" She laid the journal on the table, laughing at the idea that Black Cat and Angel had anything to do with her decision to read the diary.

After logging in fifteen books, Kimberlee set up a new mystery book display near the front of the store. At the sound of a knock, she went to the door. "Hey! Come on in," she said, closing and locking it. "I'm out of coffee, but there are cookies left from yesterday. How's your morning going?"

Dorian patted her notebook. "Someone broke into a locked glass case at the hardware store and stole a hand gun. Looked like an inside job. We interviewed all the employees last night, and I had to file my report this morning." She eyed the cookies.

"That's great. So, another Fern Lake thug who didn't have a gun yesterday has one today." Kimberlee took the lid off the tray of cookies. "Help yourself. When will our city council get a handle on crime? We hear more about it every day."

"Don't blame me." Dorian chose a lemon bar and laid it on a napkin. "We're doing the best we can. I even spoke at the teen center last week, to warn them about the consequences of gangs, guns, and drugs. Some days, it doesn't seem to make much difference, one way or the other."

Black Cat pawed up Dorian's leg. *Yowww! Pick me up, please.*

"Hi, Thumper. Are you helping Kimberlee today?"

"Keeping you up to speed, we're not calling him Thumper now. He's used to being called Black Cat, since that's what they called him in Nevada City all summer. We brought Angel this morning to explore the store."

"Black Cat? Okay, but it's not going to be easy to remember. Who's Angel?"

"You remember Grandmother's cat, Noe-Noe, from Texas? We've

changed her name, too. Her name is Angel now." Kimberlee lowered her head. "I shouldn't have said that about the crime in Fern Lake. I didn't mean to suggest you weren't doing a good job. I meant—"

"Don't worry about it. I see you changed your book table display up front."

"That's about all I've done since I got here. I spent most of the morning reading a WWII soldier's diary. It's fascinating. I stopped just before he goes into battle at Normandy. I know the kid survived because the journal continues after the war, but who knows what he went through that day? I can't wait to get back to it. If you want to read it, I'll lend it to you before I put it on the shelf."

"I don't have time to read. You can tell me about it when you're done." Dorian took a bite of lemon bar. "These are good."

Kimberlee nodded. "So, tell me about the break-in. Did you get any leads on the thief?"

"Oh, you mean at the hardware store?" Dorian took another bite. "I questioned all the employees. There was an older man; a new employee. Something about him… His voice, I think. It gave me a weird feeling that I'd seen him before, but I can't place from where."

"What did he look like?" *It couldn't be the same man...* Chill bumps raced up Kimberlee's arm.

"Why?" Dorian set her cookie on the counter and put her hand on Kimberlee's arm. "What's wrong? You look positively green."

"Do you remember Harold from Grandmother's ranch in Texas?"

"Harold?" Dorian raised her eyebrows. "I remember him. What about him?"

The possibilities continued to turn in Kimberlee's mind. "What was his name? The employee you questioned?" She held her breath.

Dorian shook her head. "I can't discuss an ongoing investigation, but if you're suggesting it might have been Harold, that's not the name he gave. For that matter, we only questioned him along with the rest of the staff. Besides, isn't our Harold from Texas in jail? What makes you think it could be him?"

Kimberlee stood and paced between the coffee counter and the cash register. "I bumped a car at the stoplight this morning. The driver looked like Harold, but when I asked his name, he yelled at me and drove off. I'm probably imagining things, but I was almost positive it was Harold, without his beard and ponytail."

Dorian checked her watch. "Well, that sounds like a stretch. Let's go down to the diner for a quick cup of coffee."

"Good idea. Let me check on the cats. They'll be fine here for a little while."

Finding the cats still sound asleep on the storeroom table, Kimberlee locked the front door and she and Dorian walked down the street to the diner.

Black Cat lifted his head. "Angel? You awake?"

"No."

"You must be awake. You answered me. Did you hear Kimberlee?"

"No. I wasn't listening."

"How could you not hear? You were lying right there, not two feet away."

"Oh, for Pete's sake, what is it? I didn't say I couldn't hear. I said I wasn't listening. I was having the nicest dream."

Angel did a lot of that lately, sleeping and ignoring everything around her. Black Cat ducked his head. "You heard Dorian. Is it possible that the man at the stop sign and the guy at the hardware store are the same man? Could it be Harold from Grandmother's ranch in Texas?"

"I don't see how. They put him in jail months ago. How could he be here in Fern Lake?"

"How should I know? Humans do strange things." Black Cat stood and shook his long black fur. "Maybe they let him go. Maybe he escaped." Black Cat flipped his tail. *Females!*

"There you go again, getting all dramatic and sarcastic. I have no idea if Harold murdered the guard, hitch-hiked to Fern Lake, stole a gun and plans to rob the First National Bank of Calcutta. Furthermore, I couldn't give a rat's *behind* one way or the other. I'm more interested in whether Kimberlee is coming back in time to take us home for dinner or if we're stuck in the store all night. I could starve to death."

Black Cat's eyes blinked. *She always has to be a smart-aleck.* Maybe if Angel understood more about him... Brett and Kimberlee often talked about Harold's secrets.

"You would care if you knew the whole story. You knew that Harold came to Grandmother's ranch over ten years ago, and Brett suspected he had a secret past."

"I know. I have my ancestors' memories, too. We are distantly related, remember? My mother was there when he came to live at the ranch. I don't hold it against him for having secrets. Everyone has secrets. I don't think he committed all the crimes they charged him with, though. He was always good to me. He's not really a bad man."

"Okay. Okay. Listen for a minute. The fact is, twenty-five years ago, Mrs. Herman's husband, Ted, faked his own death. He lived in the Cayman Islands for years before he came to Texas and changed his name to Harold."

"No! Harold is really old Mrs. Herman's husband? *Huh!* I didn't know that. Now I understand why he faked his death. He wanted to get away from her."

Black cat twitched his whiskers. "There is more to it than that, but suffice it to say, that's why Kimberlee wonders why he would come back to Fern Lake now."

"*Shh.* The girls are back." Black Cat ducked his head, closed his eyes and pretended to be asleep.

The key clicked in the lock—the door opened. "I should get back to the station," Dorian said. "Thanks for taking my mind off work for a while." She gave Kimberlee a hug and turned toward the door. "Let me know how that journal turns out. You've got me curious."

"I'll do that. Bye." She locked the door behind Dorian.

Kimberlee wiped off the coffee counter and put the remaining cookies in a zip-lock bag. "Come on, kids, let's go." She tucked the leather diary into her purse, put the cats in the car, and drove home.

Chapter Five

There is no longer an atheist among us. - Dewey's diary

imberlee slid a lasagna casserole into the oven and settled in her easy chair in front of the fire. She draped a lap robe over her legs and opened the journal to the last page she had read. Several pages later, the ink became blurred, making Dewey's army camp entries harder to read. She was right about the battle at Normandy. Dewey made entries while in a landing craft headed for the beach where the German army lay in wait for the invaders.

He wrote about how the boat rocked, how the smell of diesel fuel caused most of the soldiers to moan and vomit in the bottom of the craft. Those not already sick from the fumes became ill from the stench of vomit. Some of them buried their heads in their arms to keep others from seeing their tears. Everyone was terrified, wondering whose lives were measured in minutes. The deafening pounding of the artillery from the ships onto the beach made conversation impossible, adding to their terror. The landing craft came closer to shore.

Dewey's scrawled words were difficult to read. Kimberlee smiled at Dewey's comment. *Forty minutes already coming ashore. Everyone is scared. Mother will be pleased. There is no longer an atheist among us. Signs of the cross. Hands clasped in prayer. Almost to a man, they're "coming to Jesus." If this is my last day—no regrets. I'm ready to meet...*

Kimberlee flipped the page. Nothing. She swallowed a lump in her throat. Tears pricked her eyes. Even knowing that Dewey survived the battle, her heart ached for the boy. He faced Hell on earth that day. Eighteen years old, and like so many others from all over the U.S.A., this naïve, small-town boy carried a rifle into battle, ready to kill or be killed. What had he endured over the next few days? How many of his comrades died? Did Dewey kill a man that day? How does an eighteen-year-old boy experience such an event and not relive the Hell night after night for the rest of his life?

Brett stood in the doorway. "Is the casserole about ready? I'm starving. Are you coming to dinner?"

Kimberlee turned a page in the journal and shook her head. "You and Amanda should go ahead and eat. I'll eat later. There's a salad in the fridge. I can't put this down right now. Oh, would you feed the cats and bring me a cup of coffee?"

"Sure. We'll manage. Take your time. You'll have to tell me later what's so interesting."

"Okay." Kimberlee had already turned back to the diary.

Kimberlee read that Dewey carried the journal onto the shore. She ran her hand over the leather cover blotched with stains, more sure of their origin now. Had he tucked it into his rucksack or carried the journal inside his shirt next to his heart, hoping that the connection with his mother would see him through the day?

The entries picked up again several days later, apparently from the battlefield. The page had no date and was smeared and dirty. Dark streaks near the top of the page could have been mud or blood. Were the circular marks from raindrops…or Dewey's tears?

His next sentences were cryptic.

Guess they've left me behind thinking I died in the battle. Will I still be alive when…or if…someone ever reads this page? Everything is quiet, except for the wind. Bodies everywhere. Americans and Germans. This must be what Hell is like. Terrific headache. Bullet hole in helmet. Ate candy bar. God? Why have you forsaken me? Didn't Jesus say that on the cross?

Following the battle, the army abandoned the beach in a hurry to get the wounded to medical care, and left the dead for another nightmare day of retrieval. How long did Dewey wait before someone returned and rescued him? A day? Two days?

Kimberlee checked the clock. 6:30 P.M. "Brett. Don't worry about the dishes. I'll clean up the kitchen later."

"Take your time and don't worry about Amanda. She's playing in her room. I have to get ready for my meeting. I'll read her a story before I go."

Kimberlee turned her attention back to the journal. Dewey's writing was more legible, the pages cleaner. The date indicated several days had passed. He wrote from a hospital ward and journaled about the days before the troops returned to rescue him.

Apparently, among the dead men surrounding his location, Dewey heard and responded to a young German soldier, gravely wounded, also left for dead. Dewey dragged the lad under the truck where they took shelter. Using the scant medical supplies from his backpack, and his brief training with the medics, he tended the soldier, bound up his leg wound with his own shirt torn into strips, and gave him water and food, undoubtedly saving his life.

Kimberlee paused. Wasn't it remarkable how, even in the midst of battle, and not knowing if he would be rescued or die on that horrendous beach, this young man reached out to save an enemy's life? She turned the page, and Dewey's story continued.

The German boy spoke English and introduced himself as Hans Kreuger. Over the next twenty-four hours, as he passed in and out of consciousness, Dewey tended his wound, gave him water and kept him talking. They discussed everything from baseball to their hometowns, family, girlfriends, how they celebrated holidays, favorite snacks, movie stars, the classics, and music. Anything, to keep up their spirits and support their will to live.

Hans occasionally spoke about his dreams and hopes for the future.

Never once were the subjects of war, politics, Hitler, or Eisenhower mentioned.

The boys exchanged addresses, vowed their undying and eternal friendship. At last, the American troops returned. Dewey and Hans were taken to the hospital ship—Hans to surgery and Dewey to a hospital ward where he was assessed and released the next day to return to his decimated battalion, a little thinner, a lot older than his years, and much subdued in spirit. In spite of his attempts to inquire about Hans, Dewey never learned his fate.

Back at camp, the young men laughed, slapped each other's backs, and rejoiced for surviving the battle when so many others hadn't. No longer driven by fear of imminent death, the religious commitments made on the landing crafts almost disappeared. Slang and profanity filled the conversations of bravado and bragging about how many Germans each had killed.

Dewey kept to himself and wrote of his gratitude and thankfulness to God for sparing his life.

It's only been a few days since I last journaled, but after what I've been through, I feel ten years older and decades wiser. Will I ever again sleep through the night without seeing the bodies or hear my friend, Hans, scream in pain? Must not dwell on that. Will I ever see Hans again? They say he was likely sent to an American prison camp with other captured Germans.

Kimberlee was not surprised that Dewey wrote nothing about the actual landing on the beaches of Normandy, the assault onto sand and barbed wire, seeing his friends drop and die left and right, charging forward with bullets whizzing and shells shrieking overhead. She suspected he did not record that day because he couldn't bear to remember, or write about the horrors he had lived. She didn't need to read his account of the experience. She had seen movies and read books and reports by other veterans who survived the landing and ensuing battle. She wiped away tears and closed the diary. *Enough.*

Tomorrow, she would read about Dewey's homecoming to Oregon, and hopefully, his marriage to Betsy and the remainder of his happy life. After surviving Normandy, he deserved that.

Chapter Six

I can't change the past, even if I wanted to. - Ted Herman

tars twinkled overhead. Crickets chirped. Rental boats creaked against their pilings. A few guests came and went to their cabins. Peace dwelt among the visitors at the lodge by the lake and in the little Victorian house next door. Black Cat reached his paw toward the front door handle. *Meow! Let me out.*

Angel perched on the back of the sofa. *Where are you going this time of night?*

I want to visit Mrs. Herman. She should be feeling more like having company tonight. I want to welcome her home.

Brett came out of the kitchen, pulled his jacket from the closet, and called to Kimberlee. "I'm leaving for my meeting, honey. Do you need me to stop for anything on my way?"

"Not that I can think of at the moment. Have a good time."

Brett opened the front door. "Oh, you want out, too, Thum…*um*… Black Cat? Don't stay out too late. Nothing good happens to tomcats after midnight." He stepped out the door and gazed across the lawn at Mrs. Herman's house, "Looks like Mrs. Herman's got company. There's a new bright red SUV parked in front of her house. Nice car."

"That's nice. Drive careful. See you later," Kimberlee said.

Brett pulled the door shut behind him. Black Cat trotted out the front gate and turned toward the dock. Business before pleasure. A quick check of the perimeter was in order. He passed the bait shop, now closed and dark except for the colored lights around the front window with its lighted sign—*Boat Rentals-Sodas-Snacks-Earthworms*. His whiskers twitched every time he passed the sign. *Earthworms...*

The soft pads on his feet made no sound as he ambled down the length of the dock. The same breeze that lifted the long fur on his flank sent waves of ripples onto the shore. Boats tied to the pier sloshed in the gentle wake, with an occasional thud when one bumped against the wooden dock.

Black Cat sat and stared across the lake. He loved the solitude at this time of night. Most of the guests had returned to their cabins or gone out for the evening. The reflection of the full moon cast a glow across the dark water. Neon lights from the bar around the bend cast a colored glow across the waves. The soft thrum of a guitar came from a nearby campsite.

The sight and sound of the music renewed memories of two years past when Kimberlee first came to the lodge and searched for her father's killer. With the aid of his ancestors' memories, Black Cat helped guide Kimberlee to some of the answers. She married Brett, and with her six-year-old daughter, Amanda, moved back into her parent's Victorian next to Fern Lake Lodge.

A skittering sound pulled Black Cat back from his reverie. Another rat. No surprise to find them along the waterfront. With Black Cat away from the lodge all summer, the rodents had acquired a new toehold in the neighborhood. He and Angel would soon have the spindle-tailed vermin under control. That is, if he could get Angel off her duff to handle her share of the hunting, instead of lying around, complaining, and mooning over whatever she was mooning over.

Feeling most magnanimous, thanks to the softness of the night and no stomach for a fight, he flicked his tail and strolled back down the dock. Tomorrow, he planned to locate, stalk, and annihilate the flea-bitten critter. He would let the rogue live another night, as long as it stayed away from his family.

Black Cat approached Mrs. Herman's house, stepped onto the front porch and sniffed at the place where the jam jar had smashed. A purple stain colored the bottom step. He circled the house to the cat door Mrs. Herman installed over twenty-five years ago, where one after another of his black and white ancestors with six toes on each foot, had come and gone at will. Slipping through the plastic flap, he tip-toed across the kitchen linoleum. He could hear voices coming from the next room. Someone was with Mrs. Herman. *Ah. That's right. Brett said she had company.* Black Cat sashayed into the living room where Mrs. Herman sat in her rocker, twisting her handkerchief.

An older man with dark hair, obviously dyed, and not a very good job of it at that, sat on the sofa, his mouth pulled down in a scowl. He turned toward Black Cat and glared. The leathery skin on his forehead suggested many years in the sun. "So, what can I say?" He smirked. "I can't change the past, even if I wanted to…which I don't."

Mrs. Herman's face drained of color. "Do you have any idea what you've put me through?" Her hands trembled. "Everyone searched for your body. We all thought you were dead. Not a word for twenty-five years, and now you show up out of nowhere? What am I supposed to think? It's a wonder you don't give me a heart attack from the shock." Tears puddled in the old woman's eyes.

Black Cat rubbed against her leg in an effort to lend his support and sympathy. In a flash, another memory rushed into his mind. A picture of Mrs. Herman and a man holding a baby, standing next to another couple. Was it a picture of baby Kimberlee and her parents?

Wait. Wasn't this man the driver of the car Kimberlee bumped this morning? It all became clear. He called himself Harold in Texas, but, in truth, he was Mrs. Herman's long-lost, presumed-to-be-dead husband. Who would expect Harold, or Ted Herman, or whatever he called himself these days, to return to Fern Lake, reclaim his true identity, and harass poor old Mrs. Herman?

"So, where have you been? For years, everyone thought you drowned in the Cayman Islands. Except me." Mrs. Herman dabbed her eyes with a hankie. "I never declared you legally dead. I always held out hope you were alive and would come back to—"

"Come back to you? How noble… It's quite simple. I planned my disappearing act to avoid trouble here at home, bummed around the Islands for a while, changed my name and went to Texas. I ran into a bit of trouble there and figured what better place to hide out than in California…where I'm assumed dead and still own property." He grinned, took a drag from his cigarette, and ground it out in the candy dish on the coffee table.

Mrs. Herman's voice trembled. "After all this time, do you think you can pick up the pieces right where you left off? What do want from me?"

"I needed a fresh start and a new identity. Why shouldn't I come back? I'm your husband, and I own half of this lodge."

Mrs. Herman jerked her head. "You…what?" She wiped tears from her wrinkled cheeks. "You think you still own…? I've worked seven days a week for twenty-five years to pay off the mortgage. You don't have a right to anything."

"I beg to differ. That's where you're wrong. If you check the deed, you'll see it says 'community property.' That means we're equal partners."

"What would it take to make you go away…for good?" Mrs. Herman's pale face tore at Black Cat's heart. If only he could do something to help. Maybe he should jump on the sofa and scratch the man's eyes out. Maybe that wasn't such a good idea, considering the size of his chest and shoulders.

"Give me $150,000, and I'll leave and never bother you again." Ted lit another cigarette.

"You know I don't have that kind of money. I've been in the hospital for over a year."

"Then, I'll stay and take over the place. I'll take a draw every month from the lodge's income." He glanced around the room, eyeing the color TV and the new carpets Mrs. Herman had installed before she was hospitalized. "From the looks of things, you're doing okay."

"It's not true," Mrs. Herman protested. "Between Jack's salary and the staff and my hospital bills, there's barely enough to keep up the expenses and the taxes on the lodge. Jack made a few improvements on the boathouse and the dock this year, but—"

"*Tut...tut.* Don't worry about Jack's salary. Now that I'm back, we don't need him. I'll take the salary you paid him. That'll be quite sufficient, along with my part-time job at the hardware store."

"You can't mean that." Mrs. Herman put her hands over her pale face. "Jack's been with us for over thirty years. He's like a son to me. I don't know what I'd have done without him. I can't throw him into the street like yesterday's trash."

"Maybe you can't, but I can. From now on, we'll do things my way. I'm not planning to move back into the house just yet. I'll stay in Jack's cottage." Ted-Harold threw back his head and laughed. "From the looks of you, it won't be for long. After you're gone, I'll move back in the house, or better yet, maybe I'll sell the place." He stood and picked up his jacket.

Mrs. Herman shook her head, her face as pale as death.

Black Cat shivered. Could the stress of Ted's visit cause her to have another stroke? It must be a terrible shock to see the man she thought to be dead, threatening to turn her life upside down. He lifted his paw and touched Mrs. Herman's hand. *Meow. I'm here for you.*

Ted crossed the living room to the front door. "I'll give you some time to think things over. You'll come to see things my way. As your husband, you know I have your very best interest at heart." He chuckled and opened the door. "Good night, mommy dearest. Sleep tight." Out the door he went and slammed it behind him. His chortles could be heard all the way to his car. The car started, and gravel spewed left and right as it peeled down the driveway.

Mrs. Herman laid her head on the arm of her chair. "Whatever can

I do?" She picked up Black Cat, pressed him to her chest and wept into his long black fur. "I have no one to turn to—no one to advise me. No one cares if I live or die. I've left the lodge to Jack in my will, but, until I'm gone, he has no legal way to fight Ted." She screamed, grabbed the glass of water on the end table and pitched it across the room where it crashed into the fireplace.

Poor Mrs. Herman. Black Cat threw his heart into purring as loud as he could. Over time, her illness and quarrelsome personality antagonized all her friends. She'd even quarreled with Kimberlee. Jack was probably the only soul in Fern Lake who gave two rips for her, and now, he was in Ted's cross hairs. The old woman had to take whatever he dished out. Due to her illness and incapacity, Ted, as her husband, could legally make decisions as he saw fit, even to discharge Jack.

Mrs. Herman's sobs subsided. She dried her eyes, sighed and stroked Black Cat's back. "As long as I'm alive, there's nothing I can do to help Jack. He'd be better off with me dead. Then, he'd have legal standing to contest Ted in court." She dropped Black Cat to the floor and stood, reached for her walker and inched her way to the kitchen. "Ted's right. I haven't got the strength to fight him. I should have declared him legally dead years ago. The statute of limitations has run out on any of his previous crimes…except murder. Maybe I could fix that…" She stood in the kitchen window and stared at Jack's cabin. "I have to think."

Black Cat followed Mrs. Herman into the kitchen. He pawed at her leg. *Call Brett. He'll know what to do.*

Where would Jack go if Ted made him leave the lodge? How could Ted be so cruel? For over twenty-five years, Jack had lived in the little cabin by the lake he now shared with his dog, Chance. Black Cat growled.

"You're right. That's how I feel, too." Mrs. Herman's hand shook as she pulled a paper and a pen from the drawer beside the kitchen sink. She sat at the table and began to write. The clock on the wall ticked as she tapped the pen on her lips and stared out the window before writing again. Finally, she laid the pen down. "There. Maybe this will help."

She turned to Black Cat, sitting patiently by the back door, doing his best to lend moral support to the grieving old woman.

"Do you want to hear what I wrote?" she asked. "To Whom It May Concern. Being of sound mind, on this day, I set my hand to swear that only two people hate me enough to cause my death, Ted Herman and Kimberlee Clarke. We assumed Ted died in the Cayman Islands. I blame Kimberlee for my husband's desertion and his betrayal. Now, he has returned and is threatening my livelihood and my life.

Today, Kimberlee threatened to kill me. Should my death be under questionable circumstances, be assured that one of them is responsible. My will is filed with Haggerstrom and Ollingham, Attorneys at Law. How's that sound?" She shook the letter toward Black Cat. "I'll mail it in the morning." Mrs. Herman addressed the letter to the local police department and stumbled to her feet. Her walker scratched the linoleum as she moved, step by step, across the kitchen. She placed the letter on the sideboard and picked up her framed wedding picture. She stared at it for a moment and flung it to the floor, shattering the glass. "Why on earth did I keep that stupid thing all these years?"

Black Cat followed her into the living room. Could she be planning suicide, hoping the letter would cause trouble for Ted or Kimberlee? Had she completely lost her mind? No question about her anger with Ted considering his plans, but to think that her past history with Kimberlee and their argument was enough to include her in her threats? Had Mrs. Herman gone a little bit *cray-cray?*

Mrs. Herman swept the candy dish off the coffee table, sending Ted's cigarette stub to the floor. She heaved a pillow at the lamp, knocking it to the rug beside her rocking chair. Placing her hands over her face, tears coursed down her cheeks "Now, I've had a temper tantrum, and the nurse will have to clean it up. They'd all be better off without me."

Mrs. Herman opened a bottle of medicine and dumped the pills onto the end table. "You might as well go home, Black Cat." She dabbed her eyes with a tissue and blew her nose. "Maybe I'll take all these pills and go to bed. That would settle everything, wouldn't it? Go. Get out of here." She waved toward the kitchen.

Now, she's turned on me. Black Cat eyed the mess in the living room. Should he stay or go? His presence seemed to be upsetting her more than helping.

The end table wobbled as he hopped to the floor, knocking a thin gold chain off the table. He rushed into the kitchen and scooted through the cat door. Maybe things would look better in the morning. Halfway across the dark lawn, he stopped and sucked in the cool night air. What a relief to be out of that house and away from such despair. Far too upset to sleep, he thought perhaps a stroll back to the dock and another crack at the rat would rid him of the willy-jams before he went home.

He tiptoed down the wooden slats. Moonlight cast a yellow glow across the boats tied on both sides of the pier. As the gentle waves rippled toward shore, the boats tapped against the dock, adding to the rhythm of the night.

Now, where did that critter get off to? Somewhere right around here... Black Cat jumped onto a storage box containing glass floats and hunkered down, his ears tipped toward any movement. With the patience only a cat possesses and his head filled with the disturbing events at Mrs. Herman's house, several hours passed as he watched and waited for the rat to reappear.

Sometime around midnight, Brett's car pulled up to the house. Black Cat gave up the stakeout, raced down the dock and across the lawn to the house. As he followed Brett through the front door, a final thought crossed his mind.

With Mrs. Herman in such a weakened condition and so vulnerable, if Ted truly meant to harm her and returned during the night, the old woman wouldn't stand a chance.

Chapter Seven

Go if you must, but I plan to take a nap. - Angel

lancing at the clock over the stove, Kimberlee tapped the table beside Amanda's bowl. "It's 7:15 A.M. already. Put down your doll and eat your cereal. You need to get dressed. The bus will be here in half an hour." She took the coffeepot off its stand and refilled Brett's cup. "What time did you get home last night? I didn't hear you come in."

"About midnight, I think. You were out for the count when I came to bed. Did you finish your journal?"

"No. Dorian called, and we chatted for a while. Then Amanda woke up, and I had to get her back to sleep. I went to bed about ten o'clock. I'll find some time today to finish the journal. I got to the part where Dewey made the Normandy landing and met a German soldier. For a diary, it's pretty exciting."

"Did he fight hand to hand with the German soldier? That must have been awful."

"Actually, he saved the kid's life and they became friends. Can you imagine? Dewey was left for dead on the battlefield and then saved an enemy soldier's life. That's pretty heady stuff for an eighteen-year-old."

"I'll have to keep that in mind for my next novel. Just the concept, mind you, not his particular story."

"I can't wait to read what happens next. I stopped at the part where he and the German boy were hospitalized." Kimberlee picked up

Amanda's bowl and set it in the sink. "Run and get dressed, Amanda. I'll be in to fix your hair in a minute. I wonder if Dewey every saw the German soldier again?"

"Not likely," Brett said. "Probably a prison camp for the German and back to the states with a medical discharge for…what's his name?"

"Dewey Brooker. From a little town in Oregon."

Brett swallowed the last of his coffee. "Well, it's the computer and my own mystery for me. I better get at it."

Black Cat nudged Angel as she hunched beside the water bowl. *Pretty cool, huh? We made her read the diary.* Angel lifted her head. Drops of water dripped from her chin. She stretched and then ambled from the kitchen into the living room.

Kimberlee dressed Amanda in a black and white pinafore, white blouse, and white leggings. She donned her little *Toy Story* backpack and she and Kimberlee walked to the bus stop. She glanced toward the street as sirens cut through the stillness of the morning.

Kimberlee pulled Amanda further onto the lawn, away from the sidewalk. "Stand way back, Amanda. We don't want to get run over by a fire truck, do we?" A Fern Lake police car and a fire truck turned into the Fern Lake Lodge driveway and stopped in front of Mrs. Herman's house. "Oh, my goodness. They're coming here."

The school bus came to a stop beside the sidewalk. Kimberlee helped Amanda up the steps and waved as the bus pulled away from the curb. She hurried across the grass toward the lodge residence. Something was going on over at Mrs. Herman's house. Not surprisingly, Dorian's car was parked in front of Mrs. Herman's residence and a string of yellow crime tape stretched across the front of the house.

Kimberlee's heartbeat picked up as she caught Dorian's eye, frowned, and mouthed the words, "What's up?" From the looks of the hubbub around the house and the yellow crime tape, it appeared something bad happened there during the night.

Even from where she stood on the lawn, Kimberlee could still see the purple stain from the broken jam jar on the porch step. She should have known that coming over would irritate the cantankerous old woman. It wasn't surprising their conversation ended in a quarrel. She should have asked Brett to take the flowers to Mrs. Herman. Kimberlee shook her head. *Shoulda, coulda, woulda.* It's so easy to Monday morning quarterback after the deed is done.

Dorian stepped away from the uniformed officer and approached Kimberlee, gesturing toward the crime tape. "Did something happen to Mrs. Herman?"

Dorian's eyes opened in surprise. "What makes you ask that?"

Kimberlee shook her head. "I mean. All the police… I just guessed." No one should rejoice in someone's death, but… With Mrs. Herman out of the way, life would certainly be easier. Kimberlee peered into Dorian's face. "She's dead. Right?"

Dorian nodded. "Worse yet, we can't rule out murder. I shouldn't tell you this, but from the looks of the house, she put up a good fight. We found hair and blood on the metal doorstop, so that must be what killed her. The caregiver found her this morning when she came to fix breakfast."

"Murder?" Kimberlee stared at Dorian's stern expression. "I can't believe it. I just saw her. She seemed fine. Hateful, as usual, but fine…"

"Will you be home later this morning? Considering the quarrel you had with Mrs. Herman yesterday, I'll need to ask you some questions, or would you rather stop by the station? The nurse even mentioned it when I spoke to her this morning."

Prickles crept up the back of Kimberlee's neck. "I'm working the morning shift at the store, but I'll be home by two o'clock when Amanda gets home. Can you come by the house after that? I'd rather not discuss this at the store."

"Of course. Oh. There's Jack. I need to speak to him, too. I'll see you later. Don't worry, you're not a suspect." Dorian smirked and then turned toward Jack.

"Thanks a bunch for the vote of confidence," Kimberlee called after her. Where Mrs. Herman was concerned, she couldn't win. They never had gotten along. Thanks to that stupid argument and her own temper tantrum, now she was going to be questioned about a murder. *Why did Brett have to go out last night?*

Gravel crunched under another police car as it came up the driveway and stopped in front. Virgil Pellini, Dorian's current boyfriend, and Fern Lake's lead detective, stepped out. He waved at Kimberlee, ducked under the crime tape, and then hurried into Mrs. Herman's house.

Black Cat and Angel sat on the back of the sofa, peeking through the front window curtains at the hubbub across the lawn. He scratched at the window glass. "I should have stayed with Mrs. Herman last night. Something terrible has happened, I just know it." He flattened his ears. "Ted was there. I was afraid he might come back and hurt her. Or, maybe she did something desperate."

Angel tossed her head. "What could you have done if you'd stayed? If she intended to do herself harm, you couldn't have stopped her. You don't have opposable thumbs—couldn't make a phone call. Or for that matter, what if Ted came back? What could you have done? Really, Black Cat, you think entirely too much of yourself. You aren't invincible." Angel turned up her nose and jumped off the back of the sofa onto a velvet pillow. She turned in a circle and lay down. "I'm taking a nap. Let me know when you're over your God-complex."

Black Cat glared down at her. "I don't have a… what you said. It's not that I think I could have changed things. I'm just saying, maybe I should have stayed. Here comes Kimberlee now. Maybe she'll tell us what happened."

The front gate opened and closed. Kimberlee stepped through the front door, her cheeks rosy from her hurried walk across the lawn. "Hey, cats. What's up?" She glanced at Black Cat, still standing on his hind feet on the back of the sofa, peering out the window. "Lots of excitement out there, *huh*? Can you believe it? Mrs. Herman died last night. She might have even been murdered." She stifled a chuckle and wiped the smile off her mouth. "You're right. It is terrible, but I can't seem to muster up much sympathy." She leaned down and stroked Angel's back. "That's not very Christian of me, is it?"

A smile curved Kimberlee's lip as she peered into the mirror over the fireplace. "Imagine. Dorian is going to question me as if I'm a person of interest in Mrs. Herman's murder. Well, I should get to work. This person of interest has a store to run." She grabbed her keys and her purse, and stopped at the door. "Are you coming with me today, Black Cat? I could use the moral support."

Black Cat jumped off the sofa and ran into the kitchen.

"Guess not. Okay, then, I'll see you later." She opened the door and went out.

Kimberlee's car no sooner pulled away than Black Cat ambled back into the living room. "Didn't I tell you? I knew I should have stayed with Mrs. Herman last night. I'll bet that Ted-Harold person came back after I left and whacked her."

Angel lifted her head off her paws. "Whacked her? You're watching too much TV. And, suppose you'd stayed, and he came back to whack her, he could have whacked you, too. What, pray tell, could you have done to stop him doing whatever you think he did?"

"I could have jumped on him and bit him, like that other crook at Grandmother's ranch in Texas." He paced the living room again, his fur stiffening across his broad shoulders.

"No, if I recall, you didn't stop anyone. You only slowed him down a bit and nearly got yourself *whacked* in the bargain."

Black Cat bristled. "At least I tried. That's what counts."

Angel tossed her head. "Counts for what? Is someone keeping score?"

"You've got it all wrong. That's not what I meant. It's just… oh, now you have me all mixed up. Why are you being so mean?" Where was the sweet and adorable kitty he loved? To hear her snarky remarks lately, you'd think she regretted her decision to return to Fern Lake with him. Though, truth to tell, once Kimberlee decided to bring her back with the family, Angel really had no say in the matter.

Angel's eyes squinted. She licked her paw and drew it over her left ear. "I'm trying to make you understand that nothing would have changed if you stayed with Mrs. Herman last night. One way or another, she would be just as dead. Some things are beyond our control." She gazed across the room, a far-away look in her eyes. "To think otherwise is either egotistical or foolish.

"At this point, I think you should be less concerned about what might have been, and more concerned for Kimberlee. You heard her say she was to be questioned about Mrs. Herman's death. Thanks to their quarrel, and being home alone last night, she'll likely be a prime suspect if they're going to call it murder."

Black Cat stopped pacing. As snippy as she sounded, he couldn't argue with Angel's logic. It was not a cat's nature to worry about things beyond the moment. How foolish to feel guilty about something that happened to Mrs. Herman when he wasn't there.

He jumped onto the back of the sofa and poked his head through the curtains. What was happening across the lawn? Had they brought out Mrs. Herman's body? "Do you want to go over there and see what's going on?"

"You'll be underfoot, but go if you must. I plan to take a nap." *Nom...nom...nom.* She licked at her shoulder and worked her way down her back.

"Then, I'm out of here." He headed for the kitchen and shot out the cat door, raced around the corner of the house and streaked across the lawn to Mrs. Herman's front porch. He stopped short when the front door opened and two ambulance attendants wheeled out a gurney with a body covered by a white sheet.

Black Cat gulped down a lump in his throat. It had been quite a while since he lived with Mrs. Herman, but he still remembered many a summer evening, she and Jack would join the lodge guests out under the trees. Jack would barbeque chicken and Mrs. Herman would move among the guests, sharing jokes and stories of her childhood in Germany.

He thought back to the first night Kimberlee came to the lodge and met Brett at the barbecue. It was almost love at first sight. That was before the trouble started between Kimberlee and Mrs. Herman. That must be what folks referred to as the *good ole' days*. Back when you remember the fun times.

It wasn't fun now with the smell of death and blood hovering over the gurney as it rolled down the sidewalk. The attendants placed the gurney in the ambulance and drove away.

Black Cat slipped through the open door into the living room and glanced around the room. Two forensic technicians leaned over the furniture, dusting for fingerprints. Another dropped a thin gold chain and Ted's cigarette butt into plastic evidence bags and handed them to Virgil. A lady photographed every angle of the room, including the broken glass on the hearth and the pillows and lamp that lay on the carpet, the result of Mrs. Herman's temper tantrum.

He sauntered into the kitchen where he encountered Dorian and Virgil leaning on the kitchen counter, deep in discussion. Virgil scribbled something on his clipboard. "From the looks of the room, she put up quite a struggle before someone struck her with the doorstop."

"Poor thing didn't have a chance, considering her condition," Dorian observed.

Wait. Black Cat jumped onto the counter and ducked his head under Dorian's hand. *There wasn't any struggle. Mrs. Herman threw things around the living room after she and Ted quarreled.*

Virgil patted Black Cat's head. "They found a cigarette butt in the candy dish. Did the victim smoke?"

"I don't think so. We haven't found any cigarettes or a lighter anywhere. Maybe the killer left the cigarette. There was no sign of forced entry which suggests she knew her visitor."

"So, do we agree? Looks like murder." Virgil raised an eyebrow.

"That's my guess, but I'll leave it to the coroner." Dorian took the evidence bag containing the bracelet from Virgil and held it up to the light. "We found this on the floor. I doubt it belongs to Mrs. Herman—might have been dropped in the struggle. Maybe we can get a fingerprint off the bracelet. There's a date and something etched into the back. It looks like… I could swear I've seen something like this before."

Black Cat spotted Mrs. Herman's letter on the sideboard that implicated Ted as a suspect…but also implicated Kimberlee. He hesitated, then leaped onto the sideboard, gripped the letter between his teeth, and hopped onto the floor. *In for penny…in for a pound.* If they were going to question Kimberlee, they sure needed to question Ted Herman, too.

"Black Cat? What have you got there?" Dorian made a grab for the letter and turned it over. "It's addressed to the Fern Lake Police Department. Should we open it?"

"Don't see why not. It's addressed to us." Virgil took the envelope, tore it open and read down the page. "*Whoa!* Check this out." He handed the paper to her.

Dorian's hand shook when she finished reading the note. She glanced up at Virgil, her eyebrows hiked up into her forehead. "Ted Herman? I just had a conversation with Kimberlee about him. After being missing for twenty-five years, and presumed dead, why do you think he's come back to Fern Lake? There's more to this story than we know."

Virgil tucked the letter into an evidence bag and snapped it onto his clipboard. "Perhaps he came to kill his wife and take over the lodge. Let's pick him up for questioning. Then, there's Kimberlee. Considering this letter, it looks like she could be a person of interest, too. I'd also like to know if either she or Ted Herman smoked Camel's cigarettes."

Dorian's face drained of color as her gaze moved from Virgil's face to the note on his clipboard. "I know for a fact Kimberlee doesn't smoke."

Chapter Eight

...and the day he returns, his wife turns up dead. - Dorian

How she loved coming to the bookstore. Kimberlee unlocked the front door and clicked on the lights. She hung her coat on the rack and shoved her purse into its cubby. Her heart filled with pride every time she stepped through the door of her own business, her life's dream, now a reality. Of course, recently marrying the love of her life wasn't all that bad either. Brett seemed happy with his ready-made family, and Amanda couldn't be happier with her new stepfather. Everyone was overjoyed that Thumper, *er*...Black Cat, had come home after being missing all summer. With the addition of Angel, their family felt complete.

She frowned as she straightened a stack of new books on the front display table. She mustn't get complacent and careless. As good as things were right now, life could go south any moment. For instance, when Dorian questioned her about Mrs. Herman's murder. Not that she had anything to worry about. Other than quarreling with the cantankerous old woman, there was nothing to suggest she had anything to do with it.

With Mrs. Herman gone, life would be even better, not having to deal with a hateful next-door neighbor. She carried the coffeepot to the break room, filled the reservoir with water, and poured in a pre-measured packet of coffee she'd brought from home. She glanced at the clock on her way back to the coffee bar. Almost 9:30 A.M.

Bernard would be here any minute with her daily order of freshly baked goodies from the Fern Lake Bakery down the street. What a profitable idea Jack suggested, adding pastries and coffee in her bookstore. Customers could relax at tables and various seating arrangements with a cup of coffee and a treat while they perused the *For Preview Only* copies of new, best-selling books. New customers came seeking a cup of coffee and dessert and often stayed to buy a book or one of the lovely hand-crafted items created by local artists.

She pulled Dewey's journal from her purse and carried it to one of the comfortable sofa chairs, rechecked her watch, and curled into the chair. She had fifteen minutes to read before time to unlock the door.

Writing from his hospital bed, Dewey described how a bullet had entered his helmet, grazed his head, and knocked him unconscious. Following a brief hospitalization, he returned to his company, still suffering migraines and severe dizziness. On September 10, 1944, Dewey wrote in his journal.

Going home. Medical disability due to migraines and dizziness. Mother is happy, but I'm not sure how I feel. Hate to leave my friends, but happy to go home. Wonder if I'll ever sleep without dreams of Normandy? Must try to move on. Can't wait to see Betsy, Mom, and Jimmy.

After Dewey returned home, his entries were farther between. He occasionally made a note of the major milestones in his life. Getting back to home life, work, and family, his documentation was less interesting. Dewey married his girlfriend in November 1944.

Happy day marrying my beautiful bride, Betsy, marred only by a migraine headache later that day.

July 2 1945 Mother's cat gave birth to four kittens last month. James, a cousin from the Wilkey branch in California, is making the rounds through Oregon and Idaho on his vacation. He stopped to visit us here in Grants Pass. He plans to take the black and white tuxedo kitten with the extra toes home with him next week when he goes back to Newbury. Mother says, "Only three to go." They say the war is almost over. God grant that it be true.

Dewey wrote on September 2, 1945.

Victory. V-J Day. What a great day. Everyone is celebrating the end to the war and peace will return to the world. How many of my friends made it through alive? I wonder if the recruiting office would give me their addresses. I'd love to write and tell them about our expected bundle of joy. I suppose they'll release Hans from the prison camp. Will I ever hear from him again? I hope he can return to his family and be as happy as I am.

His son, John Dewey Brooker, was born in late September 1945. *Not even the end of war and signing the peace treaties makes me feel as great as the birth of my son. Nothing before in my life prepared me for the sensation of feeling his tiny hand close around my finger. In that moment, I knew I was not just a man, not even a soldier, or just a husband. I was a father. Imagine! Me! A father! The responsibility of it is overwhelming. I promised God I would protect him, keep him safe. I committed my life to raise him with the values my father taught me. I thanked God for this wonderful gift and opportunity and pray there will never be another war during his lifetime.*

Tears pricked Kimberlee's eyes. That's exactly how she felt when Amanda was born.

The time flew by as Kimberlee turned the pages. A knock on the front door tore her from the celebrations of V-J Day to the reality of earning a living in Fern Lake. She put a bookmark in Dewey's journal, jumped up, and hurried to the door. The aroma of chocolate crept out from under the plastic lid of the tray Bernard carried into the bookstore. "Morning, Mrs. Clarke. Mimi thought you'd like chocolate cupcakes for a change. I brought half a dozen. Is that okay?"

Kimberlee sniffed. "They smell wonderful. By the way, the shipment of *Harry Potter and the Goblet of Fire* arrived yesterday afternoon. They've been on back-order for a while."

"Great. I borrowed it from the library, but I wanted my own copy." Bernard set the tray on the counter and handed the receipt to Kimberlee to sign.

"Well, I'm putting the books on sale tomorrow. If you like, I'll set aside a copy for you."

"Thanks. I'd like that." He glanced around the shop, his gaze lingering on the array of colorful ceramic pots lined up on the far wall. He turned back toward Kimberlee. "Where's the cat? He's usually here when I come in."

Kimberlee signed the receipt for the baked goods. "He stayed home today. I expect Black Cat wanted to sit in the window and watch all the excitement next door. You probably haven't heard yet, but the lady who owns Fern Lake Lodge died last night. They think it might have been murder."

"Gee, that's really a shame. My dad and I rented a fishing boat from her a few times." Bernard folded the receipt and put it in his pocket. He picked up the tray from the previous day's delivery. At the door, he turned, gazed at the books, hand-crafted works of art, and ferns hanging from hooks near the front window. His brow wrinkled. "I love to come in here. Everything looks and smells so nice. What did you ever do to deserve such a nice store?"

What an odd question. "Believe me, I don't think I *deserve* anything. It took lots of hard work, some help from friends, and a good business plan to build a business. Why do you ask?"

Bernard stared at his feet and mumbled. "My folks worked hard, too. We used to have a bookstore in Cloverdale, but we lost it…" His lips trembled. "I gotta go. I'm on the register today, and we open in a few minutes." He reached for the doorknob. "That lodge lady who died… Do they have any idea who killed her?"

Kimberlee shrugged. "I don't know anything more about it. There might be something on the news tonight."

"*Uh-huh.* I'll come by tomorrow and pick up my book. See

you later." The bell over the door tinkled as Bernard pulled it closed behind him.

Kimberlee turned into her driveway that afternoon at 2:20 P.M. There were no police cars or emergency vehicles next door, but yellow crime tape still circled the front of Mrs. Herman's residence. She stopped her car beside Jack and Amanda, walking toward the house with Chance. "Hi, Jack. Hi, sweetheart. How are two of my favorite people? And, one of my favorite dogs?" Kimberlee opened her door, patted Chance's head, and hugged Amanda. "Sweetie, why don't you and Chance run and play on the lawn." She glanced at Jack, "I expect you'll want to talk about…*um*…things. Do you have time for coffee?"

He muttered, "Yeah, I got nothin' but time." He pulled a tennis ball from his jacket pocket and tossed it onto the lawn. "Go on, Chance. Go play with Amanda." Chance raced after the ball with Amanda close behind. Jack followed Kimberlee into the house. "I don't know what to say. I can't believe…" He spread his hands, shook his head, and dropped into a kitchen chair.

"I know. This must be hard for you. I guess you heard about my quarrel with Mrs. Herman. I should never have gone over there." Kimberlee poured two cups of coffee, popped them into the microwave, and pushed the buttons. "These will just take a minute. We can sit on the front porch if you like."

"Okay. It's nice out today."

The microwave dinged. Kimberlee pulled out the cups, handed one to Jack, and followed him out the front door.

Light rain during the night left a clean, damp fragrance in the air, and droplets still gathered on the wisteria climbing the trellis.

The swing next to the porch railing creaked as Jack sat down beside her. He sipped his coffee. "Did ya talk to the police yet? Any idea what happened? I went over when I saw the commotion, but they wouldn't let me into the house." His eyes glistened with tears. "Dorian told me she was dead, and it's possible she was murdered." His gaze followed Chance and Amanda.

Kimberlee squeezed Jack's arm. "Dorian didn't give me any details, either. Apparently, the nurse found her when she came to work this morning. It's terrible. I'm so sorry, Jack. I know you cared for her."

He blinked back tears. "We go back a long way, ya know. She was more of a mother to me than my own."

"I know."

"I never understood why you two didn't get along." He ran his hand over his face. "She thought so much of you and your parents when you were a baby. She never would talk about what turned her against you when you came back to Fern Lake last year. I asked once, and she told me to mind my own business."

"It's all too much to take in today." Unexpected death was always disturbing. It made one's own mortality so uncertain. And those we love… Her gaze moved to Amanda and Chance racing across the lawn. "If anything ever happened to Amanda…"

Dorian's police car pulled into the driveway and stopped. She climbed out, strode purposefully up the sidewalk, and joined the two on the porch. "Good. You're both here. I can kill two birds with… *uh*…I mean…" Her face flushed. "I'm sorry. Me and my big mouth. So… Amanda looks like she's having fun with Chance."

Kimberlee chuckled. "That makes one of us, right? Grab that folding chair and sit down. Do you want coffee? It's from this morning, but still drinkable."

"I'm fine." Dorian tapped her pen on a clipboard. "I'm sorry to bother you, Jack. I know this is hard. I need to ask you two a few questions. The sooner we get this out of the way, the sooner we can visit." She unfolded the lawn chair and sat. "When did you last see Mrs. Herman?"

Jack ran his hand across his forehead. "I met the van when they brought her home yesterday and helped the nurse get her settled. She wasn't at all happy with Chance being there, so I left right away. Then, I stopped by in the afternoon, but the nurse said she was asleep. I never saw her again." He turned away and took a couple of quick breaths. "I can't remember if I even told her, 'welcome home.'"

Kimberlee squeezed his arm. "I'm sure she knew your intentions."

Dorian scribbled on the report she would turn into the Chief of Police. "Where were you last night, between eight o'clock and midnight?"

His shoulders stiffened and his upper lip quivered. "Where do ya think? I watched TV and went ta bed about eleven, like I do most nights. Guess Chance can't give me much of an alibi, if ya think I need one."

Dorian stopped writing. "I didn't mean it that way, but you know it's my job. I have to ask." She sighed. "Did you see anyone over at Mrs. Herman's house last night? Maybe a car you didn't recognize?"

Jack sighed. "We didn't have any new clients after six P.M, but cars come and go all hours of the day and night. It's a lodge, Dorian. I didn't see anything strange because I wasn't looking." Jack slammed his cup on the end table and stood. "I have work ta do. Can't sit here all day answering your fool questions." He stepped off the porch and yelled, "Come on, Chance. Let's go. Tell Amanda goodbye." Chance came running and followed Jack toward the dock.

Dorian tapped her chin with the pen. "Well, that went well, don't you think? Now I've offended my friend, grieving the loss of his loved one." She turned to Kimberlee. "And, now I get to do it all over again. I should have let one of the other guys do these interviews. This is too personal."

"Don't worry, I'm not offended. I'll start. I went over to Mrs. Herman's house right after she came home. We quarreled. She knocked the basket out of my hand and the jam broke on the step. We both said some stupid stuff, and I came home. As for last night, Brett had a meeting. Amanda and I were alone, so I suppose I don't have an alibi either. You and I talked on the phone for a while, remember? But, I guess both Jack and I will have to stay on your *persons of interest* list until you find someone else to suspect. Does that help?" Feeling her face flushing, she gazed at Amanda scraping oak leaves into a pile. *I shouldn't have been so sarcastic. She's just doing her job.*

Black Cat ambled around from the back of the house, spotted Amanda, and raced toward her. He jumped into the pile of leaves. Amanda tossed them into the air where they rained down on his head. He leaped from side to side, grabbing at one leaf after another.

"Look at them. They're having fun while we sit here and accuse each other of terrible things." Kimberlee picked at a piece of lint on her slacks.

"Then, I guess you didn't see or hear anything unusual over there last night, either?" Dorian held her pen over Kimberlee's statement.

"No. After Brett left, I spent the evening reading Dewey's journal. I don't think I would have noticed anything, anyway. Oh, wait. Brett did mention a red SUV in front of her house before he left. So what can you tell me? What have you found out?"

"You know I can't discuss the details of the investigation." Dorian's face flushed "You didn't go back over there…last night after we talked, did you?" Her gaze moved from Kimberlee to the paperwork on her lap. "I mean…you'd tell me if you did, right?"

Kimberlee raised an eyebrow. "You know I didn't. I just told you. Where are these questions coming from?"

"Nothing important. Just wondered. *Um…*We are anxious to interview Ted Herman. He might have been there last night. How is it just a coincidence that he's missing for twenty-five years, and when he's barely back a few days, his wife turns up dead? That's really got us curious." Dorian sighed. "You know it was my job to question you and Jack because of his relationship to Mrs. Herman, and your quarrel yesterday. You're not mad, are you?"

"Of course not. Don't worry about Jack or me. He's hurt and lashing out."

"If you see him, please tell him I'm sorry." Dorian stood and gathered her paperwork. "Call me if you think of anything that would help. I'll check into that SUV."

"I suppose there will be some sort of service for Mrs. Herman. Let me know if there's anything we can do." Kimberlee stood and fluffed the pillow she'd been leaning on.

"They'll do an autopsy, and we'll go from there." Dorian backed down the sidewalk toward her car. "I'll see you later."

Kimberlee waved as Dorian drove away. As she finished her coffee, she watched Amanda and Black Cat play in the leaves. So much for the peace and tranquility she anticipated this morning. With Mrs. Herman's death and Ted Herman back from the presumed dead, what might happen next? Would Ted try to take over the lodge? Where would that leave Jack? He always spoke of his wish to buy the lodge one day, but now, who knew what might happen? Not to mention how unsettling it would be to have Ted living right next door.

Kimberlee shuddered. Things could get ugly around here real quick. She shook her head. Would they have to sell the beloved Victorian they worked so hard to restore? On the other hand, selling the house might be the least of her worries. *Don't be ridiculous. That's not going to happen.*

Chapter Nine

If there was meat in Kitty Crunchies, I'd be the first to know. - Angel

After dinner that night, Kimberlee put the last plate into the dishwasher. She gave the stove a swipe with the sponge and turned as the phone rang. "Hello?"

"Ms. Clarke? Mr. Ollingham here. I was Mrs. Herman's attorney. Can you come to my office for the reading of Mrs. Herman's will? You were named as one of the beneficiaries."

Kimberlee stared at the receiver and chuckled. "You must have me mixed up with somebody else. Mrs. Herman would never leave me anything in her will."

"I assure you, it includes you as one of the beneficiaries," the attorney said. "I'm unable to say more on the phone, Mrs. Clarke, except that your attendance is requested."

"Okay, but it's a big surprise to me. May I bring my husband?"

"He's always welcome. We'll see you then. Goodbye."

Kimberlee found Brett in his office, working on his latest manuscript. "Guess what? Mr. Ollingham called. He says I'm named in Mrs. Herman's will. I can't understand. She always hated me."

"No, she didn't." Brett hit 'save' on his computer and sipped from his coffee cup. "Ted and Mrs. Herman were both quite close to your parents when you were a baby. Ted was crazy about you. I imagine Mrs. Herman wrote her will years ago. Maybe she never changed it when the two of you had trouble last year. She probably didn't give it a second thought, or if she did, she never got around to it before she died."

"Maybe. I wonder who else will be—" A knock at the door interrupted Kimberlee. "I'll get it." She turned and started toward the living room.

Angel lowered her ears, slipped off the sofa, and headed down the hall. As she passed Black Cat, stretched out on the couch, he lifted his head. *Wait up, Angel. Where you going?*

I'm not fit for company. Angel called over her shoulder before disappearing into Amanda's room. *I haven't groomed myself for hours.*

"Oh, hi, Jack. Come on in," Kimberlee said. "How are you holding up?"

Jack stepped inside, Chance by his side. His hair stood on end and his eyes were red as though he'd been crying. His hands shook as he sat on the sofa. Chance flopped on the floor beside her master. "I wanted to tell ya, I got a call from Mr. Ollingham. He asked me ta come to his office. He says Mrs. Herman left me something in her will." Tears glistened in his eyes.

Brett came into the living room and sat in his rocker by the fireplace. "Hey, Jack. How's it going?" Black Cat jumped into his lap. He turned his head into Brett's hand. *Right there, scratch behind my ear. Ah...yes...that's the spot.*

Kimberlee handed Jack a tissue. "He called you, too? He just called me and told me the same thing. I can't imagine why she'd leave me something in her will. Maybe she's officially signing over Black Cat since he's lived with us for the past year or so." She grimaced. "Can I get you some coffee? There's a fresh pot in the kitchen."

"No thanks. I'm already wired enough." He sighed. "The morgue called this afternoon. They want ta know where ta release Mrs. Herman's remains after the autopsy is complete. The attorney said Mrs. Herman named me executor of her will, so I'm supposed to arrange a funeral. She's made some specifics requests for the service, so at least that will help."

"Won't Ted be in charge of things, now that he's back?" Kimberlee sat on the arm of Brett's chair.

"I guess not. The attorney said I'd be in the one in charge of the arrangements." Jack ran his hand through his hair. "Her will says she's ta be cremated and wants her ashes scattered on the lake. I don't know the first thing about funerals. I'll need your help with that, Kimberlee. I'm no good at managing things."

"That's not true. Look what a fine job you've done with the lodge. Brett and I would be happy to help. It might make up for the way I talked to her that morning. I'll call the paddle wheeler and make arrangements to hold the service there. I'm sure Dorian will give me a hand with the plans."

Jack stood. "Thanks. That's a big load off my mind. Come on, Chance."

"See you later," Brett said.

Kimberlee walked Jack to the door. "Don't worry. Dorian and I will take care of everything." Kimberlee closed the door behind him. "Well, guess I've got my job cut out for me. As soon as we hear from the morgue and the paddle wheeler, I'll call the local paper and run an announcement about a memorial service."

Brett stood and dumped Black Cat onto the floor. "Mrs. Herman has been away from the lake for so long, I wonder how many people will attend her service. There's a placard in the office that lists her as a member of the Hospitality and Lodge Organization. I'll contact them. Maybe you should confirm arrangements with the paddle wheeler before we start giving out any other information."

"What about a minister? Should we have some sort of religious observance?" Kimberlee reached for a tablet and pen on the coffee table. "It's a comfort to the attendees, even though I doubt Mrs. Herman ever darkened the door of a church in her life."

Angel ambled back into the living room and cruised against Kimberlee's ankle. *Is Jack gone? What's this about a darkened church door?*

Kimberlee is giving Mrs. Herman a big send-off. They were wondering if they should hire a minister.

Angel jumped into the rocking chair that Brett just vacated. *Ahh. It's still warm.* She kneaded the pillow and lay down. *Considering what you've told me about Mrs. Herman, and what I've seen for myself, I don't think a religious service will do her much good. Even if she knocked on the Pearly Gates, I have my doubts that Saint Peter would let her through the door.*

Black Cat's whiskers twitched. *Better question is, did she even get close enough to knock?*

Tuesday morning found the cats out and about town. Black Cat walked with Angel through the neighborhood, past the playground and the school. Around lunchtime, he took her downtown to Rajinder's delicatessen to meet his friend. Black Cat kneaded the floor with his front paws and then curled around Rajinder's ankle. *This is my Angel. Isn't she beautiful? I brought her to meet you.*

"Hey! Black Cat. Is this your little girlfriend? I heard you came home with a cream tabby sweetheart. Did you guys come for lunch? *Heh heh.* Let's see what we got in here." Rajinder slid open the door of the meat counter. "Better watch out, pretty girl. If you eat too much, you'll lose your trim figure." Rajinder reached into the meat case and pulled out the end-cuts off a roll of bologna. He chopped up a few pieces, placed them on a paper plate and set them in front of Angel. "Here you go, baby girl, a special treat, just for you. Welcome to Fern Lake."

Angel sniffed the meat and backed away. *No thanks. I'm a vegetarian. I don't eat meat.*

Black Cat sat back on his haunches. *We've discussed this before, Angel. You do eat meat. Remember? There's meat in our Kitty Crunchies.*

I'm sure that's an old wives' tale. I never tasted any meat in the Kitty Crunchies, and, if there is any, I'd be the first to know. She turned her back and sat.

Rajinder smiled. "You don't like bologna, little girl? Never met a cat that didn't like bologna. Well, never mind. I'm sure another neighborhood kitty will like it."

Angel lowered her ears and dashed through the door onto the sidewalk. She stopped beside a ceramic pot of geraniums and licked her left shoulder. Black Cat snatched a bite of the bologna and hurried after her. "How could you be so rude? Rajinder is my friend. Now, you've hurt his feelings." He sat down in a sun puddle and glared at Angel. "I wouldn't have brought you here if—"

"If what?" Up went her nose. "If I embarrass you, why take me anywhere? I don't know why I came with you in the first place. I'm going home."

Black Cat stared at his soulmate and shook his head. *Guess the romance is over and now she's a pain in the...*

Angel stalked up the street, her tail as straight as a flagpole and her ears back.

"Angel. Wait up. You're going the wrong way. Come back. I'll take you home."

The cats stopped at several docks along the lake, but Angel's favorite was the dock at Fern Lake Lodge, next to Kimberlee's house. With all the fishermen cleaning their morning catch beside the bait shop, the air reeked of fish. Angel lifted her nose and sniffed. "I love the smell of fish. There's nothing better than a trout slathered in butter and fried over a slow flame."

Black Cat's head whipped around. "I thought you were a vegetarian."

"Fish aren't meat. Meat is meat. Fish is fish."

Black Cat switched his tail. How could a guy understand a female, much less one as contrary as Angel?

Chapter Ten

I can't say that I'm sorry she's gone. - Kimberlee

nce aboard the paddle wheeler for Mrs. Herman's funeral, Kimberlee's hair ruffled in the breeze as she peered into the brilliant blue water. Her gaze moved toward Ted Herman, standing off to the side of the crowd, his head lowered, and his hands in his pockets. Neighbors, preparing to board the paddle wheeler, whispered and moved away, leaving him isolated. Kimberlee suspected many had heard of his unexpected return and questioned his motive for returning. None of the attendees appeared obliged to speak to the widower.

Surprisingly, a number of local businessmen and neighbors came to pay Mrs. Herman their final respects. The laughter and camaraderie of the guests walking up the gangplank suggested they were coming for an afternoon outing on the lake and a free lunch, more than to attend Mrs. Herman's memorial service. If truthful, most would admit their memories of Mrs. Herman were tainted by her disagreeable personality. Few could claim that, except for many years ago, they still remained friends or had stayed in touch during her hospitalization.

Black Cat and Angel hovered just beyond the folks gathered on the dock. When the last guest was aboard, the cats scampered up the gangplank and scooted behind a storage box that held life jackets. The ship's whistle blew, and the bells clanged, announcing its departure. Ropes were dropped, the deck shook as the engine engaged, and the paddle wheeler pulled away from the dock. Black Cat, undisturbed by the racket and vibrating deck, came out from behind the storage box and wandered near the buffet table, where he begged a snack from the merrymakers.

"Hey, Black Cat." Rajinder stroked the cat's furry black head. "Looks like you stowed aboard for the ride. Or did you come for the snacks? Here you go." He pinched off a bit of ham from his sandwich. Black Cat stood on his hind feet and delicately took the ham from Rajinder's fingers. His antics delighted the crowd. Conversation and laughter wafted across the deck. Perhaps folks found it better to celebrate life rather than mourn a death.

"Well, I'll be." Brett pointed toward the cats. "Look over there. Black Cat and Angel sneaked aboard. Jack brought Chance, and Dorian brought her dog, Sam. I suppose the cats thought they deserved a ride as much as the dogs."

Brett glanced around the crowd. "Mrs. Herman would be pleased to see such a nice turnout. Everyone looks like they're having a good time."

"Perhaps that's what Mrs. Herman intended when she suggested these specific arrangements in her will," Kimberlee said.

Standing alongside his friends, Jack blinked back tears. "That sounds like something the Mrs. Herman I knew and loved would do. I doubt this many people would come to see me off."

"Oh, Jack, don't be silly. You have lots of friends," Kimberlee squeezed his arm.

The breeze off the lake picked up, blowing her hair away from her face. "You should be proud of what you've done. It's a shame Mrs. Herman never thanked you for the way you took over the lodge and kept it going while she was ill. The lodge is even more successful now than before she was hospitalized."

"It's one thing to fill in while she was in the hospital. Now that she's gone and Ted is back…" Jack turned his head, hiding his face. "I don't know what's gonna happen now."

Kimberlee pointed across the deck. "Look at Amanda. Virgil is giving her a piggyback ride. I should probably go and check on her."

"I should walk around and greet the folks. See ya later." Jack walked over to Rajinder and shook his hand. Chance followed at Jack's heels, swishing her tail in greeting to her friend.

The guests sipped coffee and cold drinks and nibbled on snacks as the paddle wheeler churned up a trail of white foam, heading for Mrs. Herman's final resting place. Occasional shouts and laughter mixed with the crowd's nervous glances toward Ted. Few were sharing memories of Mrs. Herman, good, bad or otherwise.

Kimberlee sat Amanda at a little table near the cabin door and gave her crayons and coloring books. A six-year-old is entertained by water rushing along the side of a boat or a churning paddle wheel for only so long. Kimberlee stood nearby talking to Amanda's kindergarten teacher, Mrs. Baker.

The boat chugged to a stop in the middle of the lake, and the guests gathered on the top deck where Jack had placed the small cask of ashes near the rail. He stood nearby with his hand on Chance's head. In the background, the soft music Mrs. Herman requested played on a tape recorder. Dorian distributed white roses to the ladies while the caterer handed out glasses and poured champagne. A Unitarian minister read a Bible verse, pronounced a brief blessing, and asked if anyone wished to share a memory of Mrs. Herman.

The only sound was the water swishing against the hull and the screech of a passing seagull. With heads lowered and shuffling feet, none of Mrs. Herman's *best friends* or even her long-lost husband showed any inclination to speak.

Following an embarrassing few moments, Jack raised his glass. "Please join me in a farewell toast ta our friend, Beverly Herman." The crowd lifted their drinks, as Jack spilled Mrs. Herman's ashes over the side. Few tears were shed as the ladies tossed the roses into the water. The flowers seemed more of a tribute to Kimberlee's thoughtfulness than a measure of respect toward the recently departed.

Kimberlee set her glass on a nearby table and took Brett's arm. "Well, I can't say that I'm sorry." *And, won't we all be better off now that she's gone?*

Brett nodded toward Ted Herman, standing by himself alongside the railing. "I assume you and Jack are off the hook as persons of interest." He grimaced. "Dorian said the autopsy reported *indeterminate cause of death.* The coroner couldn't rule out homicide, but thought it possible Mrs. Herman accidentally fell and hit her head on the doorstop."

Kimberlee pulled a strand of hair off her forehead. "So, that's the end of the investigation?"

"I guess they still have a few questions. Like, what caused the mess in the house, and who might have been her late-night caller."

Kimberlee turned toward the shoreline. "It's not like she was firing on all cylinders there toward the end." Her lips curved into a smile. "I can attest to that more than some. Beyond that, who knows what might have occurred the night she died."

The engines sputtered and roared. The boat veered around, creating a backwash, whipping the waves into foam, sucking the bobbing roses into the paddles, ripping them asunder and plunging others beneath the water. Kimberlee shuddered as the roses churned about. Once evidence of respect for Mrs. Herman's earlier life, they now symbolized the end of her life, spent in bitterness and strife.

Within half an hour, the boat pulled up to the dock. Kimberlee and Brett stood by the rail as the crew tossed ropes to the dock workers, who quickly fastened them to the dock cleats. The passengers clustered near the rails until the vessel was securely fastened to the gangplank and they could disembark. When the last guest stepped onto the dock, Black Cat and Angel scurried off the boat and raced home.

The crew untied the ropes and threw them back onto the deck. The paddle wheeler pulled away, bound somewhere around the lake for another scheduled cruise.

The last guest left the parking lot, leaving the lodge quiet. Kimberlee, Amanda, Brett, and Dorian stood with Virgil and Jack on the dock. Kimberlee took Amanda's hand. "Do you want to come back to the house for coffee, Jack?"

"I don't think so, and. I have a splitting headache." He waved, turned and headed toward the bait shop with Chance at his heels.

Kimberlee and Brett exchanged glances as Jack trudged through the door of the bait shop. "Do you think Jack will be all right? I'm worried about him," Kimberlee said.

"I suspect he'll be fine. It's to be expected he's thinking about Mrs. Herman. Or, for that matter, now that she's gone, maybe he's worrying about how Ted's return will affect his own future."

"Let's hope not. I don't know if he can handle another blow," Dorian said.

Chapter Eleven

So many young men never came home from war. - Kimberlee

Returning from the paddle wheeler, Brett retired to his office and Kimberlee put Amanda down for a nap. Kimberlee curled up in the living room recliner with Dewey's journal. Now that he was home from the war and settling down with his family, she wondered if the diary would be as interesting as before.

She skimmed several pages of intermittent entries over the years… church picnics, coaching little league, ball games at his son's school. His brother went off to college in Idaho. Rather boring reading, as she expected. The next entry caught her eye. Her heartbeat quickened. Dewey received a letter from Hans.

July 4, 1953 - Another Fourth of July. I can't believe I got a letter from Hans Kreuger, all the way from Austria. He says he found my address in his duffle bag when he cleaned a closet. He thought he'd surprise me. It worked. Hans got married after the war and now he's driving an armored car for an insurance company.

Kimberlee touched the page, closed her eyes, and leaned her head back on the recliner. How good to know that these two unlikely friends had both survived, returned to normal lives, and connected with each other again. So many of their friends never had the opportunity.

Could they still be alive after almost sixty years? Though possible, they would be almost eighty years old. She skimmed through the next pages, looking for more news of Hans. Dewey's entries were fewer and farther apart. He only made entries for important family events and several times when he got a letter from Hans.

Hans wrote that he and his wife had a baby. Despite surviving the war and returning to civilian life, financial and domestic problems continued to plague him.

Dewey's life moved on.

October 6, 1953 - Took over the management of my uncle's car dealership.

January 17, 1954 - My oldest son, John Dewey, was hospitalized with pneumonia. Thankfully, he is recovering.

Kimberlee skimmed pages again when Dewey took up a new hobby. Page followed page as he wrote about building all varieties of WWII model airplanes. Kimberlee glanced at the clock. Almost 3:30 P.M. Amanda would be awake soon, and almost time to think about fixing dinner. She flipped the pages in Dewey's journal. Her heart skipped a beat when she saw a familiar name.

August 29 1954 - Received the strangest communication from Hans today. I recognized his handwriting on the envelope, but it had no return address. No letter either, but the envelope contained a page torn from a hymn book with some words scrawled around the border.

The next several pages were stuck together as though the journal had gotten wet. Kimberlee carefully peeled them apart. A loose hymnal page dropped into her lap.

She tipped it toward the light, better to read the faded message, written by hand. She turned the page in a circle, reading the words scribbled around the margins.

The key to the treasure is in Hopfgarten.

Press the feet of the babe beneath the King

hidden in the place where

storm clouds are frightened away by the ring.

Treasure? What an odd statement. What did it mean? She laid the fragile hymnal page on the end table and glanced back at the journal where Dewey continued to write.

I'll have to write to Hans and ask what it means. It's a mystery, all right.

Kimberlee put her hand to her mouth. *Hans Kreuger.* Wait a minute. A few pages before, didn't Dewey say that Hans drove an armored car? Her fingers flipped back to the previous pages where she found the note. *Armored car—1954 Hans Kreuger.* What was it that niggled in the back of her mind? The PBS documentary!

Several weeks before, she and Brett watched one of his favorite PBS documentary programs featuring unsolved crimes. He said it gave him inspiration for his next novels. The program highlighted a robbery in Munich, Germany in 1954. Two armored car drivers stole a truck loaded with a shipment of gold. The men were identified as *Hans Kreuger* and *Joseph somebody.* Hans eventually died in a police shoot-out. The police took Joseph into custody, but despite extensive questioning, he would not disclose the gold's location. To this day, the missing gold had never been found.

Kimberlee's hand shook as she thumbed through the remaining pages of Dewey's diary. If Dewey ever wrote to Hans about the mysterious message and hymnal page, he never mentioned receiving a reply. The name Hans Kreuger was probably as common in Germany as John Smith in the United States, and just a coincidence that the thief on the PBS documentary and Dewey's friend shared the same name.

She tossed the journal on her chair. While preparing dinner, the strange words kept intruding into her thoughts. As she repeated it all together, it almost sounded like a poem. "The key to the treasure is in Hopfgarten. Press the feet of the babe." What could it mean? Was it possible that Dewey's friend, Hans Kreuger, was the armored car driver reported in the documentary? Could the treasure Hans referred to in his poem be the gold from the robbery? All too fantastic to believe, and, yet, at the same time, too tempting a possibility to dismiss.

Chapter Twelve

*Brett's book royalties poured in, sufficient to keep
them all in Kitty Crunchies. - Black Cat*

Black Cat woke early, stretched and yawned. He gazed around the living room, his attention drawn to the shimmering colors on the wall. A slight breeze shook the oak leaves outside the window. Early each morning before the family arose, the sun glimmered through the leaded glass transom over the front door, casting a parade of dancing colors on the wall above the fireplace. What should he do today? He yawned again. *Where did Angel sleep last night?* She wasn't on the sofa, one of her favorite napping spots. *Maybe in Amanda's room?*

Black Cat dropped off the recliner and ambled down the hall. The family was still asleep and the house quiet. Before long, Kimberlee would be bustling around, fixing Amanda's breakfast and lunchbox. Brett would pour his second cup of coffee and disappear into his office. There, he would work on his next *tell-all* scandal novel about an unseemly killer who had run amuck years before. Despite illusive and scant facts, Brett could conger up 265 pages of gory details, and enough documentation to produce an almost believable theory of the guilt or innocence of the alleged killer, and how the scoundrel avoided capture or prosecution.

Black Cat thought that ninety-six, point five percent of Brett's facts were likely a result of prune juice and his vivid imagination. Regardless, the public ate it up, bought his books by the truckload, and the royalties poured in, sufficient to keep them all in Kitty Crunchies, and that's all that really mattered.

His whiskers twitched, amused by his droll assessment of Brett's writing career. Never a serious novelist, Brett made a good living pumping out drivel that appealed to the public's baser instincts. He wasn't proud of his accomplishments, but it paid the bills. He promised Kimberlee that one day he'd write a serious novel. The days and months passed without him fulfilling his promise.

Amanda stretched and yawned when Black Cat entered her room. "Hi, Black Cat."

As he guessed, Angel lay curled next to Amanda's hip, apparently seeking not only her little friend's companionship, but the warmth from her body during the chilly night.

Morning, Black Cat mewed. He leaped onto the bed and flopped down beside Angel's golden hip. *Did you sleep well?* His heart swelled at the sight of his two favorite girls cuddled together.

Angel tossed her head. *Mmmumph...I didn't sleep well at all. I kept dreaming we were on that confounded paddle wheel boat. The constant rocking made me a little sick.*

Really? I didn't know you suffered from motion sickness.

Neither did I, never having been on a boat before. Now that I have, I don't ever want to do it again, thank you very much. From now on, it's dry land for me.

Amanda giggled. "You kitties have a lot to say this morning, don't you?" She got out of bed, pulled the covers up toward the pillow and went into the bathroom.

Kimberlee peeked around the corner. "Are you getting dressed, Amanda? It's seven o'clock. I'm making waffles, so hurry. Oh, hi, Black Cat...Angel." She gave Angel a pat and ran her hand down Black Cat's back. She stepped back into the hall and called into Brett's office.

"Our appointment with the attorney is at ten o'clock, so you don't have a lot of time to mess around. Breakfast is almost ready, so whatever you're doing in there, let it go until later." Brett often lost contact with the conscious world while working at his computer, writing about the illusive encounters of some ne'er-do-well. Kimberlee retreated down the hall toward the kitchen. A few mumbled words came from Brett's office, most likely acquiescence to Kimberlee's decree.

Black Cat's head shot up as Kitty Crunchies plinked into his bowl. He gave Angel's head a quick lick and then streaked off the bed and down the hall toward the kitchen. He was never one to dilly dally when it came time to put on the feedbag.

Kimberlee and Brett stepped into the attorney's office. She nodded toward the pictures on the wall and remarked on his decorating style. They were reminiscent of the popular 1960s Danish Modern era, including golden teakwood chairs and end tables. Faded oil paintings hung around the lobby, depicting snow-capped mountains, cows knee-deep in fields of golden poppies, and rosy-cheeked children. Kimberlee pulled off her jacket and sat on the divan. She gazed from one pastoral painting to the next. The room brought back childhood memories of her late aunt's living room in her Southern California house.

Brett shrugged. "To each his own. One man's junk is another man's... Mr. Ollingham!" He stood and put out his hand as the office door opened and the attorney stepped into the waiting room. "I'm Brett Clarke, and this is my wife, Kimberlee. I believe we have an appointment?"

They shook hands. "Nice to meet you." The attorney glanced at his watch. "We're waiting for several more beneficiaries. They should be here momentarily. Can I get you anything? Coffee? Water?"

"No, thank you, we're fine," Kimberlee turned as the front door opened. Jack entered, along with another man and a woman.

"*Ah*, Jack. I see you've already met Mr. Whiting and Ms. Cummings." The attorney shook hands with the couple and then with

Jack. "This is Mr. and Mrs. Clarke. We're all here now, so if you'll step into my conference room, we'll get started. I know you have better things to do than hang around my dull office. *Heh heh.*"

When all were seated at the conference table, Mr. Ollingham handed each of them a folder. "If you'll open your folders, you'll see the regular boilerplate on pages one through six. On page seven, we begin the individual bequeaths." He waited until all the folders were turned to the correct page. "To the local Fern Lake Businessman's Association, the sum of $1,000 toward the retirement of the debt sustained for the Community Youth Center."

Ms. Cummings smiled. "How kind. On behalf of the Businessman's Association, we're thrilled to accept."

The attorney nodded to her. "Ms. Cummings, if you don't have any questions, you may leave now. The rest of the will pertains only to the others. Please leave the folder on the table. We'll be in touch with you soon with a check."

"Oh. Okay." Ms. Cummings stood and pushed her chair under the table. "My! That was quick. Thank you again." She nodded to the others and left the office.

Mr. Ollingham turned the page on his folder. "Now, let's see, who's next? Mr. Whiting. As the President of the local Boy Scouts of America group, you'll be pleased to know that Mrs. Herman also bequeathed $1,000 to your organization. We'll be in touch with a check shortly."

Mr. Whiting stood. "Thank you so much. We do appreciate Mrs. Herman's generosity. We'll put it to good use, I assure you. Some of the boys need financial help attending the Boy Scouts annual jamboree. Thank you. Good day." He waved and left the room.

The attorney turned to face Kimberlee and Jack. "Lastly, to Jack Smart and Kimberlee Lassiter, now Kimberlee Clarke, Fern Lake Lodge and all of its assets are to be split equally between you. After the probate expenses and monetary bequeaths previously mentioned are settled, and with a clear title to the lodge, each of you will own fifty-percent of the remainder of Mrs. Herman's estate. Congratulations."

Kimberlee's mouth dropped open. Chill bumps raced up her neck and into her cheeks. "Jack and I share ownership of the lodge?" She glanced at Jack. He held his handkerchief to his nose and then dabbed his eyes. "I can't believe it."

Kimberlee turned to Brett. "Whatever prompted her to leave me…? She…she… I don't understand." Tears pricked her eyes. "Why would she…?"

Mr. Ollingham pulled an envelope from his folder. "There's a letter for each of you." He handed one to Jack and one to Kimberlee. The faded letters on the envelope read June 25, 1990. Kimberlee scanned the letter. "June 1990. Right before my mother passed away. Mrs. Herman must have written this when she received Mother's letter about my biological history." She read aloud from Mrs. Herman's letter…

"'Kimberlee. It is only fair that you should share in your biological father's estate. I don't have much money, but maybe this will help. I hope you and Jack can work together or sell your share of the lodge, should you need the money to help pay your way through college.'" She dropped the letter onto the table. "What does Mrs. Herman's letter say to you, Jack?"

Jack unfolded the page and read from his letter, "You were like a son to me. Thank you for your devotion to me and the lodge for so many years." Jack stumbled on his words. "I don't know what to say."

Brett squeezed his shoulder. "You deserve it, after working there for twenty-five years. Congratulations. You're a business owner now."

"Well, only half a business owner." Jack smiled at Kimberlee. "But I can't think of anyone I'd rather have as a partner."

She patted his hand. "I'm pretty busy with the bookstore, so I don't know how much time I'll be able to give you, but Brett and I will do all we can to help." With the house, Amanda, and the bookstore, how could she manage another thing on her plate?

Bang!

The door to the conference room slammed against the wall. Cool air from the outer office rushed in as Ted Herman stomped into the office. "Hold everything. I just ran into Mr. Whiting down the street, and he says you're reading my wife's will? Why wasn't I notified?"

Tingles crept up the back of Kimberlee's neck. She turned to Mr. Ollingham. "Does he have a right to be here?"

The attorney pushed back his chair and stood. "Now, what is the meaning of this intrusion? It was my understanding that Mrs. Herman was a widow. Her husband was lost at sea many years ago."

Ted threw back his head and bellowed. "That's where you're wrong. I'm Ted Herman. I'm her husband. I've been…away…for a number of years and—"

"Pretending you were dead, you mean…for twenty-five years. You show up as soon as there's something of value to claim. Where were you all those years when your *wife* worked 24/7 to keep the lodge going? For that matter, how is it just a coincident that you showed up practically the day she died?" Kimberlee's voice shook.

Ted's cheeks flamed. He seemed to have no defense against the truth. "I…I…I don't have to stand here and take this verbal abuse. It's none of your business where I've been. The fact is…as you can see…I'm very much alive." He tossed his head. "Since my wife has passed away, Fern Lake Lodge belongs to me now. No one else has any standing in this phony will." Up went his nose and down went his mouth into a sneer.

A moan escaped Jack's lips. Kimberlee gripped the folder to her chest. "The will is void? I don't care for myself, but…Mrs. Herman wanted Jack to have the lodge. He's earned it after all these years." She glared daggers at Ted. "You may have a legal right, but you have no moral right to take the lodge from Jack after what you've done." She turned and sobbed into Brett's shoulder.

"There, there. It's okay. Don't cry," Brett murmured, patting her back.

"Is he right, Mr. Ollingham?" Kimberlee said, lifting her head from Brett's shoulder and dabbing her eyes with a tissue. "Does he own the lodge?"

The attorney flumped into his chair. "Now, Mr. Herman, please sit down and let's discuss this rationally." He gestured to the chair Mr. Whiting recently vacated. "If you are, indeed, Mrs. Herman's husband, you do have standing in this situation, but it's a bit more complicated than you think."

Ted dropped a briefcase on the floor beside his chair and sat with his arms folded across his chest. "It's not the least bit complicated. Beverly and I bought the lodge and filed the deed as community property. Now that she's dead, Fern Lake Lodge is mine."

Kimberlee dried her eyes with Brett's handkerchief. "If that's true, why did you call yourself Harold Marlowe this summer in Texas when we met at my grandmother's ranch? You certainly didn't claim to be Ted Herman then." Memories of the Texas ranch, her grandmother, and Harold, the stable master, rushed through her mind. Hadn't Brett been a bit suspicious of his true identity, even then?

"I don't owe you any explanation. Besides, my past is irrelevant to the current discussion."

Jack gazed from Ted to Kimberlee. His expression reminded her of a wild antelope watching an approaching lion.

"I think it's very relevant," Kimberlee said. "The last time we saw you, they were arresting you in connection with embezzlement and possible murder charges. What did you do? Break out of jail?" Kimberlee hid her hands beneath the table, lest he see them shaking.

Ted pushed up from the table. "Not that it's any of your business, but if you must know..." His voice lowered as he gained control of his emotions. "When your grandmother learned I'd been arrested, she refused to testify against me. The D.A. didn't think he could get a conviction without her testimony, so the charges were dropped."

Brett slapped Mrs. Herman's will on the table. "So you decided to leave Texas and become Ted Herman again in California, just in case they came up with more evidence and refiled the case?"

"What about Imelda?" Kimberlee said. "If you're Ted Herman and want to inherit *your wife's* Fern Lake property, what did you plan to do about your other *wife*, in Texas? I believe that's called bigamy."

"Then, isn't it fortunate that one of my wives is no longer with us." Ted snapped his fingers. "No more problem. One wife at a time is legal, even in California."

Kimberlee pounded the table. "So you admit you killed her? You're a low-down—"

"I didn't admit any such thing. You're twisting my words."

"Hold on!" The attorney pounded the table. "Before this conversation gets any further out of control, Mr. Herman, let me give you some free legal advice. If you wish to assert your standing in Mrs. Herman's will, you'll have to provide a number of things. First, that you are Ted Herman and were never declared legally dead during the past twenty-five years. Second, that there are no criminal charges pending against you here, or in any other state. Third, the original deed will indicate how you recorded the property, whether in joint tenancy, community property, or as tenants in common." Mr. Ollingham picked up the will and shook it toward Ted.

"Once all that is established, you'll need to hire an attorney to contest this will, and I assure you, it won't be me. In any event, should you prevail in the above-mentioned requirements, and if the property was held as community property, as you claim, you're only entitled to fifty-percent ownership of the lodge. Mrs. Herman had every legal right to bequeath her fifty-percent to anyone she chose. So, you'll need to come to some equitable arrangement with Jack and Kimberlee if you wish to obtain one hundred-percent. So, why don't you pack up your ditty-bag and get the heck out of my office? If you accomplish all that I've mentioned, have your attorney contact me. Good day, sir."

Ted opened his mouth, snapped it shut, and grabbed his briefcase.

He stomped out of the office, yanked open the outer door, and slammed it behind him.

"Well," Mr. Ollingham said, "that puts a pickle in the pie crust, doesn't it?"

Jack finally found his voice. "Does this mean that me and Kimberlee don't own the lodge, after all?" His hands tightened into fists. "What about my cabin? Do I have ta find another job and another place ta live?" Tears glistened in his blue eyes again.

Kimberlee squeezed her arm. "Of course you don't have to move. Ted is just trying to bully us. Isn't that right, Mr. Ollingham."

The attorney shuffled through his papers. He sighed. "You heard what I told him. He has some legal maneuvers to accomplish before he would have any claim to fifty-percent of the property. I'm betting he's bluffing. I doubt he'll get past those barriers. If he does, we'll cross that bridge when we come to it. In the meantime, I wouldn't change a thing at the lodge.

"Jack? You stay right in the cabin where you've been living. In fact, I looked into the lodge's financials and it appears that since Mrs. Herman's hospitalization and you've been in charge, the lodge has accumulated a $40,000 balance in the checking account. It's obviously because of better management. I'm authorizing you to give yourself and the staff a twelve-percent salary raise."

"*Gee,* thanks, Mr. Ollingham. Maybe I can afford ta buy a newer used truck."

Brett clicked his ballpoint pen. "I'll go with you and help you pick one out. Is there anything else we need to do, Mr. Ollingham?"

"Not today. I'll let you know if anything changes. In the meantime, I'll get things rolling and move ahead with probate.

"Kimberlee? It would be a good idea if you spent some time with Jack familiarizing yourself with the bookkeeping system, any advertising program, how the bait shop runs, and whatever else he thinks you and Brett need to know as business partners. Keep track of the hours you spend helping him. If we have to go to court down the road, or go to arbitration, it will be to your advantage that you two, have taken on some of the lodge's responsibilities. Do you have any questions?"

Brett and Kimberlee stood. "It's all so sudden. I don't think it's sunk in yet. I'll probably have questions tomorrow," Kimberlee said.

"Call anytime. That's what I'm here for." Mr. Ollingham shook hands with Brett and Jack and escorted them to the door. "Try not to worry, Kimberlee. Believe it or not, this isn't the most tangled will I've ever had to probate."

Kimberlee wrapped her scarf around her neck. "I'm willing to bet it's even more tangled than you realize, Mr. Ollingham. But, that's another story."

The attorney raised an eyebrow. "Is there something else I should know?"

Reluctant to bring up her complicated relationship and past history with Ted, she said, "Not today. If Ted succeeds in legally contesting the will, I'll come back and we'll talk."

Chapter Thirteen

Touch the feet of the babe… - Hans Kreuger

Brett and Kimberlee returned home from the attorney's office and parked in the driveway next to Dorian's car. Since it was a school holiday, she agreed to stay with Amanda while Kimberlee and Brett visited the attorney. Brett unlocked the front door and held it for Kimberlee. "Hello?" Kimberlee called, hearing Dorian and Amanda's voices in the kitchen. "We're home. Is my favorite girl here somewhere?"

Black Cat and Angel sat near the kitchen table, their gazes locked on the tiny plastic cherries in the Hi Ho Cherrie-Oh game Amanda had spread across the kitchen table. No longer able to control his excitement, waiting for a cherry to accidentally fall to the floor, Black Cat jumped onto the table and sent one of the cherries flying across the kitchen. He leaped after it. "Black Cat. Stop that. Oh, hi, Mama," Amanda giggled. "Dorian thinks she can beat me, but I win every time."

Kimberlee stroked Amanda's hair. "Mama needs to talk to Auntie Dorian, sweetheart. Why don't you take the kitties to your room? I'll play with you later, okay?"

Amanda's lip turned down. "We're playing…"

"I know. Now, don't be a pouty face and run on."

"Okay." Amanda scooped up Angel and carried her down the hall with Black Cat trailing close behind.

Dorian leaned down and picked up the plastic cherry from the floor. "Well, what happened? Did she leave you an old boot she dredged out of the lake?" She stood and poured another cup of coffee and placed it in the microwave." Dorian looked up and her smile faded. "What? What happened? What are you grinning about?"

Kimberlee pulled out a kitchen chair and motioned her into it. "You better sit down. This is going to come as a shock."

"Okay, what's going on? Don't tell me old Mrs. Herman actually gave you something worth having? Her bookshelf full of cookbooks? Her WWII rocking chair? Her leaky boat at the dock? I can't believe she'd actually—"

"How about half of the lodge. Jack got the other half." Kimberlee giggled. "You'd better breathe! Your face is turning red."

The microwave dinged. Dorian opened the door and handed the cup to Kimberlee. "You're kidding. She left you Fern Lake Lodge? Lock, stock, and barrel? Oh my goodness. Why on earth…?"

"I have no idea. We think maybe Mrs. Herman wrote the will years ago when I was a fair-haired child, and she never changed it. There's more. Ted Herman showed up at the attorney's office and threw a cat fit. Claims the lodge belongs to him. Why, I have no idea after abandoning his wife for twenty-five years. Can you believe it? After all he's done… or rather…all he hasn't done."

"So, what did the lawyer say?" Dorian poured another cup of coffee and slid it into the microwave. "Do you and Jack have to share it with Ted, or can he invalidate the will?"

Brett walked into the kitchen, retrieved a soda from the refrigerator and snapped off the top. "The attorney says Ted might have a claim, but he'll have to file a lawsuit to contest the will. The attorney is starting the procedure to probate the will for Jack and Kimberlee."

Dorian rolled her eyes. "It's like living in a circus around here. I'll bet Jack is over the moon. He's always wanted to own the lodge."

"Actually," Kimberlee said, "Jack's pretty upset. He's afraid if Ted prevails, he'll put him out on the street. Maybe you should talk to him and try to calm him down."

"No surprise." Dorian set her coffee on the table. "I'll go over there now and take him to lunch. Find out what he's thinking." She stood and put her cup in the sink. "What an unexpected surprise for both of you. I can hardly wrap my head around it."

Kimberlee walked her to the front door. "Tell Jack to come over or call any time he needs to talk. Day or night."

"I will. I'm sure he knows that already."

"Sometimes knowing and doing are two different things. Especially with Jack…"

The porch swing swayed forward and back. Brett laced his fingers behind his head and stretched. "We'll have to get together with Jack and talk about the lodge. We should go over the finances and that sort of thing."

"We can get together tomorrow morning after Amanda leaves for school," Kimberlee said. "I can have Mrs. Wilson come into the bookstore a little earlier."

"That might work. I'll call Jack and see if we can schedule something." Brett took Kimberlee's hand. "Whatever it takes, we'll figure it out. Don't worry."

"I'm not worried about me. I'm concerned about Jack. I don't want all this to send him into another tailspin. He doesn't handle stress very well."

"Dorian will monitor Jack. He'll be fine. He may even be glad to have someone else share the responsibilities and handle some of the pressure. He won't have to feel guilty about asking for help, especially during next summer's peak season."

The lawn swing creaked as they rocked in silence for a few minutes. Kimberlee stopped the swing. "Do you mind if I change the subject? There's something I want to talk about."

"What's on your mind, peanut?" Brett squeezed her hand.

"We haven't talked much about Dewey's journal. You know, the WWII diary I'm reading? At the point where I am now, he's back home and he got a letter from his German friend, Hans. I can't quite get something out of my mind."

"Yeah. So, he got a letter…"

"I told you about how he saved the kid's life at Normandy? Wait here. I want you to see something." Kimberlee jumped out of the swing, dashed into the house and came back with the diary. She handed him the loose hymnal page. "Look. Dewey received this from Austria in an empty envelope. No letter or explanation. He's sure it came from Hans. What do you think?"

Brett twisted the page clockwise and read the message scrawled around the border of the song. "Touch the feet of the babe that lies beneath the king… Did you notice the underlined words in the second verse of the song?"

"I hadn't even noticed the title. *Jesus, Precious Treasure*. I was reading Hans's handwritten words." Kimberlee took the paper and read aloud the underlined words from the song.

> "Let your arms enfold me:
> those who try to wound me cannot reach me here.
> Though the earth be shaking, every heart be quaking,
> Jesus calms my fear.Fires may flash and thunder crash;
> yea, though sin and hell assail me,
> Jesus will not fail me."

Kimberlee shook her head. "Why do you suppose he underlined those words? What do you think that means?"

"Maybe he thought the words suggested that day on the battlefield. That's the reason he sent Dewey the message, to thank him for saving his life. 'Though the earth be shaking, every heart be quaking… fires may flash and thunder crash…' It certainly sounds like a battlefield, doesn't it? But, why would he send the hymnal page and write those strange words around the edge, about treasure and the babe beneath the king. What does that mean?" Brett handed the page to Kimberlee.

"Maybe you'll think I'm crazy, but I think he was telling Dewey about an actual treasure he hid in Hopfgarten. Remember that unsolved crimes documentary we watched a few weeks ago about the armored car and missing gold in Germany? One of the thieves was Hans Kreuger. Dewey's friend, Hans, drove an armored car. The robbery took place in 1954, right before Hans sent this to Dewey. I think Hans and his partner pulled off the robbery. If I'm right, his message…" She shook the paper, "…refers to the stolen gold from the armored truck. He used a coded message he thought Dewey would understand. I've scanned the rest of the diary. Dewey says he wrote to Hans several times, asking for clarification, but he never heard from him again. According to the documentary, Hans Kreuger died in a police shoot-out in Hopfgarten. Maybe, that's why he never wrote back."

"*Hmmm*…" Brett reread the message. He flipped over the page and scanned the hymn printed on the opposite side. Nothing else in the diary about it, *huh*?"

"Not that I can find with a quick look, but I haven't read every page yet. If Hans was trying to send a cryptic message, Dewey either didn't understand it, or never went to Hopfgarten to check it out."

Brett laid the hymnal page on the end table. "You're taking a lot for granted. It's probably all a mysterious coincidence." He chuckled. "So, you think this could be a clue to a treasure that hasn't been discovered for over fifty years?"

"Well… I don't know. Hans has the same name as the thief, but who knows if he's the same Hans Kreuger who stole the gold. I find it very curious, that's all."

"If the gold in the television documentary is Hans's treasure, it was never found. Perhaps you've really located a clue to an unsolved mystery." The lawn swing creaked as he stood. "And, now I need to get into my office and work on my own mystery." He leaned down and kissed Kimberlee's forehead. "Too bad there's nothing you can do about it."

Chapter Fourteen

Some good news would be welcome about now. - Kimberlee

Kimberlee stepped through the front door of the bookstore. She flicked on the lights, started the coffeepot, and sat at her desk. Noticing the blinking red light on the answering machine, she picked up a pen and pushed the play button. At first, she heard static and a few garbled words. "…your response…a mistake…letter…regret…warning." Then, the next few words were audible. In a clear voice, she heard the words, "shouldn't keep what isn't yours. Don't ignore...warning."

Kimberlee's temples throbbed. Warning about what? What letter? She stared at the machine and hit the replay button. The same garbled words came through with the last few words intelligible… "warning…"

What did she have that belonged to someone else? She dialed her home phone number. "Brett? Listen. Someone's left a strange message on my answering machine."

"What kind of message?"

"It sounds like they think I'm keeping something that doesn't belong to me. I have no idea what it means. Are you busy? Can you come down and take a listen?"

"Amanda just left for school. I'll be right down. Call Dorian. It's probably a prank. She'll know if other stores made similar reports."

"Thanks, hon. See you in a few minutes." She clicked the receiver on the phone and dialed Dorian's number. Within fifteen minutes, Brett arrived, listened to the message, and walked around the store, checking the doors and windows for any attempted break-in. Finding nothing amiss, he poured a cup of coffee and was eating one of yesterday's donuts when Dorian and her partner arrived.

"Hey, guys." Dorian laid her car keys on the counter where Kimberlee stood. "What's going on?"

"Listen." Kimberlee punched the button on the answering machine.

Dorian listened to the message from beginning to end and replayed it several times. "I suspect we're hearing an attempt to disguise his voice. I can't be sure. Any idea who it is, or what he's talking about?"

Kimberlee shrugged. "As far as I know, I'm not keeping anything that isn't mine."

Brett topped off his cup of coffee and turned. "That's not exactly true, honey. You and Jack are going to inherit Fern Lake Lodge. Ted Herman claims it *belongs* to him. But, I can't believe he's so stupid as to leave a verbal threat on your phone. The police have voice identification technology. He knows he'd be the first person we'd suspect."

"Have you talked to Jack? Has he received any threats?" Kimberlee slid pencils and a tablet around the counter.

Dorian shook her head and pulled her cell phone from her pocket. "I'll call and see if he's had any trouble at the lodge. In the meantime, we'll treat this phone message as a legitimate threat. Can I take the cassette from your phone? We'll keep it on file, in case anything else comes of it."

"Go ahead. I have a spare cassette in the desk." Kimberlee opened the top of the message machine and handed the cassette to Dorian. "Hopefully, just someone's idea of a prank. Do you have time for coffee? There are several donuts left from yesterday."

Brett set his empty cup in the tray and pulled his keys from his pocket. "Listen, hon, everything looks okay around the store. Since Dorian's here, if you don't mind, I'm going to shove off. I'm right in the middle of a sting operation on my *baddie*."

"Sure. Thanks for coming down. I'll see you later."

Brett kissed her forehead and left the store.

"Smithers," Dorian said. "Why don't you take the car back to headquarters? Virgil is on a nearby call. I'll have him pick me up in a while." The officer nodded and started for the door.

Kimberlee called. "Oh, Smithers. There's a donut with your name on it. Do you want one for the road?"

The officer turned. "Sure thing. Thanks." He picked up the chocolate glazed donut, took a bite, and grinned. "Always glad to help clean up a mess. See you back at the station."

Dorian poured a cup of coffee, selected the last donut and sat at a little table near the dessert bar. "Do you want half of this? I'll share."

"No thanks. My stomach is upset. I'll make some tea."

"I have something to tell you." Dorian beamed. "It should cheer you up."

"Some good news would be welcome about now."

"Captain Ehrhardt and his wife were scheduled to go to an International Law Enforcement Conference in Munich, Germany next week. Unfortunately, his hernia is acting up again, and his doctor wants to schedule surgery right away, so they're sending me in his place. The department already paid for the airline tickets and hotel for him and his wife. If I'm going all the way to Germany, I'd like to do a little sightseeing, but it wouldn't be much fun to go alone. Do you want to go with me? We could extend the trip a few days afterward, and see the sights. What do you say?"

"*Gee.* I don't know." Kimberlee's smile lit up her face. "What would it cost? I'd have to make arrangements with Mrs. Wilson to work full-time at the bookstore, and Brett would have to…"

Her mind raced through everything involved in a last minute trip out of the country. What should she pack? Was her passport current? Could Brett handle Amanda alone? Would Mrs. Wilson consider working extra hours? What about their new commitment to Jack and the lodge? Would it be selfish to take money from their savings account for a vacation?

Oh! Oh! Her thoughts switched gears to the clues to the treasure in Dewey's diary. If Hans was really the driver of the armored car mentioned in the documentary... Munich wasn't far from Austria. Maybe they could go to Hopfgarten and investigate. Or, was it just her imagination that linked Hans's message with the PBS documentary? On the other hand... Kimberlee's heart fluttered. "How long would I be on my own?"

"I'm in class for two days. Is that a game changer?"

Two days on my own. I could rent a car and... "Not necessarily. I'd love to go...if I can work out the details, and if Brett thinks we can afford it."

"Well, great. I'm so excited! What would you do while I'm in class?"

"*Umm.*" Kimberlee's cheeks warmed. "I'll drive around and see the sights. From the pictures I've seen, the towns and churches are all fabulous. I might look up that little town I read about in Dewey's journal. Oh, Dorian, what fun. I can't wait. When do we leave?"

"In four days. Is that too soon? I'll call the airline and make sure I can change the names on Captain Ehrhardt's tickets. If, not, I'll have to go as Captain Ehrhardt." She giggled. "And, you'll have to go as my wife."

Kimberlee glanced at the empty slot in the answering machine where the cassette had been. It reminded her of a gaping mouth waiting to gobble up another cassette. *What an ominous thought.*

Dorian's invitation felt like the opportunity of a lifetime. Or was it just an excuse to avoid being *gobbled up* by an inevitable court fight with Ted over Mrs. Herman's will?

Chapter Fifteen

Putting up with stupid persons is a curse! - Black Cat

Four days later, Dorian and Kimberlee were ready to depart. Within the hour, they would drive to the San Francisco airport and board the plane for Germany. Black Cat and Angel breakfasted together in the kitchen shortly after the sun came up. While Angel took her constitutional walk through the rose garden, Black Cat went to Amanda's room to keep her company while Kimberlee finished packing.

Kimberlee fussed in the kitchen and Brett fussed over Kimberlee, making sure she tied up all the loose ends for her trip. "Have you got everything, hon? Enough money? Your credit card? Are you taking comfortable shoes? What about a raincoat? Who knows what kind of weather you'll run into?"

"I've got everything under control. Don't worry."

Brett followed her around the kitchen like a puppy, while she repeatedly opened the freezer and the refrigerator doors, checking the provisions she was leaving for Brett and Amanda. "Now, I've put several casseroles in the freezer, and there's plenty of milk and eggs, and enough lunchmeat for sandwiches." Kimberlee wrung her hands. "Oh, dear, are you sure you and Amanda will be okay? What about her lunches? She likes the crust cut off her sandwiches. Maybe I shouldn't go."

Brett snickered. "Of course you should go. When will you

get another chance for a practically fully paid vacation? Germany is beautiful this time of year. Did you pack extra batteries for your camera? I want to see lots of pictures."

Kimberlee stopped pacing and moved things around on the counter. "Have you seen my gold bracelet? The one my aunt gave me when I graduated from college? I haven't seen it for a while. Oh, dear. I wanted to take that with me to Germany."

"When did you last wear it?"

Kimberlee shrugged. "I can't remember. Things have been so hectic the last few days. Where's Amanda? I hope she understands about the trip. I don't want her to think I'm abandoning her."

"She's in her room with Black Cat. She knows you and Dorian will be gone for a while. I talked to her last night. She's fine. Now, have you checked your list? What about your passport. Did you put it somewhere you reach it easily? You'll need it when you get to Germany."

"My passport? Oh, you're right. I meant to pack it yesterday and I forgot. Now, where did I put it?" She hurried to the dining room bureau, yanked open the drawer and rifled through the papers. "It should be right here. I'm sure that's where I last…" She turned. "It's not here." Her cheeks chilled. "Where could it be? I can't get on the plane without it." Tears pricked her eyes.

"Now, calm down and think. When did you last see it?" Brett was always the sensible one.

"I think… Let's see. I think I took it with me last spring when we went to Texas. That's the last time I remember… With Grandmother's ranch so near Mexico, I thought I might need it if we decided to go across the border."

"So, did you put it back in the bureau when we got home?" Brett pawed through the papers, to no avail.

She shrugged. "I can't remember. I thought I did. Well, that settles it. I'm not going." Kimberlee crossed her arms and flopped onto the sofa, tears spilling down her cheeks. "Dorian is going to *kill* me." She glanced at the clock over the fireplace. "She'll be here any minute. What am I going to tell her? They've already paid for the tickets." She threw herself on the sofa and sobbed. "She'll ne…never forgive…me."

Hearing the sobs, Black Cat wandered into the living room and jumped onto the sofa. *What's wrong? Can I help?* He licked Kimberlee's cheek. She threw her arm around his middle and squeezed him to her bosom. "I don't suppose you've seen my passport," she whispered into his long black fur, as if asking a cat would solve her problem.

Ah! The little blue book with her ugly picture inside? I think…I saw it…. Yes. I'm sure I saw it. How could he get Kimberlee to look in Amanda's room where he saw her playing with the little book? He wiggled away from Kimberlee, pawed at Brett's leg and hurried toward the hall.

Brett sat on the sofa beside Kimberlee and patted her shoulder. "Crying isn't going to help. Get up and help me look for it. You take the living room and kitchen, and I'll go into the bedrooms. It must be around here somewhere." Black Cat hurried back to Brett and pawed his leg again.

"What is it, Black Cat? Do you want to go out? I don't have time now…" He started toward his bedroom. Black Cat ran in front of him and stopped. Brett stumbled. "What? Get out of the way. I'm in a hurry."

The cat raced into Amanda's room and jumped on her bed. *Meow! Meow! Where did you put the book? Your mom needs the little book. Look in here, Brett! Rowww. Rowww!*

Brett popped his head through Amanda's door. "Amanda! What are you doing to that cat? He sounds like you're killing him." He stepped into the bedroom.

Black Cat pawed at the bookshelf, then ran to the toy box and pawed at the box, then to the closet door. *Inferior human! How can I make you understand? Putting up with stupid persons is a curse. For Pete's sake, look in here, Brett.*

Brett stood in the doorway and stared. "What…" A smile brightened his face. "Wait. Are you trying to tell me something?"

Had he finally remembered the day, not so long ago, when he searched this same room, looking for a clue to solve a murder? Had he remembered how Black Cat showed him an important clue that day? Brett stooped and took Amanda's arm. "Have you seen Mama's little blue book?" He made a small rectangle with his fingers, about the size of the book and then started pulling books off her shelf. He turned and lifted the lid to the toy box.

"*Umm*... Book?" Amanda put her hands over her eyes. "I was playing school with my dolls…and…it was the right size…"

Brett turned. "You saw it? It's very important that we find Mama's little book. Do you know where it is? Mama really needs it right now. Can you think?" He slid open the closet door and shuffled through the toys on the floor.

Black Cat pawed at a large round Fisher Price Circus© container. "*Meow!*"

Brett grabbed the container and snapped off the lid. Inside, among the giraffes, seals, lion, and horse, he spotted the passport. "*Ah ha!* We found it. Kimberlee, come quick!"

She came running. "You found it? Oh, thank goodness. Where did you find it?"

Amanda flopped onto the bed and buried her head under her pillow. "I was playing school…"

Kimberlee sat beside her. "It's okay, sweetheart. The important thing is we found it in time. But you mustn't take Mama's things without asking. Now give me a kiss. Auntie Dorian will be here any minute. We might have time to read a story together before she comes. Sit up now." Kimberlee curled up with Amanda, her back against the headboard.

Black Cat licked the front of his furry white bib. *It takes time to train a human, but Brett is coming along nicely. Another couple years and...*

Bing... Bong...

Black Cat leaped off the bed and raced to the front door. *I'll go. It must be Dorian. Come on, Kimberlee. Chop. Chop.*

Brett followed Black Cat across the living room. He opened the door, bowed, and swung out his arm like a court jester and announced, "Come right in, mi' lady." He glanced up...into Ted Herman's face.

Ted's mouth crunched into a smirk. "I'm not *your lady*, but I'll come in, anyway. I'm looking for Kimberlee."

Brett's mouth dropped open. "Ted? She's...she's just about to leave." He glanced at his wristwatch and then down the driveway. "What do you want?"

"Your wife and I need to talk. We need to come to an understanding about *my* lodge. Is she here?"

Kimberlee backed into the living room, rolling two suitcases behind her. She called over her shoulder. "I'm ready, Dorian. Give me a minute. I want to go back for a scarf. *Hon*? Will you take these to the..." She turned. Her cheeks paled when her gaze met Ted's, standing inside the front door. "What...what are you doing here?"

"I want to talk to you about Beverly's will. Apparently, under some delusion, she thought she could leave the lodge to you and Jack."

Amanda followed her mother into the living room. Ted started as his gaze moved across the room and came to rest on the child. His mouth fell open. "My God! She looks just like you when you were a baby." His hand trembled as he reached out toward Amanda, his gaze flitting from Amanda to Kimberlee and back again. "I can't..."

Had he remembered the days he carried Kimberlee on his shoulders, proudly showed her to all the guests, tromped through the swamp searching for a frog because she asked for one? Had he remembered the parades, the picnics, the ball games he'd shared with Kimberlee and her parents before her father's death? Ted's face quivered as though he might burst into tears. He ran his hand over his mouth. "I can't do this. I have to go."

He flung open the door and nearly bumped into Dorian as she reached for the doorknob. "Excuse me." He rushed past her, jumped into his red SUV, and tore down the driveway.

"What's up with him?" Dorian looked back over her shoulder and stepped inside. She checked her watch. "You about ready? We've got a long drive to the airport."

Brett and Kimberlee exchanged glances and shrugged. Kimberlee stooped to hug Amanda. "Now, you be a good girl, and take care of the kitties." She kissed Amanda's forehead. Amanda nodded and picked up Black Cat, struggling to hold the squirming cat, almost too heavy for her to handle.

The little procession trailed down the sidewalk to Dorian's car. Brett brought up the rear, rolling Kimberlee's suitcases. He opened her door and leaned down to kiss her good-bye once she was in the passenger seat. "Don't worry about a thing. We'll be fine. Is your passport where you can easily find it now?"

She giggled and patted her purse. "Safe and sound."

Dorian slid into the driver's seat and tooted the horn. "Okay? Guess we're off, like a ruptured duck! Germany, here we come." She turned to Kimberlee with a grin.

"What does that mean? 'Off, like a ruptured duck,'" Kimberlee said.

"It's a WWII reference. The men discharged from the military were given a pin shaped like a triangular with an eagle and a gold wreath in the center. They wore it on their uniform, above their right breast pocket. Since they were allowed to wear their uniforms for up to thirty days after discharge, the pin indicated to the military police they weren't AWOL, but honorably discharged."

"That's nice, but I still don't understand what that has to do with a 'ruptured duck,'" Kimberlee said.

Brett leaned down. "Because the boys thought the eagle looked more like a duck than an eagle, so they called it a 'ruptured duck.' Since the pin signified they were going home, the nickname stuck. They were off like a ruptured duck."

Kimberlee laughed. "Oh, I get it. Then I guess we're a couple of ruptured ducks. Bye, Amanda."

Brett closed Kimberlee's door. Kimberlee waved and blew kisses as Dorian started the car and drove off. As they turned the corner, Black Cat jumped from Amanda's arms and hurried over to lie under a rose bush beside Angel. "Well, she's off. I'll bet they have a good time."

"I expect Kimberlee will find more than she bargained for in Hopfgarten."

Black Cat's eyes opened wide. "Why do you say that?"

"Let's just say… I had a funny feeling that first day in the bookstore when I spotted Dewey's book. I wanted her to look at it, because it's important, but it scared me a little bit, too. I don't know why I felt that way, but I did. I hope she doesn't rue the day she laid eyes on that book…"

"That's ridiculous. I won't listen to such nonsense." Black Cat jumped up and bounded back to the house.

Chapter Sixteen

I wish I could take you with me, but I can't. - Kimberlee

Eleven hours after boarding the plane in San Francisco, but a day later on the calendar, Kimberlee and Dorian arrived in Munich, Germany. They caught the shuttle to the conference hotel where they collapsed on feather beds and slept until 6:00 o'clock the following morning. Dorian's conference was to start at 8:30 A.M.

Dorian plugged her hairdryer into the 220 adapter. "Glad you reminded me to bring this thing. What would I do if I couldn't dry my hair?" The hair dryer hummed as her long blonde hair blew around her face. "Are you sure you want to take off alone today? You could stay in town and visit the sites here in Munich. At least we could have dinner together tonight."

Kimberlee stood in front of the mirror applying lipstick. She smacked her lips and dropped the lipstick tube back into her makeup case. "I think this is exactly what I need. Some time alone to make a plan for how Brett and I can balance helping Jack run the lodge, and still keep up our other responsibilities. I'm actually looking forward to being alone. I haven't spent a day by myself since our wedding day, though I do miss Amanda. I'll be fine."

Dorian leaned over to dry the back of her hair. "If you say so... Try to be back before dark tomorrow and don't forget to call me tonight. So, what are your plans?"

"There's a glass-blowing factory in Munich that makes beautiful hand-blown Christmas tree ornaments and vases and things. It only makes sense to visit the factory while I'm here. I want to set up a distributorship and sell some of their products in the bookstore."

"That's a great idea." Dorian frowned. "Wait. Why don't we go to the factory together after I've finished my conference?" She sighed. "Save some of the wonderful stuff for me, okay? Then we can drive on into Austria."

"All right. I'll take the map and see where the road leads. Take lots of notes." Kimberlee picked up her small overnight bag and waved good-bye.

After consulting an area map, and deciding on a particular route, she drove through Munich and took the freeway ramp, heading for Salzburg. Without a particular timetable, she planned to stop any place she found interesting along the way.

Her thoughts returned to last night, when she and Dorian discussed their plans for the week. When Dorian completed her conference, they would drive together to Austria, visit Hopfgarten, and try to locate Hans Kreuger's relatives. They were too close to the location mentioned in Dewey's diary, not to visit Hopfgarten and investigate. One way or another, they wanted to learn more about the mystery in the diary. Was it a fable or a treasure still waiting to be found?

Kimberlee gripped the steering wheel. Dots of perspiration popped out on her forehead as she kept a careful eye on the autobahn traffic. Driving was intense, with cars zooming past at 100-miles-an hour in the fast lane. Even in *the slow lane*, she had to keep up with traffic, averaging 70 mph or more. How did people ever get used to driving at such speeds? She played one of her soft music cassettes to calm her anxiety.

An army vehicle zoomed past her car, reminding her of their first impressions of Germany at the Munich airport the day before. Departing the plane, they had walked across the pavement toward the customs building, looking forward to getting their passports stamped with a foreign stamp.

They no sooner entered the building when they came face to face with soldiers carrying machine guns, strolling among the waiting passengers. Beyond the front windows, military tanks rolled through the parking lot.

Dorian grabbed Kimberlee's arm. "Whatever you do," she whispered, "don't make eye contact with those armed guards. Something's going on, and I don't want to get in the middle of it."

Kimberlee caught the attention of a porter pushing a stack of suitcases. "Excuse me? What is happening? Is there some trouble? Do you speak English?"

The porter grinned and nodded. "Ein biten. (*Just a little.*) English not too much."

"Why are the soldiers patrolling the airport?" Kimberlee glanced at the other passengers hurrying past, none of whom seemed particularly perturbed by the sight of men armed with rifles roaming through the terminal.

"Is for guard…for terrorist." The porter waved his hand toward the tarmac. "Is Al- Qaeda. Always watch. Excuse, please." He hurried on.

Dorian took Kimberlee's arm and walked straight ahead. "They need guns and tanks to protect the airport? I don't like it. Keep walking. Let's get our rental car and get out of here as quick as we can."

Kimberlee remembered how nervous the extensive airport security made Dorian, something only beginning to happen in the U.S. Were the soldiers expecting a terrorist attack in the airport? How could such things happen? The whole world had gone mad. Better safe than sorry.

She forced the sights at the airport out of her mind and put her full attention on driving at a speed that made her uncomfortable, keeping an eye on the Mercedes and BMWs that passed as though her car was standing still.

Around noon, Kimberlee pulled off the freeway into a small town. Window boxes filled with golden geraniums in full bloom decorated the windows in the picturesque village houses. A horse-drawn cart pulled in front of her at a stop sign. She couldn't keep from smiling. She rolled down her window and listened to the clip-clop of the horse's hooves on the cobblestone street. Several blocks later, she stopped at a petrol station. An attendant rushed from the building and leaned toward her car window. "Willkamen. Kann ick di hulpen?" (*Welcome. Can I help you?*)

Kimberlee lifted her purse and gestured toward the gas pump. "Petrol?" She held up two Euro bills. *How much does it cost to fill the tank?*

The attendant nodded, disengaged the nozzle from the pump, and plugged it into the gas tank. How refreshing? When had an attendant ever pumped her gas in California? Another young man appeared by the car window with a rag and squirt bottle. He whistled as he attacked the bugs on her windshield.

An air-raid siren shrieked, cutting into the peaceful surroundings. Kimberlee cringed. *Now, what's happening?* Nothing appeared amiss. There were no armed guards here to protect the village. Her heart pounded as she glanced anxiously around. Seeing Kimberlee's concern, the young man hurried over. "Don't worry, Fraulein. It is nothing to fear. The siren is tested every day at noon."

The siren shrieked for about thirty seconds and then stopped, its shrill sound still echoed in her head. Again, the siren illustrated the country's heightened preparedness against disaster or attack. After the recent events in the news, it made sense to be vigilant in airports and public places. She took deep breaths to calm her nerves as she got out of her car, needing to stretch her legs and visit the washroom.

Alongside the building, she paused to stroke a little black cat with a bulging belly, digging through a garbage can. Definitely *mitt kitten*, she appeared soon to give birth. With her long black fur and white stocking feet, she looked so much like Black Cat, that Kimberlee could imagine the little cat to be one of his cousins from across the sea.

Kimberlee returned to her car and retrieved a small bag containing a strip of beef jerky, broke it up in small bites and tossed it to the cat. "There you go, kitty. Good luck with your new family. Looks like you're going to need it." Some problems were universal. Germany, as well as the U.S.A, neglected to curb the birth of unwanted pets, and too many homeless cats wandered the streets. Kimberlee stroked the little cat's soft black fur. "I wish I could take you with me, but I can't." She gestured to the young station attendant. "Is this your cat?"

"Nee. (*no*) Is stray." He set the spray bottle and rag beside the gas pump.

"Who feeds her? She looks hungry." Kimberlee ran her hand over the kitty's head.

The young man shrugged and blushed.

"Please, wait a minute." Kimberlee returned to her car and retrieved her purse. She handed the attendant the Euros for the gasoline. "Is that enough for the gas?"

He nodded.

"Will you do something for me?" She pulled a U.S.A. twenty-dollar bill from her wallet. "Will you buy some cat food and see that she's fed? She's going to have kittens soon. Is this enough to take care of her?"

The young man took the bill and nodded. "I will take care. She is good cat. Keeps away rats."

After a quick visit to the washroom, Kimberlee reluctantly gave the cat a final pat before getting into her car. Pulling onto the street, she glanced in the rearview mirror. The little black cat ran behind her car as if she knew someone had compassion for her. It took all of Kimberlee's will power not to stop the car, grab the little cat and toss her into the back seat, as she had done with Black Cat the first summer she came to Fern Lake.

As Kimberlee passed through the countryside, the terrain varied. The road rose and fell through hills and valleys. Around every corner, another picture-postcard vista appeared. With no particular agenda, Kimberlee stopped often to take a photograph.

She stopped the car in a green meadow, where the only sound was the breeze shaking the leaves on the shrubs alongside the road. The tinkling of brass bells hanging from the collars of a flock of sheep and black and white cows grazing nearby stirred her captivated heart.

Around another corner, the gentle terrain rose up through the pasture to a hillside shaded by a fine mist. The sound of tinkling bells suggested more animals hidden among the distant trees.

Fewer vineyards dotted the hillside as Kimberlee approached Salzburg; the town where Mozart lived, played his harpsichord, and wrote melodies. Several hundred years later, his name still a household word, millions of people continued to enjoy his music.

She reached the center of Salzburg, parked along a cobbled street, and started down the sidewalk past ancient ivy-laden buildings and colorful courtyards. Church spires peeked out from behind red tile rooftops. She paused to read the dates carved on a church wall—1200-1400. How incredible.

Faint music drew her toward the town square where a street musician stood on the steps of an ancient church, playing Ave Maria on his violin. While tourists clustered nearer, pigeons softly cooed and flew from rooftop to rooftop. How often did they pause and listen? Perhaps a daily occurrence, they appeared mesmerized by the haunting melody.

Kimberlee drew nearer. The lingering notes echoed off the surrounding ancient buildings and filled the courtyard with music such as one might imagine hearing in Heaven. Her thoughts drifted back to another time. She imagined the cobbled streets filled with horse-drawn carriages. Perhaps one held a princess and her ladies-in-waiting. Over there, a knight in shining armor on his trusty steed, ready to joust with a dragon. A court jester danced to amuse the children.

As the musician drew his bow across the strings, the final note hung in the air and then faded into silence. He lowered his hand. Too moved even to applaud, the audience stood motionless. Someone coughed and broke the spell. Applause and cheers broke out. Generous visitors tossed money into the violin case at the musician's feet, and then moved away, eager to experience more of the wonder that Salzburg could offer.

Kimberlee opened her purse and dropped a few euros into his case. "Absolutely lovely. Thank you so much. I can't tell you how much I enjoyed your music."

She ran to catch a tram climbing up a hill to a medieval castle overlooking the city; a cold and barren place with multiple staircases reaching in all directions. Inside the castle, armor, ancient guns, javelins, chains and torture devices covered the stone walls, once instruments of torture, now intended to amuse the tourists. Stepping through a doorway onto a balcony, she looked over the entire city and valley. Tiny buildings, streets, and church spires far below reminded her of a picture from Amanda's storybook. Rainy mists on the distant mountains beckoned hikers upward into the cold crisp air. To the left were rivers, towers, cathedrals, graveyards, and church spires. To the right, horse-drawn carriages filled the cobblestone streets. Street vendors hawked their wares beneath colorful awnings and the sidewalks were shared by cafes, musicians, and artists. She raised her camera to snap a picture, knowing it could never do justice to the real experience or convey to the viewer, the feelings generated by the sight of so much beauty. After wandering through the castle for an hour and taking dozens of pictures, she boarded the tram and returned to the city.

On a particular sidewalk, she came upon a street artist, sitting on a short stool, his backpack and watercolor paint palette by his side. He leaned into his easel and applied the finishing touches to a painting of a musician on the steps of the ancient church she recently visited. Could it be the musician she heard earlier that morning? Could the tiny red blob in the midst of the adoring tourists be her red sweater? Unable to resist the appeal of the drawing and the memory of the exquisite performance, she purchased the painting. She would frame it and hang it in her bedroom, a reminder of the poignant melody that had stirred her heart.

What a magical city. After a hearty meal and very strong coffee in a sidewalk café, Kimberlee returned to her car. On the outskirts of town she looked for a *pension* where she could spend the night. She couldn't wait to call Brett and tell him about all the things she experienced today. How she missed him and wished he could share her wonderful day.

Chapter Seventeen

What a mess. Looks like there was a cat fight in here. - Black Cat

The morning sun lit up Brett's bedroom. Exhausted from a poor night's sleep, he had buried his head under the pillow. Despite knowing her mother would return in a few days, Amanda cried herself to sleep when Kimberlee wasn't there to tuck her into bed. Even Black Cat couldn't comfort her. Troubled by bad dreams, she awakened several times in the night.

Black Cat lifted his head when the telephone jarred him awake. He jumped off Amanda's bed and raced into Brett's room. *Where's Angel?*

Brett rubbed his eyes, glanced at the bedroom clock and reached for the phone. "Hello?" He cleared his throat. "Hello? Oh, hi Jack, what's up? The bookstore? Oh, good grief! You've called the police, right? I'll be right down."

Brett slammed down the phone and threw back the covers. He stifled a yawn as he pulled on his pants and called down the hall. "Amanda, sweetheart. Come on now. You have to wake up. Daddy Brett has to… Oh, shoot! I'll have to get her dressed." He glanced at this watch. 5:45 A.M. Way too early. "What am I going to do with her at this hour?"

Amanda rubbed her eyes and whined as Brett pulled the covers off her. Her face brightened when Angel wandered into the bedroom. *"What's all the commotion? The sun's barely up. Is something wrong?"* Angel yawned, stretched out her legs, and arched her back. *Morning, sleepy-head.*

Black Cat jumped onto Amanda's bed. *Jack called. Sounds like trouble at Kimberlee's store. Brett's going down. Do you want to come with us? There might be police cars or fire trucks.*

Angel hopped off the bed and headed for the kitchen. *Now that I'm awake, I might as well go with you. Can we eat something before we go? I'm hungry.*

Black Cat followed her to the kitchen. *How can you think about food at a time like this? Who knows what we might be missing?* Angel crouched in front of her bowl. At least Brett remembered to keep it full. Usually Kimberlee's job, there were always snacks whenever the cats felt hungry. Angel munched on a Kitty Crunchie while Black Cat danced by the cat door. "I'm going to leave if you don't hurry up."

She stretched. "Go ahead and leave then. Now that I've eaten, I think I'll go back to sleep. You can tell me all about it when you get back."

"Angel! You are so frustrating." Black Cat raced through the cat door and ran the five blocks, past Rajinder's deli. *That female drives me crazy.* He turned the corner and skidded to a stop in front of the bookstore.

Jack and Chance were on the sidewalk, looking through the broken front window. "Hey, Black Cat. Where's Brett?" Jack knelt to stroke Black Cat's head.

He's coming. He's dealing with a sleepy six-year-old.

All three Fern Lake detectives responded to Jack's call. Any break-and-entry before six o'clock in the morning was enough incentive to roll out the entire police force. Straight off Mrs. Herman's questionable death, adrenalin still ran high in the police community, and they almost welcomed the report of a burglary to fill the boring night and early morning hours.

Black Cat walked beneath the yellow crime ribbon stretched across the front window, stepped over the broken glass littering the sidewalk and followed a policeman through the front door. *What a mess. Looks like a catfight in here.*

Shortly, Brett's SUV pulled up in front with a sleepy Amanda. "Had to bring her," Brett said to Jack. He lifted the child from the back seat and carried her as he followed Jack into the store. "Good grief." He stopped and stared. "Looks like there's been a catfight in here."

That's exactly what I thought. Black Cat's whiskers twitched as he cruised around Brett's ankles.

Books lay scattered across the floor. Broken pots, plants, and dirt covered the little tables where on the previous afternoon happy customers enjoyed coffee and strawberry scones buried in whipped cream. A pile of mail lay beneath broken glass in front of the mail slot at the front door.

"Watch where you step, sweetheart." Brett set Amanda in one of the sofa chairs. "You stay here until we get the glass swept up, okay? I'll get you a book to read." He picked up the mail from the floor, shook off the glass shards, tossed the junk mail and circulars into the wastebasket, and paused at an envelope hand-addressed to the bookstore. Post office markings stamped across the envelope indicated a delay in delivery due to mishandling at the post office. Brett tossed the letter onto the counter.

Amanda sat curled up in the corner of the chair. "Black Cat." She reached out to the cat. He hopped onto the chair, circled, and flopped into her lap. *Hey. Amanda. Pretty exciting, huh?* Amanda wrapped her arms around his middle and pulled him to her chest. She stroked his back until her head nodded and within a few minutes, her eyes were closed.

Brett strode from one side of the store to the other, surveying the damage. Broken handcrafted items lay among books strewn on the floor. For some reason, the cash register didn't appear to be harmed. Not that the thief would have gotten anything, since the evening clerk always placed the day's receipts into a small wall safe every night. It looked like a case of pure vandalism.

Brett turned to face Jack. "How did you happen to be here so early?"

"Chance and I were out walking and we passed the bookstore. I called you and the police as soon as I saw the broken window." He glanced at a message spray-painted on the mirror behind the counter. *Bad things happen to good people.* Jack nodded toward the mirror, and then to the policeman writing his report. "Did ya see that? What do ya think that means?"

The police officer looked up. "I suspect it means what it says." His pen tapped his notebook. "Could be a veiled threat. Any idea what's behind this, Mr. Clarke?"

Brett's feet shuffled through the dirt from the broken plants. "It sounds somewhat like the message left on Kimberlee's phone the other day. A warning or a threat, but we're not sure."

Jack interrupted. "We have a pretty good idea who did it. It's that Ted Herman, you can bet yer bottom dollar. He thinks if he gives us enough grief, we'll let him have the lodge."

The officer's pen hung over the notebook. "I don't understand. What does Ted Herman have to do with this or the lodge?" He pushed back his cap and scratched his head.

"Mrs. Herman left the lodge to Jack and my wife in her will," Brett said. "Her husband, who just hit town, thinks the lodge should be his. He's contesting the will."

"I see. But, both of these threats were left at the bookstore, not the lodge, so I'm not sure how that fits with your theory. Have there been any problems at the lodge?"

Jack shook his head "Not yet, but maybe I'll be next."

The officer made another note. "I'll pass all this along to Detective Yates. He may have more questions for you."

Brett reached for the broom beside the counter. "Can we start cleaning up?"

"Go ahead, but stick with the stuff on the floor," the officer said.

"We got pictures, and the fingerprint guy should be done pretty quickly. We'll need Jack, you, your wife and your employees to come down to the station and give us prints for elimination purposes. Sometime later today would be good."

"I'll notify the staff. Jack and I can come, but Kimberlee is in Germany. She won't be home for another week."

"Then we'll have to work with what we've got. There have been several break-ins around town. They might be connected, but if your suspicions are right, it sounds more personal."

"Did the other break-ins leave a written message like this?" Brett asked.

"I haven't worked the other cases. You'd have to talk to Detective Yates about that."

Brett ran his hands through his hair and turned to Jack. "I need to inventory the damaged items for insurance. Maybe you can help me clean up a little?" He glanced at the clock over the counter. "I should call Mrs. Wilson and let her know what happened. I doubt we can open today, but she could come in and help clean up."

Jack took the broom from Brett and swept the broken glass beneath the front window into a dustpan. "You gonna tell Kimberlee about all this?"

"Not on your life. She just got to Germany. If she knew what happened, she'd be on the next plane home." He thumbed through the telephone book, found the number for a local glass repair, and dialed the phone. At the speaker's direction, he left a message. "Hello? This is Brett Clarke, at the Book Nook on Main Street. Our front window was smashed last night. Could you send someone this morning to replace it? It's about eight foot by four... Give me a call as soon as possible. Thanks." He left his phone number and returned to the task of cleaning up.

Black Cat kept Amanda distracted while Brett called Mrs. Wilson and helped Jack clean up the broken art objects. So many lovely things.

The artists would receive full compensation from the insurance, but what a hateful thing—destroying something beautiful for no good reason. Human failings. It always gave him pleasure to know cats were above such behavior. And yet, humans claimed to be the superior race? *What a joke.*

Jack dumped a dustpan full of broken glass into the large waste barrel. "That's about all of it. So, I've been thinking. If it was Ted, why do somthin' like this?"

"I can't imagine. What would he gain by threats and destroying property? You and Kimberlee aren't going to give up the lodge because of a broken window or a threat on the answering machine. I don't get it. Not that I wish trouble on you, but why single out Kimberlee's store? You inherit as much as she does. It doesn't make sense."

Brett checked his watch and then looked toward Amanda, awake again, and reading a storybook to Black Cat. "Listen. I need to get Amanda home and ready for school."

"Give me yer house key," Jack said. "I've got this. You stay here and deal with the store. I'll take her home and get her off ta school." He snapped his fingers. "Come on, Chance." The golden Lab rose from the corner where she'd been napping and ambled across the room.

"Are you sure? I didn't have time to get her stuff together this morning. She'll need her lunch made and her teeth brushed and she only ate a piece of toast before we left."

"I've got this." Jack checked the wall clock. "There's almost an hour before the bus comes. Back in the day when Kimberlee was a toddler, I usta get her ready for daycare. Some mornings her mom would call me early and…" He gazed through the broken window with a faraway look, as though remembering the days he took care of the child he loved. He glanced back at Brett. "Don't worry, okay?"

"You're a saint. Kimberlee would kill me if she knew I'd shifted my responsibility onto you…but someone's got to wait here for the window guy, and Mrs. Wilson will be here soon. We'll need to take an inventory and contact the insurance company and—"

"I'll get Amanda off to school and meet her bus this afternoon. You do what you gotta do here. We'll see you later." Jack walked over to the sofa. "Let's go, punkin.' Jack's gonna make you some pancakes and get you ready for school, okay?" He leaned down, picked her up and put her on his back. "This is how I usta carry yer mom. You comin', Black Cat, or are you gonna stay with Brett?"

Coming. Black Cat hopped off the chair and followed Jack and Amanda to the front door. He paused to look back. Brett was trying so hard to take care of Amanda and handle everything for Kimberlee. There he stood beside the cash register, staring into the waste container filled with plants, ceramics and broken glass—an attack on his wife's dream. Black Cat studied Brett's face. What was going through his mind? Meet the glass man, complete an inventory, contact the insurance company, and visit the police department for fingerprints. He looked sad and determined, and at the same time, angry. Did Ted Herman do this?

A shiver wrinkled the fur on Black Cat's back as he raced down the sidewalk behind Jack and Amanda. He couldn't wait to share the exciting happenings with Angel.

Chapter Eighteen

Every residence in Germany appeared to be designed by the same architect, or so it seemed as Kimberlee drove through the Germany countryside. The houses were quite unlike any in the USA, designed by a thousand different builders. The typical German house was often two stories with a balcony across the front, bordered by wooden flower boxes overflowing with orange and yellow geraniums. If only one story tall, the colorful flower boxes were under the front windows. Often, the larger houses had a barn attached at one end to house cows or sheep.

The multitude of flower boxes added a splash of color to contrast with white stucco walls. Though the cookie-cutter houses looked alike, they varied in size, depending on the wealth or size of the family. Often, an entrepreneurial family with an extra bedroom or two, or perhaps empty-nesters, posted a notice—*pension*—on the front fence, advertising willingness to accommodate tourists for the night and include a light breakfast, all for a fair price.

On the outskirts of Salzburg, Kimberlee stopped at an endearing *pension*—a charming stucco, two-story building. She followed the path to the front door and rang the bell. A stout, older woman answered. "Wilkomen. Kumm in. (*Welcome. Come in*).

Kimberlee held up her overnight case. "Do you have a room? Do you speak English?"

The woman smiled. "Ya. I hef nice room. This way, please." She led Kimberlee to a room next to the garden filled with pink and yellow tulips and tall gladiolas. The room contained plain, solid, wood furniture without elaborate carvings or decoration. A thick feather comforter and feather pillows lay atop the double bed. A vase of fresh flowers adorned the nightstand, as though Kimberlee had been expected. French doors led to the garden. "Is good?" The woman's friendly smile warmed her face.

"Yes, it's lovely." Kimberlee opened her purse. "How many Euros?" She pulled out several bills.

The hostess took two bills from her hand. "Is enough. Breakfast is 7:00 A.M. Is good?"

"Thank you. That will be fine." Kimberlee set her overnight case on the floor and took off her jacket. She opened the French doors, stepped into the garden, and was immediately enveloped by the scent of flowers. A green, carved wooden bench sat beside a fish pond where, upon her approach, red and black koi fish bobbed to the surface. How she wished Brett could see this. Wouldn't it have been better to wait and share this beautiful experience with a loved one? Her first day alone in this beautiful country already presented so many wondrous sites. Tears pricked her eyes. Surely, she and Brett would have to return together someday.

Poor Dorian. Coming all the way to beautiful Germany and stuck for two days in a stuffy conference room, listening to boring lectures. *And here I am visiting castles and fairytale towns.* Dorian would be so jealous when she heard about all the lovely sites in Salzburg. Kimberlee thought that she should write down her feelings and experiences.

She sat on the bench and watched the koi glide back and forth across the pond, stopping momentarily to nibble at a mossy rock and move on, occasionally pausing to bask in a ray of sunshine. As she watched the fish move about, her thoughts drifted. Would she have experienced the sights and sounds of the day the same way if Brett or

Dorian had been with her?

The spacious, green, lush meadows, the sense of *oneness* created by the similarity of the houses, the tinkle of the cows' bells in similar pastures and the serene agelessness of the castles high atop the hillsides. The way the church bells rang every hour. She sighed. How the peaceful countryside affected her. The violinist's song had touched her heart. The fairytale town transported her to another time and place. In truth, the day's events left her feeling as though she had stepped away from earth and into another dimension. Her soul felt refreshed and her faith reaffirmed. She felt she had gained the strength to face the challenges that awaited her upon her return to Fern Lake.

A sudden thought. Spending the day alone provided such unexpected and personal reactions. As pleasant as it would be to share with a loved one, would she have experienced the day in the same way? Perhaps, once in a while, a day spent in solitude could be as rewarding as when shared by another.

She revisited the events of the day, from meeting the little cat, to the musician on the church steps, to the castle on the hill, to the mists in the meadows and the cows in the field. And, finally, to a bench beside the koi pond, remembering each beautiful moment in the beauty and stillness of the garden.

She closed her eyes, breathed in the scent of flowers, and delighted in the sound of a bird twittering overhead. In the distance, a church bell chimed. Resolving that she should not forget a minute of the day's events, Kimberlee picked up a pen and filled her journal with all the sights and feelings of this wondrous day.

Kimberlee opened her eyes. *Where am I?* Of course. The pension near Salzburg. She glanced at her watch. 7:10 A.M. What time would it be in California? She did a quick calculation of the time difference.

It must be about 4:10 P.M. in Fern Lake. *Amanda should be home from school. I could call Brett.*

She folded the feather comforter, dressed, and left her room. The hostess had provided an array of cheeses and sliced meats, muffins and various kinds of jam spread out on the dining room table. A bowl of bright red apples and the aroma of strong coffee completed the inviting repast. "Good morning."

"Gut morning. You did sleep well? Sit. Eat. You would like coffee?" The hostess poured a cup of very dark coffee and set it in front of Kimberlee.

"Thank you. I slept very well. Your garden is lovely." She chose a muffin, broke it in half and spooned a dollop of jam onto her plate. "Excuse me. Can you help me make a long distance call back to my home in the states?"

"Ja. I will help you with phone call. Now is good time. Is now afternoon in your country."

"Yes. I thought so, too." Kimberlee sipped the coffee. Her mouth puckered. "Your coffee is very strong, like our French Roast, but I like it." She added cream from the little pitcher. Kimberlee finished her meal, and with the help of the hostess, placed the call. The phone rang twice.

"Hello? Clarke residence." Brett's voice, so welcoming.

"Hi, sweetheart. It's me."

"Kimberlee. Is everything all right?"

"Sure. I missed you. Just thought I'd let you know we got here safely. Oh, Brett. Everything is so beautiful. We must come back some day."

"Sounds great. Let's do that."

"Is everything okay there? How's Amanda? The cats? Is Ted giving you any trouble?"

"Everything's fine. Amanda's right here. Do you want to say hi?" His voice faded. "Mommy's on the phone. Say hello."

Amanda came on the line. "Hi, mama. Guess what? We went downtown with Black Cat, and we saw glass on the floor and then Jack made pancakes."

"Really? That's nice. Now, you be a good girl and mind Daddy Brett, okay? Let me talk to Daddy Brett now. I love you."

"Mama says she wants to talk to you." Unintelligible mumbles came over the line and then Brett came back. "I'm here."

"What is she talking about? What glass on the floor?" Kimberlee wiped a sweaty hand on her pants leg. Maybe she shouldn't have left them alone, after all.

"Oh, it's nothing. You know how kids are. I went to the bookstore early this morning, so Jack got her ready for school. Guess that's what she's talking about."

Kimberlee wrinkled her brow. "Oh, okay. I'd better go. The house mom here says it's really expensive to call the states. I'll call again in a couple of days, okay? I love you."

"Love you more. Have fun, and don't worry about a thing."

Kimberlee hung up the phone. Had Brett told her the complete truth? Why would he need to go to the Book Nook so early that Jack had to get Amanda off to school? She shrugged. Whatever happened at the store, she felt sure Brett could handle it.

Chapter Nineteen

Don't hold your breath if you don't hear from me. - Brett

*B*ing-Bong!

Black Cat's ears perked up. *Who would be coming to visit so early in the morning?*

"Finish your cereal, Amanda," Brett called as he hurried into the living room. "The bus will be here in a few minutes." Brett nearly tripped over Angel, who scooted toward the bedroom when she heard the doorbell. He opened the door. "Yes?"

Ted Herman? Black Cat's ears went down.

Ted smiled. "Morning, Mr. Clarke. We need to talk. Is this a good time?"

Brett glanced at his watch. "You've got some nerve showing up here. I suppose you'll tell me you have no knowledge about the mess at the bookstore yesterday morning."

Ted spread out his hands. "What mess? What about the store?"

"Someone broke in and trashed the place."

Ted shook his head. "Don't look at me. I wasn't anywhere near Fern Lake yesterday morning or the night before. I went to Cloverdale and stayed overnight. Didn't get home until five o'clock last night." He reached into his pocket to pull out a business card. "Go ahead. If you don't believe me, call my lawyer. He'll confirm my story."

Brett took the card. "I'll give it to the police. They can sort it out. So, what are you here for? I'm trying to get Amanda ready for school."

"I want to talk to you and Jack about the lodge. We need to work this out. None of us need to go to court and fight over Beverly's will."

Brett shook his head and glanced over his shoulder. "This isn't a good time. I seriously doubt there's much point talking, any time. My wife is out of the country and nothing you could say will make Jack give up his interest in the lodge."

"I understand about Jack, but listen. According to Mr. Ollingham, I'm entitled to half the lodge. If I contest the will, we're both out a bundle in legal fees. If we sit down and discuss the matter rationally, maybe we can work something out without going to court. My attorney and I have come up with a plan. You should at least hear me out."

Brett glanced at his watch again. "I don't think Jack wants to talk with you. Why don't you discuss your proposal with Mr. Ollingham? If there's anything to consider, he can tell us."

"Oh, I don't think the attorneys need to get involved. We can settle this without any fuss. Give me a chance to tell you what I have in mind." Ted scribbled his phone number on a piece of paper and handed it to Brett. "Here's my number. Give me a call."

"Don't hold your breath if you don't hear from me."

Ted scowled. "If you're interested in your wife's financial well-being, you'll call and at least hear what I have to say."

"Call my attorney. I'll listen to anything *he* has to say." Brett closed the door in Ted's face.

Black Cat rubbed against Brett's ankle. Now, what game was Ted playing? He denied breaking into the bookstore. Did Brett believe him? He couldn't imagine what offer Ted could have cooked up to make Kimberlee and Jack willing to give up half of the lodge.

Chapter Twenty

This could be next year's Christmas card. - Kimberlee

After breakfast, Kimberlee packed her bags, thanked her hostess for a lovely stay in her charming pension and set out across the countryside. With the full day ahead before she was to meet Dorian that evening back at the hotel, she planned to explore leisurely as she made her way back to town. She checked the map and chose a general direction between Salzburg and Munich. *I'll stop whenever something looks interesting.*

The road she chose rambled over green hills, valleys, rivers, and past churches. Cows grazed on the flowered meadows beneath craggy mountains. Every few miles, she passed castles in various stages of disrepair. After the fifth or sixth stop to take a picture, she pulled up alongside a meadow. Several cows gathered near the road, their bells tinkling as she stepped from the car and approached the fence. Were they used to travelers stopping to take pictures? Maybe they thought they would get a treat.

"Hey, cows. Good morning." She slowly lifted her camera, adjusted the lens and focused on the lovely face of a black and white heifer. "Wait until Amanda sees you. I love your bell. You're a beauty, aren't you?" She clicked the shutter. "I'm sorry I don't have anything to give you." Startled by the camera's click, the cow jerked away from the fence and a black cow moved into her place.

Kimberlee stepped onto the rail of the fence to focus her camera on the herd and centered the black and white cow against a forest in the distance, and a charming white pension off to the side. "This could be next year's Christmas card. Thanks, girls. Have a lovely day." She waved, and got back into her car.

Not far down the road, she spotted a beautiful castle at the top of a hill. A narrow lane curved off the main road and headed toward the castle. She turned up the lane and ascended the steep road. Switchbacks curving left and right climbed higher and higher to manage the terrain.

After many twists and turns, Kimberlee stopped the car and gazed at the left side of the road where a canyon yawned. A sobering thought. With no side rails or fencing, should a mishap occur, it seemed possible for a car to disappear into the shrubs and rocks below. It occurred to her that no one knew exactly where she was. What if her car went off the road? *They might never find me.* Her heart pounded. *This isn't fun anymore. I need to go back.* She glanced in her rear view mirror. The road was too narrow to turn around here. Should she drive on and hope to find a wider place in the road, or should she back down the steep and crooked road? Neither option appealed to her.

She sat in the car, gripping the steering wheel. What to do? Up or down? *Breathe.*

If she went up the hill and found no place to turn around, she would be even worse off than now. If she tried to back down the hill, the car could easily go off the cliff if she turned the wrong way. Sitting on a steep, winding road with her heart pounding was not her idea of a great adventure. The joy of the morning's drive had quickly taken a turn for the worse. *I can't just sit here. What if another car should come down the hill or come up behind me?*

Going up seemed safer than trying to back down. Perhaps further up, she'd find a place wide enough to turn around. Her engine grumbled as she shifted into low gear and crept up the narrow, winding road. At several places along the way, the road widened, which might have allowed another car to pass, should it have been necessary. But, with no fence on the canyon side, she was afraid to try and turn around. *Surely, at the castle on top of the hill, there must be a parking lot.*

Up she went, traversing the numerous twists and turns so tight that a truck or a bus would have trouble making the turn in one pass.

Perspiration beaded her forehead. Her lips moved in constant prayer as she inched the car forward. Despite her uncomfortable situation, the view was spectacular. The sight of the valley below, sprinkled with little white houses, church steeples, and fields dotted with black specks that she knew were cows, looked like a Christmas card without the snow. She kept talking to herself, "I'm enjoying this. I'm having fun. Buck up, Kimberlee. You're not going to plunge off the cliff. Really. This is an adventure. You'll laugh with Dorian tonight when you get back to the hotel. You'll…" *What is that? People singing? Where…?*

She slammed on the brakes. Coming around the corner, heading downhill, a tour bus appeared, loaded with passengers bellowing at the top of their lungs, *Oh, Susanna! Oh, don't you cry for me.* The bus stopped and flashed its lights.

What did he want her to do? Surely, he didn't think she should back her car down three twists in the road to the wider spot a quarter of a mile down the hill. She remembered the spot barely wide enough for two Volkswagens to pass, but only at the risk of scraping a layer of paint off one of them. Wasn't the vehicle headed downward supposed to back up the hill in such a case? Or was that only in California? Maybe things were different in Germany. She stared at the bus driver, shook her head and raised her hands as if to seek advice.

The bus flashed its lights again and honked. The driver shook his fist. Apparently he expected her to back down.

Her heart felt as if it would leap from her chest. How could this day get any worse? Tears pricked her eyes. Maybe if she explained to the bus driver that as a tourist, she was unfamiliar with this type of road… Then what might he do? From the look on his face, the jubilant seniors were on his last nerve, and his day had gone about as well as hers. If the situation wasn't so dire, it would almost be funny.

OK, Kimberlee, get a grip. That bus wasn't going to back up. She would have to back her car down to a place where the bus could pass. She would hug the cliff and let the bus pass her on the outside. Why had they made a public road so impossible to traverse?

She wiped her sweaty palms on her pants, took a deep breath, put the car in reverse and turned to look back over her left shoulder. *You can do this. A little gas and straight back...* The car jerked and lurched to the left toward the canyon. She hit the brake. *Not so much gas.* She straightened the wheel and tried again. Better this time, but then she reached the first switchback curve.

A wave of despair surged through her chest. How could she traverse this *hell on the side of the mountain* with its twists and turns for a quarter of a mile? And, even when she reached the miniscule wider spot in the road, how could the bus pass? Did he expect her to back all the way to the main highway? Never in her life had she felt so incapable of dealing with a situation.

Kimberlee swiped the back of her hand across her face and dashed a tear from her cheek. She gritted her teeth and pressed the gas pedal, jerked the wheel to the left and prayed the car would stay on the road as it twisted sharply to the right. Waking up this morning in the pension with its beautiful garden outside her window hadn't prepared her for this mountain top nightmare with a bus barreling down on her.

Her rental car swung around the corner. She whipped the wheel back to the right to straighten out and then pressed the brake. Now in the center of the curve, she could see the bus creeping slowly down the road. It stopped, the door swung open, and an elderly gentleman stepped off. Were her prayers about to be answered? Did he intend to help her back the car down the road?

She clutched the steering wheel as the old man trotted down the road. *Praise the Lord!* Maybe he would drive her car far enough down the hill for the bus to pass. Kimberlee rolled down her window and waved. "Have you come to help me?"

"Ja! My name is Heinrich. I tell the bus driver. This lady cannot drive down this road. I will help." He pushed his long grey hair behind his ear and reached for the door handle. "I will make your car to a place where the bus can pass, ja?" He opened the door.

Kimberlee shifted into neutral and pulled on the brake. "Oh, thank you! You're an angel. Could you turn the car around so I can go back down the hill? I didn't know the road would be so steep and narrow." She stepped out of the car and laughed nervously. "Go ahead and drive. I'll walk."

"Ja." He slid into the driver's seat and released the brake.

Kimberlee stepped away from the car. "Thanks ever so much." She felt as if a burden was lifted from her back.

Heinrich put the car in gear and looking back over his shoulder, steered it around the twist in the road and out of sight. He made it look so easy, as though he traversed forwards and backwards around treacherous curves every day of his life.

Kimberlee stepped to the side of the road as the bus rumbled parallel to her and stopped. The door opened and the driver yelled, "You want to ride down the hill, lady?"

Kimberlee shook her head. "No, thanks, go on ahead. I'll walk. It isn't far." It felt so good to have her feet on solid ground and her car in the hands of an expert.

Her breathing returned to normal, and her racing heartbeat slowed as she hiked down the road. The seniors singing voices faded, and the swish of leaves blowing in the breeze grew louder. Off to the right in the distance, snow-covered mountains reached skyward. A green meadow stretched out far below the road, curving across the plain. In the center of the meadow stood a small abandoned building…perhaps a shepherd's hut. It appeared God was in his Heaven, and all was right with the world. How she wished she'd thought to grab her camera before she relinquished the car to the elderly gentleman.

She turned another corner. There sat her car, parked close to the hillside, turned and pointed toward the highway. *Bless his heart.* The bus had gone on down the hill with the old man aboard. Not wanting to linger and receive her gushy thanks or even a reward, he must have encouraged the driver to move on to their next tourist stop. *I should have gotten on the bus. At least I could have thanked Heinrich properly.*

Warm gratitude washed through her chest as she hurried toward her car. What would we do without the kindness of strangers? To honor Heinrich, she vowed to *pay it forward* at the first opportunity and lend a helping hand to the next person she met, in need.

Kimberlee hummed a little tune from *The Sound of Music* as she trotted the last few feet. She slid behind the wheel, and her gaze swept across the seat and onto the floorboard. *What...?* Where was her camera? And why was her wallet lying next to her purse on the floor? She held her breath, picked up her purse and looked inside. By the grace of God, her passport was still tucked inside the zipper pocket, but when she opened her wallet, her credit card, every Euro, and three $100 bills were gone.

Chapter Twenty-One

Okay, I get it. I was naïve and stupid. - Kimberlee

Munich, by the shortest route possible was Kimberlee's goal, as her car turned onto the main highway. What if she ran out of gas, had a flat tire, or car trouble along the way? Without any money to buy a sandwich or deal with an emergency, she was nearly overwhelmed with stress. She kept her thoughts on the beauty and pleasure she experienced the day before in Salzburg. Any thought of her current situation brought tears to her eyes.

Between the map and remembering the sights from the previous day, Kimberlee drove straight through without stopping and arrived at the Munich hotel in the middle of the afternoon.

At 5:00 P.M., when Dorian returned from her meeting, she found Kimberlee collapsed on her bed, faint and light-headed from hunger and worry. Many tears later, Kimberlee sat on her bed with a sandwich and a cup of coffee. Between bites and sips of coffee, she shared her unfortunate encounter with the smooth-talking *gentleman* who drove her car down the hill.

"It's all gone." Kimberlee dabbed her eyes with a tissue. "Every dollar. Heinrich took all my money. Thank God he left my driver's license and passport." Kimberlee threw herself face down on the bed.

Dorian listened to Kimberlee's sad story as she paced from the lace-covered window curtains to the arched doorway of the bathroom and back again. "I can't believe you let that man drive off in your car without a second thought. What were you thinking? And, to leave your purse and your camera right there on the seat? That was extremely foolish, Kimberlee."

Kimberlee sat up and swiped the back of her hand across her tear-streaked cheeks. "You don't need to scold me. I know it was stupid, but he seemed so nice. I was scared to ride in the car while he backed it around the corners."

"Then, why didn't you get on the bus when they offered you a ride?"

Kimberlee shook her head. "I know, I should have. I was so relieved that someone came to help me and…and I thought the fresh air would clear my head." She sighed. "Okay, I get it. I was naïve and stupid. Now, what am I going to do?" Tears dripped from her chin into her coffee cup. She dried her cheeks with a napkin.

"You're right. I shouldn't scold you." Dorian patted her shoulder. "I can imagine how scared you were, driving all the way back to Munich without any money. It must have been terrible. You couldn't even call me. Here's what we'll do." She sat on the bed and took Kimberlee's hand. "Brett can wire you some money through Western Union. It will be here in a few hours. In the meantime, don't worry about a thing. I have enough money for both of us.

"Here now, cheer up. Look what I got this afternoon before you got back." Dorian opened her purse. "Tickets to a ballet tonight and afterward, we'll go to that fancy restaurant down the street. Now, stop crying and go wash your face. Then you can tell me all about Salzburg. I know you must have had a good time there."

"Oh, I did. Everything is so beautiful." Kimberlee's smile returned. "The churches. And, the castles, and all the shops. I stayed in the most precious pension last night. It had a feather comforter on the bed. No sheets, mind you... just a big fat comforter. And, the garden…" She frowned and shook her head. "I can't even show you the pictures I took. They're all gone with my camera. I saw the most precious black and white cows." She stood and crossed the room. At the door of the bathroom, she turned. "You're the best, Dorian. I'll give Brett a call. What time is it in Fern Lake?"

"Well, actually," Dorian checked her watch, "it's one-thirty in the morning over there. Better wait until after dinner to call. Say, about… ten o'clock tonight? That will be about seven in the morning in Fern Lake, before he takes Amanda to school. Then he can go to the bank. The money should be here by the time we get up tomorrow morning. *Viola!*" She snapped her fingers. "Easy-peasy."

"Easy-peasy for you. What'll Brett say when he hears how gullible I was to let Heinrich take my car?"

"He'll say he's glad the only thing you lost was your money, and he'll be super glad that nothing bad happened to you. That's what's important."

"You're right. I'm sorry to cause so much trouble. Thanks for not being mad."

"Don't be silly. If it happened to me, would you be mad?"

"If it was the other way around, you wouldn't have let it happen."

"Oh, you." Dorian shooed Kimberlee into the bathroom. "Go check out that fancy bathtub. There's bubble bath on the counter."

Kimberlee filled the tub, gathered her hair in a ponytail, and spoke to her reflection in the mirror. "She's right. It's only money. It's not that important." The hot water crept up her back as she lowered her body into the tub and laid her head against the edge. "*Ahhh!*"

The tensions of the day melted away as the hot water swished over her body. Kimberlee put aside the unfortunate day's experience, and closed her eyes. In her mind's eye, she could see and hear the violinist on the Salzburg church steps. All too soon, the water cooled. She stepped out of the tub and dried off with a soft towel. Wiping the cloudy, steamed mirror, she smiled at her streaky reflection. Her smile wavered. "Now, I have to figure out what to say to Brett." Leaving the warmth and comfort of the previous moments behind, she dressed and stepped into the cool bedroom.

Chapter Twenty-Two

*Don't worry about a thing, sweetheart, and take
lots of pictures. - Brett*

Pacing between the living room and the kitchen, Black Cat anxiously awaited the arrival of Attorney Ollingham. He wanted to be on hand to lend Jack and Brett moral support if the attorney brought distressing news from Ted Herman. He joined Brett and Jack in the kitchen.

Brett picked up the coffee pot and raised it. "Do you want a warm up?"

Jack's face suggested lack of sleep as he hunched over the breakfast table. His hands clutched the coffee cup as if it was the lifeline that would get him through the day. "This is fine."

Bing-bong

"There he is now." Brett went to the door. "Good morning. Thanks for coming by so early."

Attorney Ollingham stepped inside. "Not a problem." He pulled off his jacket and hat and handed them to Brett. "It worked best for me, too. I have an eight-thirty court appearance this morning." He rubbed his hands together. "It's a bit chilly out."

"Come on in. The coffee's hot." Brett hung the attorney's items on the hall tree and led the way into the kitchen. "Is it okay if we sit at the kitchen table and talk?"

Mr. Ollingham nodded, set his briefcase on the table, and pulled out a chair. "Good morning, Jack." The attorney's eyes widened when he noticed Black Cat crouched on the floor near his water dish. "What a beautiful cat."

Black Cat eyed the attorney. Short, stout, balding, intelligent blue eyes, bulbous nose… Not the best looking man he'd ever seen, but he supposed attorneys never won many beauty contests. He certainly looked capable. Hopefully, he'd help Brett and Jack reach an equitable agreement with Ted Herman.

Mr. Ollingham opened his briefcase. "What a surprise to receive a call from Mr. Herman's attorney. I really didn't expect to hear from Ted again, but sometimes it happens that way. His attorney actually came up with a reasonable proposal that would eliminate the need to fight an expensive court case." He glanced between Brett and Jack. "It's in your best interest to give it some serious thought." He drew papers from his briefcase and laid them on the table. "First, let me reiterate what I mentioned the other day in my office. Ted has *standing* to contest Mrs. Herman's will, as they held the deed to the lodge as community property." He slid a copy of the original deed to Jack and one to Brett. "If Ted contests the will, the law is on his side. He will acquire fifty percent of the estate. Kimberlee and Jack would be awarded the other fifty percent, according to Mrs. Herman's bequeath. They may even be required to pay all the court costs."

Brett shook his head. "That isn't going to work. There's no way Jack and Kimberlee could be partners with Ted. There's too much history between them…facts that you don't understand." He stood and paced to the kitchen sink, filled a glass of water, and took a long drink.

"Now, wait. Sit down, Brett," Mr. Ollingham said. "That's not what Ted's proposing. He's asking you to buy him out. He wants $150,000 for his share. That's far less than the value of half of the lodge, if the court assessed the property. As the lodge is debt-free, you'd have no trouble borrowing that amount. Jack and Kimberlee would then own it lock, stock, and barrel. This offer negates the need for a drawn-out and testy, not to mention, expensive court fight."

Jack stood and crossed the kitchen. He ran his hand down Black Cat's back. After a moment, the lines in his brow relaxed. "If we give Ted the money, do ya think we can trust that he won't be back askin' for more? He's not very trustworthy. In fact, it's possible he's behind the trouble at the bookstore."

Mr. Ollingham raised his eyebrows. "What kind of trouble?"

"The bookstore was vandalized," Brett said. "Ted denies responsibility, but with all this business about the will, we're not sure what to believe."

Attorney Ollingham nodded. "Be that as it may, it doesn't change Ted's legal right to challenge you for ownership of the lodge. His attorney claims Ted has no interest in staying in Fern Lake and wants to return to his wife in Texas. We only have his word on that, of course."

Jack rinsed his hands at the sink, dried them on the tea towel and sat down at the table. "Cat hair." He grinned. "So that's it? All it's gonna take is $150,000 to get him to leave town? I wish Kimberlee was here. She'll have to agree."

Mr. Ollingham held up a paper covered with figures. "Considering the value of comparable Fern Lake lodges, if Ted contests the will and wins, you'll have to take out a much larger loan to buy him out, or sell the property and divide the proceeds 50/50. Not that I'm saying you should accept his offer, mind you, but, this is about the best you could hope for."

Mr. Ollingham stood. "Why don't you talk it over with Kimberlee? Ted has given you ten days." He checked his watch. "I hate to rush off, but, like I said, I have to be in court..." he checked his watch..."in a few minutes. Let me know what you decide, and I'll draw up the legal documents."

Black Cat followed the men into the living room. Brett handed the attorney his coat. "Thanks for coming, Mr. Ollingham. We'll talk it over and let—"

Ring...Ring.

"Jack. Will you see Mr. Ollingham out?" He turned. "Gotta get that. Thanks again." Brett waved and hurried to the phone. "Hello? Kimberlee? You're crying. What's wrong, babe? Are you okay?" Black Cat jumped onto the end table and pushed his head under Brett's hand, demanding attention.

Amongst sniffles and tears, Kimberlee spilled out the whole sordid story of the crooked road to the castle, the bus on the hill, the kind old gentleman who offered to move her car, and the disappearance of her money and camera.

"Oh, honey. I'm so sorry. Now, stop crying. I'll wire you some money right away. Where should I send it?" He ran his hand over Black Cat's back and up his bushy tail. "Hand me a pen, would you Jack?"

Kimberlee gave him the information she acquired from the hotel, and with a few more assurances that Brett wasn't angry about the mishap, they ended the call.

"What's wrong?" Jack hovered in the door way, having heard only Brett's half of the conversation. "Is she okay?"

"I have to find a Western Union Office. Apparently, she was robbed." Brett shook his head. "I was worried about her going off alone for two days. At least she'll be with Dorian the rest of the trip."

"I noticed that ya didn't tell her about Ted's proposal."

"What was I supposed to say? By the way, babe, sorry you were robbed, but we had a break-in and the Book Nook got trashed. Ted plans to sue us if we don't buy him out, which isn't a half-bad idea, but we'll have to borrow $150,000. Now, don't worry about a thing, sweetheart, and take lots of pictures." A snarky grin creased his jaw.

Jack chuckled. "Yeah, I guess I see yer point."

Brett followed Jack to the front door. "There's no need for her to stew about anything. She's upset enough about losing her money." He glanced at the clock over the mantle. "Goodbye, Jack. I'll see you later. I have to get Amanda off to school. Come on, Amanda," Brett called down the hall. "Are you ready? The bus will be here pretty soon." He strode down the hall to her bedroom.

Black Cat hopped off the table and scooted past Jack's legs, onto the porch. *It boggles the feline mind how these humans get themselves into the most exasperating predicaments.*

Chapter Twenty-Three

I'm game if you are. Lead on, Sherlock. - Dorian

reams of switchbacks on a mountain road and her car plummeting over the edge of the canyon haunted Kimberlee's slumber. Her dream changed to the kindly, smiling face of the old gentlemen, only to have his smile become a sneer. After tossing and turning through most of the night, she awoke with a crick in her neck to the aroma of strong coffee.

"Good morning, sleepyhead." Dorian leaned over her bed, sipping coffee from a paper cup. "It's 6:30. I thought I'd let you sleep in. Want some coffee?" She handed Kimberlee a covered paper cup.

"6:30 is sleeping in? When did you get up?"

"I've been up since five o'clock. I took a little walk around town and watched the sunrise from the café down the street. That's where I got the coffee."

Kimberlee threw back the covers. "Thanks." She took the cup and took a sip. "I need to check downstairs and see if Brett sent me some money, else I'm a leech and a pauper for the rest of the day."

"I already checked. There's a cable waiting for you, so stop worrying. *Pauperdom* is not in your immediate future."

"I knew I could count on Brett."

"Hurry and get dressed, so we can get something to eat and decide what's on the agenda for today."

Kimberlee stood and slipped on her robe. "I'd like to visit the Franz Mayer Glass Factory today, if that's okay. I sent the sales manager an email and told him we'd be here this week. He agreed to give us a back-room tour of the glass-blowing process whenever we came by. How does that sound?"

"Sounds interesting, but why this sudden interest in art glass? You've never mentioned it before."

"I thought it would be fun to ship some pieces back to Fern Lake. Don't you think the tourists would love genuine hand-blown pieces from Germany?"

Dorian shrugged. "Guess it depends on the item and the price. I don't think Fern Lake tourists who come to fish and boat will pay hundreds of dollars for a blown-glass vase."

"True, but I'd like to talk to the factory salesman and see what they have to offer. What do you say? Do you want to go today?"

"I'm game. We can be there by midmorning if we hurry."

Within the hour, the girls breakfasted, collected the Western Union money Brett sent, and headed across town to the Franz Mayer and Company Glass Factory.

From brochures handed out at the door, Kimberlee learned the business, housed within the imposing six-story building, had been owned by the same family for over 150 years. At the height of their popularity in the late nineteenth and early twentieth centuries, they manufactured a majority of the Catholic Church's stained glass windows in both Europe and the United States.

The lead sales manager escorted Kimberlee and Dorian to the workroom where the glass art pieces were made. As they entered the workshop, the heat of the furnaces considerably raised the temperature. Overhead fans ran full blast to cool the various workstations where pairs of artists worked together to produce a single piece of art glass. Kimberlee's guide waved to one of the artists. "I'll leave you with Johan." The guide stepped away.

The workman handed off his piece to another team member and approached. "Hello. I'm Johan Burger. Welcome to Mayer's." He shook hands with Kimberlee and Dorian, and then led them to a row of shelves where finished vases and figurines were displayed.

"This is all so exciting, Dorian. Look at the purple fish. Isn't it precious? Now, that's something my customers might be interested in buying."

Johan smiled. "Good choice. That's one of our popular production pieces. It can be made in a variety of colors and styles, and the price is reasonable." He pointed to another shelf. "There's one in light blue."

Dorian and Kimberlee followed Johan to another two-man team work station.

"David, the lead glassblower, is called the *gaffer*," Johan explained. "His assistant, Dirk, has a pre-heated, hollow iron or steel pipe called a *blowpipe*. He dips it into a *crucible*, or pot of molten clear glass to obtain a *gather* of molten glass on the end of the blowpipe."

Kimberlee stepped closer, "I see."

"Now he's rolling the *gather* into colored glass chips called *frit* to add color. He needs to return it to the *glory hole,* or oven, for about fifteen seconds between each step to maintain the proper heat." Steam rose from the molten glass as Dirk spun the blowpipe and twisted it through a thick wad of newspapers he held in his hand.

Dorian scribbled the descriptive words in her notebook as Johan continued to narrate the process. "He isn't wearing gloves. Doesn't the blowpipe get hot?" She took a step away as Dirk inserted the glass-coated blowpipe back into the oven.

"The heat doesn't transfer into the four-foot long steel pipe," Johan said.

Dirk removed the steel pipe from the *glory hole*, turned, and handed it to David.

"Now, David is rolling the molten glass over the steel table, called a *marver. (marvering)* This cools the piece and forms an exterior skin, as well as helps shape it. Dirk then blows into the blowpipe, again, to create a bubble in the *gather*," Johan said.

David picked up the narration, explaining the process as Dirk blew more air through the blowpipe, stretching the piece into a larger shape. Glowing red hot, and spinning, the color chips (*frit*) swirled around the perimeter of the molten glass.

David took back the blowpipe and holding it at arms-length, swung it back and forth, to stretch the hollow molten glass, creating a vase shape. He formed the base by cutting a flat piece off the molten glass with a steel pincher device, (*crosscuts* or *diamond shears*). David placed a water-soaked fruitwood paddle against the bottom of the spinning molten glass to further cool, flatten, and shape the base. "Now we must transfer the piece from the blowpipe over to this shorter, solid rod *punty.*"

"So, the vase starts out on the blowpipe, upside down?" Dorian asked.

"You could say that," David said. He applied a tiny bit of molten glass to the base of the vase. With a sharp tap, he separated the vase from the blowpipe and transferred it to the *punty.*

"*Wow!* How often does it break at that point?" Kimberlee asked.

"Not as often as you'd think. These guys are experts," Johan said. "To keep the piece above 950 degrees, the piece is reinserted into the glory hole multiple times through the process."

Kimberlee closed her eyes. The spinning vase and the heated room made her feel dizzy.

David continued to spin the pipe, using jack clamps to shape the neck much like a potter works with a lump of clay. A thin stream of glass was dripped around the lip of the vase as the *punty* continued to spin. "This prevents the color from bleeding over the lip." David made his final touches with his jacks to create the desired angle.

As he slowed the spinning rod, Kimberlee exclaimed. "Oh! Look! The colors are changing." She wiped perspiration from her forehead.

"The frit changes colors as the piece cools." Dirk donned a clear plastic face shield and thick gloves.

In the final step, David added a drop of water to the bottom of the vase, gave it a quick rap, and the vase fell from the *punty* into Dirk's hands. He then carried it to the *annealing* oven.

"We keep the annealing oven between 940 and 950 degrees. This piece will cool for about fifteen hours. This anneals the glass and keeps it from cracking or shattering. I know it's a lot to take in." David moved slowly toward the door. "Unless you have questions, I'll send you back to the show room."

"I saw some pieces in the display cabinet with intricate patterns. How is that done?" Kimberlee asked.

"We showed you the basic process. For more complex patterns, we can add colored glass rods, *frit, cane* or rods cut in a various manner to reveal patterns, called *murrine*. By compound layering, gold and silver can be added to the pieces. You'll see some of that in the showroom."

Over the next hour, Kimberlee and Dorian *oohed* and *ahhed* over the showroom pieces. Kimberlee ordered several varieties and colors of blown-glass fish to be shipped to her Fern Lake bookstore.

As they stepped through the glass door into the parking lot, Kimberlee squinted into the blue sky and donned her sunglasses. "*Wow!* What a lot of information. Could you follow all those steps?"

"Not really." Dorian clicked the key to unlock the rental car. "It was fascinating, but I'm hungry. Let's find a café and get some lunch."

Kimberlee nodded. "I really enjoyed watching the process. I can't wait for the first shipment to arrive in Fern Lake. Won't the tourists love those blown-glass fish?" She opened the car door and slid inside. "When we get to the café, I want to tell you about the part I'm reading in Dewey's journal." She wiggled her eyebrows Groucho-style.

"The WWII journal? I had a feeling it had something to do with your interest in coming over here." Dorian left the factory parking lot and drove several blocks through the city.

"You're right, but I wanted to wait until we got here to go into more detail about the treasure in Hopfgarten."

"There's a cute place." Dorian nodded up the street toward a chalet-style cafe with sidewalk tables. "Let's stop here." She pulled into a parking space and turned off the motor. "It's so nice out, we can sit outside. Aren't those umbrella-covered tables cute?" Large ceramic planters filled with blazing red geraniums lined the edge of the patio. Wooden baskets overflowing with pansies and ivy hanging from the eaves created a charming garden atmosphere. Music from a jukebox followed a customer through the door as he exited the café.

Dorian snapped a picture of Kimberlee standing next to the ceramic planters. "If we're going to talk about a lost treasure, we couldn't find a more picturesque place to do it." She laid her camera on the table and sat.

Kimberlee retrieved the diary from her purse and opened it to a book-marked page. "Here's where Dewey writes about the note from Hans. There's a poem that has clues to a treasure supposedly in Hopfgarten. We're so close to Austria and Hopfgarten. We have to go there and see if any of Hans's relatives are still there and—"

Dorian raised an eyebrow. "Tell me again. Who's Hans?"

"You remember. He's the German soldier that Dewey met at Normandy when they were both left on the battlefield. After the war, they exchanged letters. Hans sent Dewey the coded message about the treasure. I thought I told you about Dewey and Hans and the documentary we saw about the lost gold coins."

"I guess you told me, but now that we're here, I see why you'd be more intrigued by the mystery. From the look in your eye, I think you've cooked up some hair-brained scheme to try and find the treasure. You get me into trouble every time, but I suppose I'm game if you are, so lead on, Sherlock." She winked and greeted the waitress who came out to take their order.

Chapter Twenty-Four

I can't open my mouth, without sticking my paw into it. - Black Cat

eaves drifted from the oak tree and twirled in the breeze. Black Cat sat on the back of the sofa, peeking through the lace curtain. Fall was upon them. Soon it would be Thanksgiving and then Christmas. Maybe the bustle of the holidays would brighten Angel's spirit. His heart ached, realizing she wasn't happy.

He closed his eyes, remembering the day they left the Nevada City emu ranch. Angel was reluctant to leave their new caretakers, John and Cindy, but it was even harder to leave her kittens. She had been depressed ever since their return to Fern Lake. Nothing seemed to improve her mood. He turned toward the hallway where he'd last seen Angel heading for the bedroom. What more could he do to cheer her up? Perhaps she'd like to go for a walk and chase the falling leaves. *That's always fun...*

His gaze snapped back to the window as a car stopped at the front gate. *It must be one of Brett's friends.* Several minutes passed, but no one got out of the car. The hair on the back of his neck stiffened. Something didn't feel right. Five more minutes passed, and then the driver side door opened and a woman stepped out.

Oh no! It couldn't be...*her*. Black Cat leaped off the sofa. "Angel! Angel! Where are you?" He raced into Amanda's bedroom. "Hide. She's come to Fern Lake." *Where is she?* He raced down the hall to Amanda's room where Angel usually napped in the early morning, but she wasn't there. Maybe she was in the porch swing? The woman would see her when she came up the sidewalk. He dashed back into the living room. "Angel! Where are you?"

Bing Bong

Black Cat froze, and stared at the front door. His heart beat like a base drum against his furry white chest. What a relief to know that Angel wasn't on the porch. She must be in the house…maybe under Kimberlee's bed?

Memories from Texas filled his head. *Horses. Green fields. A long dirt driveway lined with stone fences. The stable master, who now called himself by another name, and a killer stalking through the house.* Black Cat shook his head. He couldn't think about that now.

With Amanda at school, and Brett already headed for the bookstore not ten minutes before, there was no one here to protect them. If the old woman broke into the house, she could find Angel.

Bing Bong

Black Cat crouched on his belly and slunk across the carpet. He sniffed at the crack beneath the door. Thank goodness, Kimberlee was out of the country.

Bing Bong! The sound of the doorbell thudded through his head again.

Angel wandered into the living room, yawning. "Somebody's at the door."

Black Cat's head whipped around. "Angel? Where were you? You need to hide. It's her. She's come to take you away." He rushed across the room, knocked his head against Angel's shoulder and tried to herd her into the hall.

"Stop pushing. Who's come to take me away?"

"Grandmother Lassiter, from Texas. She's at the door."

"Really?" Angel's nose went up. "It is her. I can smell her perfume. Why is she here? I thought she and Kimberlee didn't get along."

Black Cat shrugged. "I suspect she's up to no good. Be still. We don't want her to know we're in here."

"Why not? I'm not afraid of her. She's never done anything—"

"How quickly you forget. Kimberlee didn't exactly ask permission when she brought you home with us from Texas. Brett says that Grandmother Lassiter called last month. She wants you back. Though I can't imagine why she'd come all the way to California just to fetch a cat. I suspect it has more to do with making trouble for Kimberlee."

"Gee. Thanks. So, I'm not worth a trip to California? Well, for your information… Oh, never mind." Angel hopped onto the sofa and peeked through the curtains.

"Don't be mad," Black Cat said. "I didn't mean it that way. I'd come to California for you. I just didn't think that she thought that much…" That hadn't come out right, either. *I can't open my mouth, without sticking my paw into it.*

"She left something on the front door, and now she's leaving."

Black Cat hopped onto the sofa beside Angel in time to see Grandmother Lassiter walk down the sidewalk, open the gate and get into her car. She drove around the lawn and stopped in front of the lodge registration office. "I'll bet she's planning to stay at the lodge. We haven't seen the last of her yet." He glanced at Angel. "Really, I didn't mean to insult you. I'm sorry. You mad?"

Angel stared out the window until Mrs. Lassiter disappeared into Jack's office. "I'm going to Amanda's room. I don't want to talk to you right now."

Black Cat's heart raced. After all they had been through this summer in Nevada City and finally back in Fern Lake; he hoped things would return to normal. But, he was wise enough to know that hearts want what hearts want, and sometimes it doesn't coincide with the heart wants of others.

Now that Grandmother was in town, would Angel want to return to Texas with her?

Black Cat cruised under the table while Brett opened a piece of paper. His hand trembled as he picked up the telephone and punched in a number. He pushed the speaker button as he slid the paper around the table. "Hi, Jack, you busy?"

"I have a few minutes. What's up?"

"I just got home and found a note on the front door from Kimberlee's grandmother. Apparently, she's in town and wants to meet with me." He glanced nervously toward Amanda's room.

"Yeah, I know." Jack's voice lowered a level. "She rented a cabin. I thought I recognized the name. She claimed she came ta visit her granddaughter. Guess she doesn't know Kimberlee's in Germany, *huh?* What do ya suppose she wants?"

"No doubt she's come to cause trouble. We didn't exactly ask her permission to take Angel when we left Texas. It was sort of a spur-of-the moment thing. Mrs. Lassiter was in the hospital and the cats were together. We sort of…took her. It's too late now, but I'll admit, I regret the way it happened." He scowled into the telephone.

Meow! Black Cat leaped into Brett's lap and pawed at his face. *You made the right decision, Brett. Don't let her take Angel. I'll die if she takes my Angel.*

"Get down, Black Cat. I don't have time for you now." Brett pushed Black Cat off his lap. He stood and paced the floor.

"Do ya think she came all this way ta get her cat? That doesn't make sense—"

"No idea. How can I say no if she demands we give her back? After all that happened in Texas, Kimberlee will have a cat-fit, herself, if I let Angel go. Not to mention Amanda. She'd be heartbroken. The old dame must have something else on her mind. By the way, which cabin is she in?" Brett reached down and stroked Black Cat's head. Was he sorry for shoving the cat off his lap?

"She's in cabin six, by the lake. Her car is parked out front now."

Black Cat lifted his feet onto Brett's legs and leaned into his hand.

Don't worry, Brett. I'll protect Angel. The only way the old lady will take her is over my dead body.

Brett stood. "I think I'll walk over there and see what she wants. Will you come with me? I might need a witness. She's a good one for making things up to suit her purpose. Besides, I don't want to talk to her here. I don't want her to see Angel."

"Sure." Jack snapped his fingers for Chance "Let's go, girl. Can't let our buddy face the old lady alone. I'll meet ya out front." He hung up the phone.

I'm coming too. Black Cat growled and raced out the front door at Brett's feet.

Jack met Brett as they crossed the lawn. "Now try ta stay calm, Brett. Don't let her goad you into something you'll regret. Ya know if ya touch her, she could file assault charges."

Brett nodded. Perspiration beaded his forehead. He took a breath and knocked on the cabin door. "This is the cabin where Kimberlee and Amanda stayed last year when we first met," he whispered. "I hate thinking Mrs. Lassiter is in there."

Black Cat hunkered at his feet, his fur puffed out.

The door swung open and Grandmother Lassiter stared at Brett. Her mouth twisted into a sneer. "Oh. It's you." She glared at Jack. "What do you want? I paid for the cabin."

Jack blushed and ducked his head. "No problem. I'm…*uh*… friends…*uh*…I better get back ta work, Brett." He scurried toward the dock.

Brett's gaze followed him across the lawn. He turned back to the door. "I saw your note. Kimberlee's in Europe. So…"

"So, you'll do. Probably better to talk to you, anyway." Grandmother Lassiter threw back her shoulders and took a breath. "Last year, when I signed over the deed to that house," she nodded toward the Victorian house Brett and Kimberlee worked so hard to restore. "I assumed I was giving it to my *granddaughter*. I've recently learned otherwise."

Black Cat lifted his head and gazed at Brett's pale face. Never in their wildest imagination had they ever imagined that information about Kimberlee's birth parents would affect their home. Hadn't they taken the run-down Victorian house where Kimberlee was born and remodeled it from top to bottom? Hadn't they spent thousands of dollars and hundreds of hours to upgrade the kitchen and the bathroom, replaced the roof, repaired the fence, replanted the lawn, and changed a falling-down wreck into a beautiful home?

Black Cat growled, and glanced at Brett. *First, Angel. Now, our home? Should I kill her, or do you want to do it?*

"Really, Mrs. Lassiter, even from you, this is beyond the pale. Kimberlee was your son's child in every way humanly possible. He's the only father she ever knew, as brief a time as they had together. She only learned the truth surrounding her birth by accident last year after you signed over the house deed to her.

"That wreck of a house probably should have been torn down. Instead, we completely restored it from top to bottom with our own money." His hands knotted into fists. Beads of perspiration trickled off his brow and followed the wrinkle grooves beside his eyes.

Mrs. Lassiter's shoulders relaxed. Her lips curved into a twisted smile. "I'm filing a lawsuit, declaring Kimberlee coerced me into deeding the house to her under false pretenses. I'm reclaiming the title to my house."

"What? That's ridiculous. You haven't got a legal leg to stand on. There's not a court in the land…" Brett's cheeks flamed.

"Kimberlee played on my sympathies for financial gain, falsely claimed to be my granddaughter, and cajoled me into signing over the deed," Mrs. Lassiter shouted. "That's fraud across state lines, in fact. I think I have a very good chance in court." She smirked. "I have a witness, you know, who will back up my claim."

"Ted Herman, previously known as Harold Marlowe, I assume?" Brett said.

"A rose is a rose, by any other name. Before long, I'm sure you'll see things my way. Perhaps Kimberlee will even escape prison if you sign over the deed to the house. My attorney will be in contact. Good day." She slammed the cabin door.

Brett looked down at Black Cat. "Well, that went well, didn't it?"

Black Cat swished his tail. *You blew your chance, Brett. All you had to do was say the word. I offered to kill her.*

Chapter Twenty-Five

Okay. If it makes you feel any better, you're a hero. - Angel

hat was that sound? Black Cat bolted awake. Something was wrong. The yellow half-moon sent a streak of moonlight through the window. Black Cat's pupils widened, better to see in the dark living room. He rose and trotted into the kitchen, out through the cat door and around the house. He stopped by the garden gate and tilted his head. *There it is again.* Glass breaking. He squeezed through the picket fence and loped toward the lake. The sound came from the direction of the dock. Perhaps the intruder who broke into the bookstore had come to rob the bait shop. Odd that Jack's dog, Chance, hadn't awakened, since their cabin was nearer the bait shop than Kimberlee's house. On the other hand, he wasn't surprised; cats being superior to dogs in so many ways.

Black Cat tiptoed on. He could see through the bait shop window—a human figure, wearing dark clothes, sneaking around inside. Black Cat hunkered on the wooden planks at the end of the dock. What to do? His head jerked toward Jack's cabin. *Better wake up Jack.* He raced to Jack's cabin and scratched on the door. *Meow! Meow!* "Wake up Jack! Hurry. Chance. Can you hear me? Wake up."

Woof. Woof!

Jack opened the door, rubbing his eyes. "Black Cat? What's goin' on out here?"

Meow! Meow! Come quick, Jack. Someone's breaking into... Black Cat raced toward the dock...stopped and looked back. *Are you coming? Meow!* He hurried back to Jack's cabin. *Chance. Come quick. Someone is in the bait shop.*

Chance bolted past Jack's legs and followed Black Cat toward the dock. *Ruff! Ruff! Ruff!* A figure rushed from behind the building and ran toward the street. Chance took off across the lawn after the intruder.

Jack dashed from his cabin with a flashlight. "Chance. What's goin' on?" He shined the light toward the retreating figure. "Hey, you! Stop!" The thief jumped into a waiting car. It roared down the dark street before Chance reached the sidewalk.

The lights came on in Brett's house. A door slammed and Brett ran down the driveway toward the lake. "What's all the shouting about?" He stopped at the bait shop. "What's wrong?"

Jack whistled and Chance sprinted back to his side, whining. "Good girl. You ran him off, didn't ya?" He patted Chance's head and then leaned down to stroke Black Cat.

Brett followed Jack to the rear of the building. "Look at this. He's jimmied the lock. Good thing Chance woke you."

Jack stepped inside the shop and flipped on the light. "*Nuh-uh.* Black Cat woke me scratchin' on the door. Someone was breakin' into the shop. Then Chance took out after the guy. Guess we got here before he could do too much damage. The display case is smashed."

Brett stroked Black Cat's head. "Well, I'll be. Good job, Black Cat. We better call the police."

Yeah. It was me. Heard a noise and came to investigate. Good thing. The thief was...

"I'm freezing," Jack said. "Gonna run and get dressed. You want to stay here for a few minutes while I call 911? At least you're wearin' a bathrobe." He shivered, his bare legs a mass of chill bumps. "If ya don't mind..."

"Go get dressed and make the call," Brett said with a chuckle. "I'll look around and see if there's any more damage. You'll need to inventory the merchandise tomorrow."

Jack returned, fully dressed by the time the police arrived and went through the bait shop. All they found was the broken glass cabinet and several missing fishing reels. Jack whispered to Brett. "What do you think? Ted Herman again?"

Black Cat hopped onto the counter. *It couldn't have been Ted Herman. Looked more like…*

Brett shrugged. "I doubt it. What would he have to gain? He wants us to buy him out. Doesn't make sense he'd be giving us all this grief. First, the bookstore, and now this?"

"I guess you're right. I wish Dorian was here. She knows about this stuff."

"Listen. I need to get back to the house," Brett said, shining his flashlight back toward his front door. "I left Amanda alone."

"Sure. You go ahead. I'll finish up with the police. If they need ta talk to ya, they can call back in the morning."

"Right." Brett hurried toward the house with Black Cat close behind.

"Meow." *Wait for me. I can't wait to tell Angel I caught the thief single-handed. If I hadn't wakened Chance, the thief might have done a lot more damage. Brett? Are you hungry? I'm hungry. Do you think we could have a little snack when we get inside? Meow. Meow.*

Brett rubbed Black Cat's head. "You've got a right to brag. You're my hero, for sure."

Black Cat twitched his whiskers. "And, then I heard a noise, so I went outside and thought someone was messing around in the bait shop." *Because I'm a hero.* "So I woke Chance and Jack, and he chased the burglar to the street."

Angel stretched and yawned. "Why did Jack chase the burglar all the way to the street?"

"No, silly. Chance chased the burglar. That's about all dogs are good for. They bark and chase things. I took Jack to the bait shop and then Brett came and they found the back door lock broken. We got there before... Angel? You're not listening..."

"Not really. I'm sleepy. You woke me up."

"I thought you'd want to know how I saved the bait shop, and—"

"And, there you go again, thinking you're some kind of superhero. You're not, you know. You're a light sleeper and you heard a noise. That's all." She yawned again.

Black Cat dropped onto the floor. His head flopped to his paws. *She's not impressed.* He tried so hard to make her proud of him... Ever since they came to Fern Lake... Nothing made her happy. Not the mouse, not meeting his friends, or walking around town, or playing in the leaves, or lying on the porch swing watching the sunset over the lake.

He'd tried everything to make her appreciate the beauty of the lake and enjoy living with Brett and Kimberlee. He wanted her to love all the good things he loved. Maybe it *was* a mistake to take her away from John and Cindy in Nevada City. But, how could he have prevented it? Would she ever be happy in Fern Lake?

"Oh, get that hang-dog look off your face." Angel lifted her head and flicked an ear. "Okay. If it makes you feel any better, you're a hero." She turned her head.

Black Cat rose from the rug and slunk toward the kitchen. *Guess that says it all...*

Down at the dock, the paddle wheeler blew its whistle and bells clanged, ready to take off on its sunrise tour.

"Wait! Come back." Angel hurried after Black Cat. "Don't go away mad. I'm sorry. Really, I am. I don't know what's wrong with me. I don't know why I say such mean things. You were really brave, and you saved the bait shop and you ran off the thief." Her head bumped against his shoulder. "Come sit with me on the porch swing. We'll watch the sunrise together. Please?"

She does love me. Black Cat bolted through the cat door and followed Angel around the corner of the house to the front porch. He hopped onto the swing, turned in a circle and flopped down. Angel jumped up beside him and lay down. "Told ya. Isn't this nice?"

"Yes," he purred. "All the leaves will soon be off the trees and sometimes we get a sprinkle of snow in the fall. That's when Brett makes a fire in the fireplace and Kimberlee makes popcorn balls. Oh, and then it's Christmas and she decorates a Christmas tree and we all get presents. You'll love it. Kimberlee hangs stockings by the fireplace and fills mine with toys and a new catnip mouse."

"Sounds nice. Grandmother Lassiter used to have a Christmas tree, but she didn't buy me presents." She leaned over her shoulder to nibble at an itch.

"I know you're having a hard time adjusting." Black Cat gave the top of Angel's head a lick. "Before long, you'll love Fern Lake as much as I do."

Warm purrs rumbled through Angel's golden body. "I'll try harder. Look. You can see the sun peeking up over the trees." A bright pink glow lit the sky over the Aspen trees at the end of the driveway.

"Red in the morn...sailors warn. I remember that from an ancestor," Black Cat said, "a pirate ship's cat that lived off the Coast of Maine...ever so long ago. Means there's a storm brewing. It's likely to rain today."

Angel shivered. "You can say that again. I feel a storm coming, in more ways than you know..."

Black Cat's eyes opened wide. "Whatever do you mean by that? What kind of storm? A rain storm, or is our family in danger?"

"You're not the only one with *the sight.* I'm not quite sure what will happen, but, trust me. I know there are trials and tribulation on the horizon. I feel it in my bones."

Tiny droplets of rain began to fall. As the rain sprinkled the yard, the scent of damp grass rose up from the nearby lawn. Like so often in the past, the porch swing faded from Black Cat's sight and his thoughts moved back in time to another day, to the memories of a distant ancestor, a ship's cat off the Coast of Maine...

Storm clouds gathered over a coastal city and ships at anchor bobbed in the churning water next to the dock. The sky darkened and the pirate ship's red sails whipped in the wind.

Nearby church bells pealed a warning to batten down and seek shelter from the coming storm.

A small black cat huddled on the dock as men hastened to lower and tie down the canvas coverings on the sails. A sudden gust of wind blew against the little cat, sending her scurrying behind a stack of boxes ready to load aboard a merchant ship.

The sky opened and drops of rain the size of pumpkin seeds pounded the wooden slats. The cat hunched lower and fluffed her fur. Rain spattered off the boxes and onto her head, leaving silvery droplets clinging to her whiskers. She shivered and lowered her head against the onslaught. Soon, the storm would pass, her fur would dry, and the harbor would be bathed in warmth and sunlight again. Perhaps a kind sailor would share his supper...

Black Cat blinked and shook his head as the harbor scene faded. His vision was likely due to the rain, or...was it a result of impending trouble, as Angel suggested?

Drops of rain plinked from the railings to the porch floor. Puddles stood on the sidewalk. Soon they would dry in the warmth of the rising sun. Angel had long since abandoned her pillow beside him. Black Cat lay on the swing, staring out at the yard, washed clean and left smelling of damp earth and summer's last roses.

Chapter Twenty-Six

If it's treasure we're after, let's be on our way. - Dorian

Umbrella tables outside the café dotted the patio with spots of red and yellow. Kimberlee and Dorian chose a table. Kimberlee gathered her hair and fastened it into a pony tail at the nape of her neck. She opened her purse and pulled out Dewey's diary. She drew in her breath as her fingers tingled at the touch of the leather. Something about the journal made it feel alive, full of unseen adventures, emotions, discoveries, and mysteries yet to be discovered.

She opened the book, licked her finger and flipped to the book-marked page. "Here it is. This is where Dewey writes about the message Hans Kreuger sent with the clue about the treasure."

"Likely story." Dorian turned and stared at the cobbled street beside the cafe.

"Listen. If we follow the clues in the poem, maybe it will lead us to the hidden treasure. We can't be this close to Hopfgarten and not even try." Kimberlee shared again, the story of the stolen armored car she had heard on the PBS station. She was convinced that Dewey's friend, Hans, was the armored truck driver, and that his letter to Dewey referred to the stolen gold.

"I've already agreed to go to Hopfgarten with you. But, you already said the clues in the diary don't make any sense." Dorian turned back to Kimberlee, her eyebrow raised. "If you really think Hans Kreuger hid the gold in Hopfgarten fifty-five years ago, don't you think someone would have found it by now? So, what's the point?"

Kimberlee shrugged. "According to the television documentary that aired just a month ago, the gold was never found. They only broadcast stories about lost treasures. I don't know what I expect, but, I think since we're this close, it would be crazy not to at least go to Hopfgarten and look around. Maybe Hans's poem would make sense if we saw the town the same way he did when he sent the note to Dewey. Don't you see? We have clues to the hiding place that no one else has ever seen, from the person who hid the gold. How can we not go and investigate?"

A crinkle crept across Dorian's cheeks. "You're right. I love an adventure as much as the next guy. If it's treasure we're after, b'gore, matey, let's pull up anchor and be on our way. *Arrggh!*"

Kimberlee brought her hand to her mouth and gasped. Dorian glanced at Kimberlee's face. "What's wrong?" She turned in the direction Kimberlee was staring.

"Over there. See that old man by the corner of the restaurant? He's been eavesdropping ever since we sat down. I'm sure he overheard us talking about Hans Kreuger and the treasure. When he realized I saw him watching us, he ran away."

Following a hasty lunch, Dorian slid into the driver seat, while Kimberlee took the role of navigator. She folded the Germany-Austria map once again, and glared at the passing street signs, trying to determine if they were headed toward the Autobahn, and Hopfgarten. "The waitress said, 'six blocks up, turn left at Strasburg, and the freeway should be there.'" She crinkled the map and peered closer. "I think we're close. Maybe another block? There it is. Strasburg Autobahn."

Dorian swung the car onto the ramp and pressed the gas. Within minutes they were racing along the modern two-lanes-wide divided freeway where cars in the slow lane drove seventy-mph, while the cars in the fast lane drove ninety-to-a-hundred mph.

Dorian's shoulders hunched as she gripped the steering wheel with both hands. "Everyone drives BMWs, Mercedes, or Volvos. I don't think there are two Volkswagens in all of Germany. These folks are either very wealthy or the price of BMWs and Mercedes is a lot less here than in the United States. Look." A Mercedes truck passed their car like they were standing still.

"Whatever you do, don't go into that far lane or we'll end up a couple of grease spots on the pavement." Kimberlee grimaced. "Now you can see what I was up against coming home yesterday. Not only a pauper, but feeling like I was pedaling a go-cart on the International Speedway. If you stay in this lane you'll be okay. Try to keep it between seventy and eighty miles an hour."

Dorian nodded. "*Yikes*. How long are we on the autobahn before we turn off?" Her gaze stayed riveted to the road. Perspiration dotted her forehead as another car whizzed past in the fast lane. She pressed the gas pedal, maintaining the seventy-mph required to keep up with traffic.

Kimberlee glanced at the map. "In about twenty miles, we turn onto another freeway. It's not marked as an autobahn, so it probably won't be so bad. Can you believe this is how people drive every day? How do they do it?"

Whoosh! Another car appeared from far behind and whizzed past their car like someone had left open a crack in Hell's front gate. Within seconds, the car almost disappeared from sight.

"I'll be so glad when this nightmare is over." Dorian wiped her sweaty palm on her pants leg. "Thank goodness, our esteemed leaders haven't decided to go this route in the U.S."

Kimberlee opened Dewey's diary. "I'll read to you. Maybe that will help you relax." She flipped a few pages. "This is the part about Hans's letter to Dewey," she said, glancing nervously between the book and the cars racing by in the left lane. For the next fifteen minutes as Kimberlee read, Dorian's shoulders relaxed and her death grip on the steering wheel eased.

Kimberlee reached the page where Dewey received Hans's letter. She held up the hymnal page and turned it in a circle, reading the words printed in the margin. *"The key to the treasure is in Hopfgarten. Touch the feet of the babe beneath the king... in the place where the storm clouds are frightened away by the ring."*

"You're right. It is intriguing. What do you suppose it means?" Dorian said, glancing quickly at the hymnal page and then back to the highway. "So, we know the treasure is in Hopfgarten. But, how do we find the babe beneath the king? And, what do storm clouds have to do with rings? Rings of what? Crazy."

"That's why we're going to Hopfgarten. Once we're there, the words might make sense or someone may understand what they mean."

"What's your plan when we get there?" Dorian reached for her water bottle, took a sip and replaced it in the cup holder. "It's not as if you're going to find a heap of gold lying on the sidewalk. Or babies and rings, for that matter."

"Let's start by trying to locate Hans's relatives. If we read the poem to them, they might understand what some of the terms relate to. Like, maybe it refers to a family secret or a family tradition or something."

"Don't you think if they knew what he meant, they'd have found the treasure themselves?"

"They didn't have the benefit of seeing what he wrote. I suspect if they had, they might have found it already." Kimberlee pushed the button on the door panel and lowered the window a few inches.

"You know, the word *treasure* also has a different meaning to different people, anywhere from gold, to health and happiness, or even peace and prosperity…like after a war. Even a *place* can be a considered a treasure." Dorian glanced to the right. "Shouldn't we be getting close to that turnoff?"

Kimberlee checked the map and looked up at the road signs over the freeway. *Innsbruck.* See?" She pointed. "We're not too far. Highway

E45, three kilometers."

Several minutes later, they turned off the autobahn. At the first opportunity, Dorian pulled over at a vista turnout. She wiped her sweaty brow with a tissue. "What a relief. Let's get out and stretch our legs," she said, grabbing her camera and opening the door. "I didn't think we'd live to see another picture postcard view." Dorian staggered toward the rock wall at the edge of the pull-off and sat, fiddling with her camera. The vista overlooked a green valley. Another car eased off the highway and stopped near the edge of the turnout, but no one exited the car.

Dorian raised her camera to capture the scene. A distant church lay nestled between a stream on one side and a green meadow on the other. The faraway tinkle of bells suggested cows hidden from view in the surrounding trees. Snow-capped mountains rearing up against a sapphire sky completed the striking view. "This is pretty." She turned and snapped another picture of Kimberlee beside their car.

"Postcard views are about all there are in Austria, no matter which way you turn." Kimberlee flexed her arms and legs and drank from her water bottle. "I have to buy a disposable camera next chance I get. Either that or you'll have to make two copies of all your pictures."

"I can do that. Though I expect you'll want your own camera."

After a few minutes, Kimberlee said, "Are you about ready to go? I'll drive for a while and let you rest." She took the wheel and glanced into the rear view mirror, then pulled onto the road. She noticed the car that had parked nearby in the parking lot, eased onto the road and then slowed, placing some distance between them.

Chapter Twenty-Seven

I believe Kimberlee would prevail in a lawsuit. - Attorney Ollingham

Twenty-two pastures filled with cows wearing bells, six small hamlets, dozens of pensions offering down-filled comforters and muffins for breakfast, numerous churches with steeples and at least forty-seven picture-postcard vista sites later, the girls entered the city limits of Hopfgarten.

On any other day, the planters, cobblestone streets, multi-colored awnings in front of lace-curtained windows, horse-drawn carriages, and snow-capped mountains would have had them *oohing* and *aahing* in wonder, but after driving through Germany and Austria, the multitude of magnificent sights had dulled their senses.

Spotting another café with red and white striped umbrella tables on the sidewalk and flowerboxes in the windows bursting with geraniums and petunias, Kimberlee parked a half-block away. "I don't think Austrians can build anything without flowers under the windows."

"I read last night that as pretty as the geraniums are, their purpose is to repel mosquitos. Who knew?" Dorian exited the car, stretched, and reached into the back seat to retrieve her purse and camera. "After lunch, let's locate a pension for the night and then we can come back and look around town." She clicked a picture of the church across the street, and then pulled out a chair from beneath the sidewalk table. She picked up the menu and chuckled.

Kimberly took a seat across from her. "What's so funny?"

"That church across the street has two bell towers. Do you think the townsfolk are hard of hearing, or so lazy, it takes two bells to call them to worship?"

Kimberlee glanced at the church towers. "Maybe the second one is just for good measure." She motioned toward the shop next door. "Look at the curtains in the windows. They're either hand-crocheted or cleverly machine-made with flowers and figures woven into the design. I can see a valance like that over my kitchen sink."

"Too girly for me. Give me venetian blinds and I'm happy." Dorian peered at the menu. "They make crepes. *Yum!* That's what I'm having."

"I think I'll order the clam—"

An elderly woman leaned over Kimberlee's shoulder and whispered, "Excuse me, miss. You are tourist and we must not make bad name with American tourist. I see you get out from that grey car down the street…?" She jerked her head toward their rental car. "That old man is making fuss on your car. I think he trying to break in." She turned and scurried away.

Dorian's blonde ponytail bounced as she jumped up and raced down the sidewalk. "Hey. Get away from there." Hearing her yell, the man turned and hurried across the street, yanked open his car door and jumped inside. Dorian dodged between two cars and raced across the street. Before she reached the other side, the car sped past the café where Kimberlee sat. She pushed back her chair and stood. *That looks like the same car...*

Somewhat out of breath, Dorian returned. "Couldn't catch him." She flopped down. "He got into a beige sedan. There's no point trying to follow."

"It passed the café like a bat out of Purgatory." Kimberlee shaded her eyes and gazed down the street where the car squealed around the corner. "It looks like the same car at the vista point where we stopped to take pictures. Do you think he followed us all the way into Hopfgarten?"

Dorian shrugged. "Could just be heading the same direction. Did you get a look at the driver?"

"I can't be sure. He looked older, with long grey hair…like…" A shiver raced up the back of Kimberlee's neck, "…like the man who was eavesdropping where we stopped earlier for lunch."

"If that's true, maybe he heard you talk about Dewey's diary and the clues to the treasure. You mentioned Hopfgarten. He probably assumed we left the diary in the car."

Kimberlee pulled the dairy part way out of her purse. "You're right. He's probably heard gossip about a lost treasure in Hopfgarten for years. Maybe he connected the gossip to what he overheard me say and followed us to get more information."

"We better watch what we say in public. We don't need any more treasure hunters on our trail."

"Let's grab something to eat and find a pension. We need to keep a lower profile. Not to mention, I'm tired."

Bumping along the cobbled streets, they passed little shops on left and right with colorful awnings over the sidewalk. Their car crossed a train track and wound up a narrow road past fields of cows. At the top of the hill, Kimberlee stopped the car in front of a guest hotel. Much like many of the structures they passed approaching Hopfgarten, the pension sported window flower boxes and brightly colored shutters. A birdbath sat in the middle of a small garden beside the driveway.

Dorian exited the car. "I'll go in and register. You can wait here, if you want to take some pictures. My camera's on the seat."

"Sounds good." Kimberlee pulled into a parking spot, got out, and wandered to the edge of the low wall overlooking the valley. She drew in her breath. The town below looked like a fairytale town in Amanda's storybooks, surrounded by rolling hills and distant mountains.

Off to the right, far below the pension, the train curved toward the town. Off to the left, she could see the lace store with the bright blue awning and flower-laden window boxes.

The church bells tolled the hour. 4:00 P.M. Kimberlee's gaze moved past the shops to the twin church towers. The sound of the chiming bells bounced off the base of the hillside where a small group of cows ambled through the mist. As the echo of the bells faded, the faint sound of the cow's bells took up the harmony. The music of the meadow and the mist and the beauty of the moment warmed her heart and radiated through her soul. She shivered. *Oh, the majesty of Your creation, Lord. This must be what it's like in Heaven.*

Dorian's words came back to her. It would be easy to believe the beauty and the splendor of Hopfgarten was the real treasure Hans spoke of in his poem, and not a monetary treasure of stolen gold.

"Are you daydreaming?" Dorian stood beside her, pulling her away from her reverie, and back to the present.

Kimberlee shook her head. "What? Oh. You're right. It's so beautiful here. Do you hear the cow bells in the distance?"

Dorian tipped her head and nodded. "Our room is on the ground floor facing the valley, so we can sit on the patio and enjoy the view. The hostess is bringing us a pot of coffee." She opened the tailgate and pulled out Kimberlee's suitcase. "Take yours. I'll get the other two. Once we're settled, we'll figure out how to find Hans's family."

"I think the first thing is to go to the county clerk and see if we can locate any of his relatives."

Dorian held the door while Kimberlee brought in the suitcases. "Sounds good. Let's freshen up and go back downtown. I want to take some pictures and then find the restaurant our hostess, Frau Hoffman, suggested for an early dinner." She stepped beneath a pair of vintage skis crisscrossed over the front door.

"And, I want to visit that lace shop and buy a valance for my kitchen window."

Dorian rubbed the chill bumps on her arm. "Let's hope we don't run into the old man and give him a second crack at our car. Let's not hang around any dark alleys. As far as I'm concerned, it's back to the pension right after dinner and a relaxing drink on the patio in time to watch the sunset."

"Sounds like a plan," Kimberlee agreed. "I'll keep the diary with me, just in case."

As usual, at the sound of the doorbell, Angel scooted down the hall toward the bedroom. Always wary with unexpected guests, it was more a matter of personal vanity, rather than shyness. Black Cat lifted his head. *Ah! Company's coming.*

Brett opened the door. "Come on in, Mr. Ollingham. I know you're busy, so thanks for dropping by again." He took the attorney's hat and coat and hung them on the hall tree. "We're both here, as you requested." He nodded toward Jack.

Jack stood and shook the attorney's hand. "Hello, sir."

"Glad you're here, Jack." Mr. Ollingham sat on the sofa and opened his briefcase. "With both of you here, it's easier to bring you up to speed. I have something to show you."

Brett gestured toward the kitchen. "May I offer you a soft drink or a cup of coffee?"

"No, thanks. I can't stay. I'm on my way home, and the missus is holding supper. I just wanted to drop by the proposal I received from Ted Herman's attorney." He handed a folder to Brett and one to Jack. "As we discussed the other day, it outlines the request for $150,000 in lieu of lengthy and costly litigation. It's not ideal, but I feel it is the best solution to your situation."

Black Cat jumped onto the arm of the sofa chair beside Brett as he flipped through the proposal.

"I know that Kimberlee is in Austria, but the offer is time-sensitive," Mr. Ollingham said. "Have you discussed the matter with her yet?"

Brett shook his head. "Jack and I are ready to approve the offer, but I haven't discussed it with Kimberlee. I didn't feel I should bring it up on a long-distance call. She'll be home before the proposal deadline. I expect her to agree to the terms, considering the alternative."

"That's good. Do you have any other questions or concerns?"

Brett's hand ran down Black Cat's back. "As a matter of fact, there is another personal matter I'd like to discuss, if you have a few minutes,"

Jack stood and moved to the door. "I'll go and give you some privacy. Thanks for dropping this by, Mr. Ollingham. I'll look over the papers and call ya if I have any questions. See ya tomorrow, Brett." He waved his copy of the document and went out.

Mr. Ollingham glanced at his watch. "What's on your mind?"

"It's Kimberlee's grandmother. She's in town, making wild accusations and threatening to take our home."

Over the next few minutes, Brett outlined the story of how Kimberlee acquired title to the house the previous year and the circumstances in Texas that created the conflict between her and her grandmother. "Now, Mrs. Lassiter is claiming that Kimberlee knowingly deceived her and coerced her into signing the deed to the house. It couldn't be farther from the truth. In fact, we had already replaced the roof on the house when Kimberlee discovered the secret details surrounding her birth."

After hearing Brett's story, including the circumstances of acquiring Angel without Mrs. Lassiter's permission when they left Texas, Mr. Ollingham offered his legal opinion. "If you have given me all the pertinent facts, I believe Kimberlee would prevail in any kind of litigation her grandmother might bring regarding the house. I suspect Mrs. Lassiter is a lonely old woman. She's striking out in bitterness against the injustice of her son's death. She could be suffering from Alzheimer's as well, considering what you've told me about her bizarre behavior last summer."

"How should we proceed if she comes back, raving about a lawsuit?" Brett asked.

Mr. Ollingham stood and drew a business card from his briefcase.

"Call her bluff. Give her my card and tell her to have her attorney contact me if and when he files charges. I doubt any legitimate lawyer would take such a case, but of course there are some..."

"Thanks. That's reassuring. Wouldn't you know the minute Kimberlee leaves town, all heck breaks loose. First, Ted asking for compensation for the lodge, and then crazy Granny showing up and threatening another lawsuit."

Mr. Ollingham chuckled. "Keeps me employed. Let me know when Kimberlee gets home and how you want to proceed." He stood and patted Black Cat's head. "Nice cat."

Brett walked him to the front door. "Thanks for coming. I appreciate your time and your advice."

"Good night, Brett. Call me anytime."

Black Cat hopped onto the back of the sofa and watched through the window as Mr. Ollingham walked down the sidewalk and through the gate to his car.

Humans. When they set out to cause trouble for someone they were supposed to love, they seldom stopped until they achieved the maximum amount of hurt possible.

Mr. Ollingham said Grandma couldn't hurt Kimberlee with a lawsuit. But, it was doubtful she would stop trying, considering her determination and the evil in her heart.

Chapter Twenty-Eight

If we don't have it, you don't need it. - Kimberlee

Morning sun streamed through the pension's patio doors, directly onto Kimberlee's face. She shivered, pulled the down comforter over her bare shoulder, and snuggled deeper under the feather coverlet. Dorian stirred in the single bed next to her. Kimberlee threw back the covers and tiptoed across the rug to the patio, stepped out onto the cold pavement, and peered over the rock wall. One shouldn't waste such a beautiful day lying in bed.

Unlike the glow of the sunset on the valley the previous evening, the colors of the streets below looked brighter. The chugging train running through the center of town sent plumes of smoke into the cloudless sky, and the church bells pealed even louder in the cold, crisp morning air.

A red-headed, black and white bird landed on the rock wall, almost close enough to touch. "Well, look at you, you pretty thing," Kimberlee whispered. "What's your name?" She stretched out her hand. The bird fluttered to a nearby bush. "I'll bet you're hungry."

She hurried back inside and returned with a package of rye crackers from last night's dinner. The cellophane crinkled as she tore it open and spread crumbs along the top of the rock wall. She stepped back. Would the bird return? Her red-headed visitor hovered above the wall and then drifted down, snagged a crumb, and flew back to the branch.

"I see you've made a friend," Dorian whispered from inside the patio door.

Kimberlee turned. "I'm sorry. Did I wake you?"

"I heard you get up. By the way, that's a Hirundo Rustica you're flirting with."

"A what?"

"Barn Swallow to you, my ornithologically challenged friend. It's Austria's national bird."

"And, you know this…how?" Kimberlee tossed several more cracker pieces to the bird, now hopping across the pavement, devouring the treat as though it was his last meal.

"I read it in the travel guide on the desk." Dorian giggled. "Do you want to go to breakfast? It's after seven."

"I do, but first, I want you to come over here. Close your eyes." Dorian closed her eyes, reached out her hands, and crossed the patio. Kimberlee put her hands over Dorian's eyes. "Listen." The tinkle of bells in the distance suggested a gathering of small animals—perhaps goats or sheep—grazing on the rich grass, hidden by the fog clinging to the nearby hillside.

Dorian opened her eyes. "Beautiful."

"I've got to find another camera today."

"We'll do that first thing, right after breakfast."

It didn't take long to locate the equivalent of Hopfgarten's County Clerk's office in a white stucco building on a side street. The required flower boxes overflowing with pink petunias and bright orange geraniums framed each side of the front door. A tiny sign in English and German identified the building to be a combination of the county seat, hall of records, city hall, county court house, and jail. A barred window on the far side of the building suggested only one jail cell—probably sufficient, considering the unlikely overabundance of crime in the little town.

"Sort of like, 'one-stop-shop,' back home," Dorian said.

"Or, if you can't find it here, you don't need it."

"Pretty much." Dorian pushed open the door. "Now, be careful what you say," she whispered. "We don't want to arouse any unnecessary interest in the '*whatsit*.'"

The stark white hallway had several doors leading off to the left and right. A photograph of the current mayor hung beside the front door. His mutton-chop sideburns extended from his hairline, across his lower jawline and chin. He wore a high-collared shirt and bowtie. Kimberlee ran her fingers down the English translated words on the left side of the directory board. "What do you suppose? Hall of Records? Room D?"

"It's as good a place to start as any."

A magazine lay on one of the two wooden benches nestled between Room A and B. Perhaps this was where litigants waited during court proceedings. An ash tray and a phone directory sat on the small table between the two benches. Several dead geraniums hung limp in a vase on the table. Kimberlee stopped outside Room D. "Here goes nothing." She pasted a smile on her face and pushed open the glass door. Inside, she stepped up to a long counter where a woman sat at a computer.

The woman stopped typing. "Gutt morning. Kann ich dir helfen?"

"I'm sorry. Do you speak English?" Kimberlee asked. "We're from the U.S.A." She set her purse on the counter.

"Ya. What help can I matter you for?" The clerk produced a big smile, appearing proud of her command of the English language.

Dorian leaned forward. "We are looking for the family of a man who knew an old friend of ours. They fought together in WWII. Our friend requested we try to locate this man's relatives and—"

"And, here we are." Kimberlee interrupted. "We're hoping to honor our friend's wishes. The man's name is Hans Kreuger. He would be elderly now, perhaps even passed on. We'd like to meet him, if he's still alive, or pay our respect to his family."

Kimberlee's heart pounded as her forced smile wavered. The clerk's brow furrowed. "I think you wish to find family of perhaps old dead Hopfgarten citizen?"

"Yes. That's it. Hans Kreuger's family. Do you know them?"

The clerk folded her hands on the desk and smiled. "Kreuger is same name which of many in our town gave."

"Hans Kreuger would be about eighty years old. Perhaps his children or grandchildren still live here?" *Keep smiling.*

The clerk opened a book. "Here is book of registered voter peoples in city limits." She turned to the page containing last names starting with "K." She ran her finger down the list. "Here is Kreuger. There are six names, but is not one Hans. Do you wish list of each with address?"

"Thank you. That would be lovely. Also, their phone numbers?"

"I give you list. You can look." She made a Xerox of the page, brought back the copy, and with a black marker, crossed off all except the Kreuger names, and handed Kimberlee the paper.

"Thank you. You've been most kind."

"Good luck with wishes for you." The clerk smiled and waved.

Once in the hallway, Kimberlee scanned the list of names. "That didn't help much. We could have gotten the same information from the phone book."

Dorian pushed open the outside door and stepped out. "At least it's a place to start. Shall we call or visit the addresses in person?"

"Probably easier to call, since we don't know the area. If they don't speak English, we're out of luck, anyway. Let's find a phone and—"

Dorian tossed her head toward the beige Mercedes across the street. "Don't look now, but our *friend* who tried to break into our car yesterday is sitting in his car across the street."

Nausea swept over Kimberlee. The fresh-baked croissant she so enjoyed with dark rich coffee and thick cream an hour before, suddenly felt like a garlic pickle drowning in sweet cream.

Chapter Twenty-Nine

Her porch light is on, but nobody's home! - Angel

umping off the back of the sofa, Black Cat tiptoed to Amanda's room, one of Angel's favorite napping places. *Where's Angel? I haven't seen her for hours.* He peeked into Kimberlee's bedroom. *Not here.*

Back in Nevada City, Angel had often napped on John's bed, but in Fern Lake, she seldom entered Brett and Kimberlee's room, a self-imposed taboo, despite Black Cat's assurances that she would be welcome. Black Cat checked the kitchen and the laundry room. Maybe she was in the yard, or perhaps on the porch swing where they occasionally enjoyed a morning nap or watched the evening sun sizzle into the lake's murky water.

Black Cat plunged through the kitchen cat door, and padded around the house, his heart full of warm and fuzzy thoughts of his love. He wanted to tell her about Brett's birthday next month and how Kimberlee would decorate the house for a surprise party. She would invite Dorian and her dog, Sam, and her boyfriend, Virgil, and Mrs. Wilson, and Jack and Chance, and maybe even Rajinder and his wife and their little girl who attended school with Amanda. There would be balloons and a big chocolate birthday cake with cherries in the middle. Brett would pretend to be surprised, even though he would know…

Black Cat reached the corner of the house and skidded to a stop. *Who is that? What is she doing? She looks like…*

A woman wearing dark glasses and a large black hat that shaded her lower face crept through the front gate and gently pulled it closed behind her. Rosebush stickers on the fence caught at her sleeve. She paused, unhooked the thorns and then, hunched over, she tip-toed down the sidewalk toward the house. Did she imagine she couldn't be seen from the house? *All two hundred pounds of her?* Black Cat lowered his ears and crept past the corner of the house. *What is she up to?*

On the other side of the gate, the woman's car motor rumbled, its driver side door hanging open. *She's up to no good, that's for sure.*

Where was Brett with all this tomfoolery going on in his front yard? Probably in his office, writing another salacious chapter to his novel.

Black Cat's heart thudded at another thought. *Where's Amanda?* Didn't this woman look like someone who might steal a little girl from her own yard? He glanced toward the front porch swing. Empty. *Good.* Amanda must be in her room, or maybe down at the lake with Jack.

The pounding in his heart eased a bit. His family was safe. Perhaps this woman intended to steal something from the front porch. He crept forward. He would have to stop her and protect the family's belongings. He could almost see the front page headlines in tomorrow's Fern Lake Gazette. Plucky Local Cat Foils Attempted Grand Larceny. *Despite overwhelming odds, the daring and plucky feline protected his master's valuable front porch rhododendron plant from the clutches of a 200 lb. female assailant determined to…so forth and so on…* Perhaps even his picture and…

His gaze swept toward the Wisteria vines at the far corner of the porch. Angel's gold tail swished back and forth beneath the hanging purple flowers. *Angel!* She had chosen a new place to nap in the shade of the…

The portly woman stepped over Amanda's doll, then sprinted the last few steps up the sidewalk, leaned down and yanked Angel by her tail, out from under the bush.

Meow!

Clutching the struggling cat to her breast, the woman turned toward her car. Angel writhed and twisted. "Oh no, you don't, my pet."

In the scuffle, the woman's hat tumbled off and spun across the grass.

Grandmother Lassiter? Black Cat raced across the lawn. *Angel!* He leaped at the woman's arm, teeth bared. Grandmother jerked away. His fangs caught the edge of her sleeve and ripped through the material. Having missed his target, he tumbled to the grass with a shriek. *Brett! Brett! Help! Help! Grandmother Lassiter is stealing Angel.*

Grandmother Lassiter waddled down the sidewalk with the wriggling cat. She struggled to open the front gate with one hand while grappling with the thrashing cat. "Stop fighting me, you little... You belong to me, and I'm taking you back."

The front door flew open and Brett stepped onto the porch. His gaze moved across the yard to the car at the curb. "What's going on out here? Grandmother Lassiter? What...?"

Once she reached her open car door, Grandmother flung Angel onto the passenger seat, and flopped into the driver's seat.

Not my Angel... Black Cat sprinted through the gate, leaped over the hood of the car, and scrambled around the car door.

Grandmother reached for the handle, but before she could slam the door shut, Black Cat leaped into her lap. She grabbed her purse and struck at his head, knocking him sideways. His head struck the dials on the radio and he fell to the floor, momentarily stunned. As though through a haze, he heard Brett yelling. Angel huddled on the front passenger seat, her nails clinging to the vinyl seat, frozen with fright, mewing pathetically, *Black Cat! Black Cat!*

Grandmother Lassiter hit the gas and the car plunged down the driveway, spewing gravel. She reached the street and gunned the engine. Her tires squealed, leaving patches of rubber as she roared past the lodge and headed for the outskirts of town. The car swayed as it sped around corners, tossing Black Cat forward and back. Grandmother Lassiter threw back her shoulders. "Thought she could get the best of me, did she? How's she gonna like it now that I've snatched her ill-gotten cat out from under her nose. What goes around comes around."

Black Cat lifted his head as the dizziness faded. *She's stealing Angel to get even with Kimberlee?* Kimberlee *had* taken Angel from Texas without permission, but what sane person would come all the way to California, sneak into someone's yard in broad daylight and snatch a cat? She probably thought no one would see her and Angel's disappearance would be chalked up to another missing cat…the object of a brief search resulting in acceptance and another kitten taking her place within a fortnight.

She hadn't counted on Black Cat mucking up her plan or figured he'd end up aboard the getaway car. Certainly, her next thought would be to get rid of him…the stowaway with teeth and a vengeance…as soon as she got away from the scene of the crime.

Within minutes, they were beyond the city limits, headed for Highway 101. The car careened around a corner, sending Angel tumbling to the floor beside her mate. *Oww! Black Cat! I'm scared.* Black Cat shook his head, clearing the last bit of dizziness. He reached out his paw and touched Angel's head. *Don't be scared. We've gotten out of worse things.*

Angel struggled to sit upright. *What could be worse than this? She's flipped her lid. Her porch light is on, but nobody's home.*

We have to get out of the car before she gets so far from home, we'll never find our way back.

Ohh! Angel put her paws over her head. *I don't want to be lost again. I want to go home.*

Despite their dire circumstances, Black Cat's heart surged. Angel wanted to go home. Had she finally accepted Brett, Kimberlee, and Amanda as her *persons* and the little house on the lake as home? If they ever got out of this mess, perhaps they could live in peace at last. First, they must deal with a car racing farther from town every minute, with the Witch of Endor's great-aunt at the wheel…

He glanced up at Grandmother Lassiter. Her shoulders were hunched and her jaw clenched tight enough to crack a molar. No way could he let her vengeful heart ruin his hard-won victory over Angel's new-found acceptance of Fern Lake.

He jumped onto the passenger seat and looked out the window. *Where are we?* The lake town was far behind and they were somewhere in the remote wooded area between Fern Lake and Highway 101. Manzanita shrubs and Aspen trees lined the road. The white line in the center of the road raced toward them as their car barreled toward… who knows where? It looked like they were approaching the kind of wooded location where Grandmother might stop and try to throw him out of the car.

Black Cat looked down at Angel. *I've got to make her stop the car. As soon as she opens the door, jump out and run back the way we came. I'll be right behind you. Are you ready?*

Ohh! Be careful, Black Cat. I love you.

I love you more. Black Cat's heart swelled as he gathered his feet under him, fixed his gaze on Grandmother's face, and prepared for the attack. *Get ready, my love.* His ears went down and his tail switched from side to side. He fastened his gaze on Grandmother's throat.

As the car approached a curve in the road, Grandmother Lassiter glanced down at Black Cat. Seeing his stance and the look of hate in his eyes, she couldn't help but guess his intent. Her attention left the road as she leaned down and scrabbled around on the floorboard for her purse to fend him off.

Black Cat leaped.

Grandmother flung up both arms to protect her face, and jammed her foot on the brake. The car skidded and careened through the wooden barrier, plunged down an embankment, flipped sideways and crashed into a tree, slamming her torso against the door and the steering wheel.

Another day flashed into Black Cat's mind. The day that Kimberlee's car crashed on the way home from Texas and their cat carrier was thrown from the vehicle. Not even protected by the walls of the carrier, as they were on that other fateful day, Black Cat and

Angel were thrown around the car, striking the cushioned seats, and the driver's side window.

Angel came to rest with her head leaning against Grandmother's lap, where she had probably spent many hours back in Texas, but this time there was no hand to stroke her golden head, and no purr to acknowledge the touch.

Black Cat lay stunned against the window and the dashboard, beside Grandmother's head. Shards of broken glass from the car window were scattered across his black fur, and blood trickled from a cut on his head. He awoke to the hum of Angel's anxious purr, her rasping tongue gliding across his cheek, washing away the blood that oozed from behind his ear. He blinked to clear the hazy vision of Grandmother's body slumped in a heap against the steering wheel. The car lay on its side in a gully while its air conditioner still whirred, pumping a cool blast of air across his aching body. Angel hunched beside him, shaking in terror. "Black Cat! Are you all right? Grandmother won't wake up."

He lifted his head, replaying through his mind the previous minutes. Leaping into Grandmother's face—the car crashing through the guardrail. *We have to get out.* He struggled to get his feet under him. His body swayed as broken glass tumbled off his fur and crunched beneath his feet. "Crawl out through the window. Be careful. It's a tight fit."

Angel crawled through the small space in the crumpled window frame and onto the ground. "Now, you come. Watch where you step. There's more broken glass out here."

Black Cat sucked in his breath and squeezed through the narrow opening, brushing against a jagged piece of metal protruding from the broken window frame. *Oww!*

"What about Grandma? We need to help her." Angel peered back through the shattered window at Grandmother's motionless body.

"Do we have to? She tried to steal you." Black Cat swayed. "Still dizzy…"

"We can't leave her like that."

"There's nothing we can do. Maybe if we go back up to the road, someone will stop."

"Come over here." Angel stepped away from the car. "Lie down there and rest. I'll go. Maybe I can…" She started up the incline, stepping through the stickers, and looked back over her shoulder. "Get that look off your face. I'll be careful."

"No. Wait." *She shouldn't go alone. It's too dangerous.* Black Cat struggled to his feet and slipping and sliding in the sandy loam, he followed Angel up the sloping embankment toward the road. He stopped at the top of the knoll and lay down beside the broken guardrail. *Any minute now, someone will stop and help.*

Angel stepped onto the pavement and looked down the road toward Fern Lake. Surely, someone driving by, and seeing the broken guard rail, would stop to investigate. The sound of a truck rumbled in the distance. If someone didn't help Grandmother soon, it might be too late. Angel moved into the middle of the road and sat. Perhaps she thought sitting in the middle of the road was the quickest way to get a car to stop, but she hadn't considered the risk. A truck rounded the corner. Its tires squealed in an attempt to stop as it skidded toward her.

Black Cat jumped to his feet. "No! Angel. Get out of the road. That's too far…"

Angel hunkered, frozen with fear as the truck careened closer and closer. Rubber tires shrieked against the pavement. Black Cat closed his eyes and held his breath. *No! No!* Was it to end like this? After all they'd been through together and finally to escape from Grandmother, surviving the crash, only to have his precious Angel mowed down by a bread truck? No. He would not have it. He tensed his muscles and with every ounce of the power of love, he willed the truck to stop. *It should have been me. I should have gone into the road. Why do I always fail my loved ones?*

Silence. Black Cat couldn't look. His heart crumbled, and he fell over in a heap of utter despair. If a cat could weep, he would have drowned in his own tears of shame and self-reproach. For a few seconds, he lay shaking on the ground, unable to open his eyes to what he feared would be the sight of his mate, crushed beneath the wheels of the bread truck. Then a door slammed, and boots thudded on the pavement. He opened his eyes and lifted his head.

A man crouched in front of the truck's bumper, blocking Black Cat's view from all except a patch of reddish-gold fur being pulled from beneath the truck. *What will the driver do with my Angel? Toss her body into the ditch?* Weakened by loss of blood from his head wound, and overcome with grief, he staggered to his feet and stumbled onto the pavement. *Meow!*

The man turned at his cry, "Another one. You must be together." He stood with Angel cradled in his arms. "Then, you'd best come with me, too. We need to get your friend to the doc."

She's still alive? With Black Cat trailing close behind, crying piteously, the man opened the truck's passenger door, wrapped his jacket around Angel, and laid her on the seat. "Come on, old fellow. You look like you could use some help, too."

Angel stirred and tried to lift her head. *Grandmother?* Black Cat sucked in his breath. Indeed. Grandmother was to blame for all this. Grandmother—still lying in the wrecked car in the gully. If the Good Samaritan knew about the car over the hill, how much time would it take to pull her from the vehicle and summon help, when Angel so desperately needed medical care?

But, what was his responsibility to Grandmother? Should he make the man aware of the car in the ditch? Who would be the wiser if he did nothing to impede Angel getting to the nearest veterinarian where time could be factor in saving her life? Who would expect him to be self-sacrificing for the old woman's sake? He certainly wasn't responsible for Grandma Lassiter, who held evil in her heart for Kimberlee and her family. Shouldn't his first loyalty be to Angel?

Black Cat jumped into the truck beside Angel and licked her ear. *I do love you, but...*

Oh, snails! I will so regret this tomorrow, but I can't do it. I can't leave her... I'm not that kind of cat.

He jumped down from the truck before the driver could shut the door and dashed to the side of the road. He set up a howling such as might only be heard on Halloween night at the sight of the Headless Horseman. *"Yowww... Owww... Owww!"* He looked back at the startled driver and then took a few steps over the hillside, came back to the side of the road and howled again. *"Yowww! Come on, stupid human. Over here. There's no time to shilly-shally. Save the old bat and let's get on our way."*

"What?" The gears in the truck driver's head must have finally clicked—the broken guardrail and two cats on the side of the road. "Is there a car…?" He rushed over and peered down the embankment. "No wonder you're having such a fit. It must be your beloved master." He ran back to his truck.

Certainly, not beloved. I don't even like her, but she is family. What choice do I have?

The driver grabbed his two-way radio and made a call. "Don't worry, kitty. I'm calling for help. Someone will be… Hello? 911? There's an accident on River Road, about six miles outside of town. We need an ambulance…"

Black Cat ceased to listen, leaped back into the truck and lay down beside Angel, to comfort her and keep her warm. *How long must we wait before help comes?*

After closing the truck door, the driver climbed down the embankment toward Grandmother's vehicle.

"Grandmother?" Angel's voice trembled. As usual, she thought of others before herself.

"Shhh. Now, you've done enough. The driver will help her, my sweet," Black Cat crooned. "Now, you rest. I'm right beside you. Help is coming soon." The ache in his heart swelled, and he felt as if he would choke on the lump in his throat. *Soon, yes, dear Angel. But, will it be soon enough?*

Chapter Thirty

Dorian, where are you when I need you? - Kimberlee

Keeping an eye on the stalker in the car across the street, Dorian hurried Kimberlee away from the courthouse and into the car. She pulled away from the curb and headed for Hopfgarten's main street. Overhead, the sky darkened and storm clouds gathered. Kimberlee turned and peered out the back window. "He's following us. What are we going to do?"

"Write down the license number," Dorian said, glancing in the rearview mirror. "Let's call his bluff and pretend we don't see him. There's not much he can do in broad daylight if we stop at a phone booth. He won't know who we're calling."

"Up there, on the left. There's a phone booth on the corner. You can park there."

Dorian parked the car and glanced back over her shoulder. "He stopped about a half block behind us. Go call a couple names on your list. I'll wander down the street past his car. Maybe I can give him a scare." She chuckled. "Or better yet, grab him by the collar and ask what he's up to." She opened the car door and walked around to the sidewalk.

While Kimberlee headed for the telephone booth, Dorian sauntered over to the store window, stood gazing at the display, and then ambled down the street, pausing at each window, slowly approaching the stalker's car.

Kimberlee opened the phone booth door and stepped inside, took the paper from her purse and dialed the operator. Maybe this wasn't such a good idea. How would she know which coins to use? Not to mention, she couldn't speak a word of German. She hung up the receiver before the operator answered and opened the phone booth door. Wouldn't it be better to return to the pension and have Frau Hoffman help them make the calls? Any charges could be added to the room bill. No fuss, no muss. She looked up and down the street. Now, where was Dorian? She had gone down the sidewalk to spook the treasure hunter, but now, she was nowhere in sight. Even the car was gone. Kimberlee walked to the end of the block and turned in a circle, scanning the sidewalks. The old man must have driven away and Dorian followed him. *I suppose she thought I'd be on the phone for a while.* Still. It wasn't very considerate to drive away and leave her standing on the street.

Should she wait for Dorian to return or walk back to the pension? She glanced again at the list of names from the courthouse. *Father Johan Kreuger.* The church should have information about him. Kimberlee crossed the street, approached the heavy double church doors, and grasped the handle. Locked! Just then, the door opened and a woman stepped out. "Good morning." Kimberlee grabbed the door and held it as the woman nodded and hurried down the steps. Kimberlee entered the church. She sucked in her breath at the sight. How could such a tiny village of less than 5000 souls create such a masterpiece of beauty?

Carved statues throughout the church depicted the Christ Child, Mary, Joseph, and the saints. A mural on the ceiling depicted angels surrounding the throne of God. Beautiful flowers, burning candles and gold-covered statues of the Holy Trinity adorned the altar. Burnished wood carvings of flowers and vines decorated the ends of each padded velvet pew.

While the countryside in its grandeur touched her heart, it couldn't compare to the emotions that surged through her breast as she gazed at the splendor. It felt as though she was standing at the Seat of God. A lump in her throat threatened to erupt in a burst of tears.

"Gutt morning. Kann ich dir helfen?"

Kimberlee started and turned. "Oh, good morning. I'm sorry. I don't speak German. I'm looking for Father Kreuger."

"I am Father Kurt. The father will be back soon. Can I help?"

"I hoped to speak to Father Kreuger on a personal matter. Your church is beautiful."

Father Kurt's smile glowed as he gazed around the church. "Yes. Very beautiful. Many fine artists gave time to make it beautiful."

Thunder rumbled outside. A spear of lightning lit up a stained glass window representing one of the Stations of the Cross, making the colorful figures appear to come alive.

"Storm comes soon. You must visit our graveyard before rain falls. It is very lovely with flowers and statues. If you have no need of me, I will leave you to your prayer and return to my duties." The priest hurried off, his black robes rustling in the silent church.

Kimberlee bowed her head, said a quick prayer, and then tiptoed toward the side door she assumed led to the graveyard. The words of Hans's poem rang through her head. *The key to the treasure is in Hopfgarten...* Well, she was in Hopfgarten, but no closer to deciphering the meaning of the words than before they left Fern Lake. So far, all they had done was attract the attention of a crazy old man bent on stealing the journal.

Perhaps it was silly to pursue this puzzling situation. She shook her head. She'd look through the graveyard and walk back to the pension. Dorian would be back soon. Maybe they should chalk up the treasure hunt as a lark, and visit the castle they passed outside of town.

Stepping through the chapel door into the ancient graveyard, Kimberlee sucked in her breath. Another amazing sight. And, here she was, without a camera.

The graveyard looked like a cherished garden, unlike cold and often little cared-for cemeteries in the states. She gazed over marble tombstones, some with dates as early as the mid-1800's. On some headstones, faded glass-framed photographs of the deceased were embedded in the stone, many with costumes and hairstyles representing fashion from the 1800's. She imagined traveling back in time, seeing the faces of parishioners whose lives were often cut short by illness or cruel circumstances.

Well-tended flowers, begonias, geraniums, ivy, pruned and trimmed and watered with care covered the graves; as though the dearly departed had recently passed, and not ancestors who lived and died many years before.

On several graves a wrought-iron cross stood near the headstone and a metal picket fence circled the plot, its blackened iron contrasting with the stark whiteness of the gleaming granite headstones and the red and yellow flowers covering the grave.

Hanging over the gate to the street, a magnificent work of wrought iron, curved into gentle arches and intertwining circles, like wedding rings. *Rings? The rings in the poem? Where the storm clouds are frightened away by the ring...* Her heart raced. Was this the right place, after all?

She walked among the graves, reading the names and dates and noted that in many cases, the complete family—father, mother and children, were all interred under one headstone. Many headstones noted the names of several children who died in infancy. Her heart went out to the mother from long ago who buried five babies within eight years, all under the age of two. How difficult it must have been to be a mother dealing with frequent infant mortality.

Again, the words of Hans's poem flashed through her mind. *Press the feet of the babe that lies beneath the king.* Could it be that simple?

Her head snapped up toward the intertwined rings over the entrance gate. *In the place where the storm clouds are frightened away by the ring.* The intertwining rings over the wrought iron gate? Her stomach lurched. Was the treasure buried here in the graveyard, perhaps beneath the headstone of a baby buried beneath a headstone of a person named

King, enclosed within the wrought iron gate? It seemed to make sense.

To find the German word for king, she flipped through her handbook of German words and phrases and paused at the K's. She ran her finger down the page. King: *Kaiser Konig.* Her gaze swept across the nearest graves, searching for a baby's grave with the name of King, Kaiser, or Konig. She'd have to read every headstone. "Dorian, where are you when I need you? This could take all day." She crouched beside a grave to pull away the flowers that covered the name.

Lightning flashed overhead again and thunder rumbled. How quickly the sky darkened. At that moment, the church bells pealed and a downpour of rain drove her to her feet. She rushed to the side door of the church she had recently excited. *It's locked.*

Holding her purse over her head, she fled through the carved wrought iron gate, down the short stone stairway and onto the street. Somewhere, there must be an awning or a covered area where she would find shelter from the sudden torrents of rain sluicing down, drenching her clothes. *There. Next to the church. A store with an awning.*

Thoroughly wet through her shirt, Kimberlee plunged down the sidewalk. Rain dripped off her hair onto her shoulders. She tried the door of the shop. Locked. The sign on the door said, *Closed 11:00 A.M. to 1:30 P.M.*. How inconvenient for tourists caught in the rain.

Kimberlee huddled against the wall, taking advantage of the slightest bit of shelter the awning offered from the storm's assault. How on earth had such a squall come seemingly out of nowhere on a sunny day? The giant drops of rain smashing against the canvas awning overhead sounded as loud as a freight train. The clanging church bells continued to peal as if the world had come to an end. She put her hands over her ears to block out the thunder and the bells.

She wrapped her arms around her body and huddled closer to the wall. *Calm down. It's only a sudden rainstorm.* Despite her self-talk, her imagination soared. Between the bells and the wind and the rain and the thunder, it felt as though she was transported to another world, or dumped into a Hollywood spy movie, seeking a hidden treasure and pursued by an evil-doer like Sherlock Holmes's Moriarty, or…

It occurred to her that she was, indeed, in *another world* and seeking a hidden treasure, and the old man following them might very well be an evil-doer, capable of anything, if he thought the diary would lead him to the treasure. Where on earth was Dorian?

Chapter Thirty-One

Touch the feet of the babe who lies beneath the king. - Dewey's diary

he wind shifted and now the rain blew under the canopy and soaked her feet. A siren wailed and rain ran in sheets across the cobblestones in the street. As the bells clanged, sirens screeched, firetrucks raced past, and water squelched from beneath their tires, spraying the sidewalk.

Was she in the midst of a national disaster? Perhaps a dam nearby had burst? Her heart pounded. She had to find better shelter than this simple awning offered. She remembered a Sweet Shop nearby. With her purse over her head, she made a mad dash across the street. There would be people in the shop and hot coffee. Perhaps they'd have some idea what happened. At least she could seek refuge from the impending disaster.

The rain pelted her face as she ran through puddles toward the warmth and safety of the Sweet Shop. She flung open the door and rushed in, her chest heaving. The low buzz of conversation stopped. *No wonder. I look like a drowned rat, dripping onto the tile floor.* The customers stared for a moment, and then turned back to their coffee, seemingly unconcerned that it appeared life as we know it could end momentarily. They were more interested in their apple strudel than the disaster right outside the door. She flinched as lightning flashed and thunder clapped directly overhead. Had she slipped into a parallel universe where Mother Nature's nightmare, aided by run-away church bells, was a common occurrence and, without concern, people accepted whatever she had in store for them?

Feeding Kimberlee's sense of impending doom, Mother Nature played her next hand, and chucks of hail the size of marbles rapped at the window like tiny ghosts from the graveyard across the street.

A waitress rushed up and handed Kimberlee a towel to dry her face. She helped her pull off her wet sweater and hung it on a coat rack beside the door. "Thank you." Kimberlee dabbed the rain from her face.

The waitress took her arm and led her to a nearby table where a young woman sat. "You sit with this lady, please?" She pulled out a chair and gestured for Kimberlee to sit. For some reason, neither the customer nor the waitress seemed concerned with whatever national disaster had occurred.

Another odd Austrian custom? Sitting me with a stranger? Kimberlee hesitated, her hand on the chair. "May I join you," she said. "I don't want to disturb you."

The young woman nodded. "Please. You are tourist?"

Kimberlee smiled at the waitress. "May I have a cup of coffee, please?" She turned back to her tablemate. "Yes. I'm from California." She gazed at the hail striking the window and the torrents of rain sluicing down. "I'm visiting here with my friend…who seems to have temporarily abandoned me to the forces of Mother Nature. It's horrible outside. I've never seen such a storm. And, the bells and sirens! What's going on? Aren't you worried?"

The young woman shrugged. "You should not to worry. Is summer storm. It will pass." She looked up and nodded toward the church across the street. "The bells will frighten away the clouds and soon will be sunshine."

Kimberlee chuckled. "Well, that's a nice idea, but it isn't working. It's been raining steadily for about fifteen minutes."

"Oh yes. Is working fine. But, the next village also ring their church bells, and clouds confused. Go there. Hear the bells, return to our town. Soon they will find quiet place and not come back again." With a reassuring smile, she took a bite of her chocolate éclair.

Kimberlee sat for a moment, politely digesting the quaint but sincere folklore this young local woman believed as truth incarnate. *Imagine. Bells scaring the clouds to the next village...* Goosebumps quivered from her head to her toes as the words of Hans's poem popped into her head. *...contained in the place where the storm clouds are frightened away by the ring...*

Not a ring of gold, nor a wrought iron ring on a graveyard gate. Hans had referred to the ringing of the church bells. The treasure must be in the tower where the bells were *frightening away the storm clouds* or in the *place* where the bells were contained. Within the church itself? Of course. The babe and the king were the Christ Child and God, his Heavenly father. Why hadn't she seen it? Had she solved the puzzle? Or at least, located the correct place to look.

"Oh! It was so nice to talk with you, but I must go." Kimberlee tossed down some bills and stood, nearly toppling the table. She grabbed her wet sweater from the rack, threw open the door, and raced back across the street. By now, the rain had slackened and true to the promise of the young woman's fable, it seemed as if the bells had, indeed, frightened away the clouds, as they gradually drifted toward the hillside where they might find a quiet place to dwell.

Filled with new confidence, Kimberlee dashed through the puddles toward the church. A sobering thought. How was she to recognize the treasure when she saw it? One cannot remove things from the church. But, the treasure couldn't be a religious relic that belonged to the church. She was convinced Hans referred to the stolen gold from the armored car. That's why he sent Dewey the message in the first place, telling him where to find it. But, how could it still be in the church, undiscovered for over fifty years? Maybe Father Kreuger would be back by now and have some answers to her questions. Her hand shook as she pulled open the front door of the church, now mercifully unlocked, and stepped inside. She stopped by the back pew. Which way should she go? And, what was she searching for?

Dark wood confessional booths sat beneath stained glass windows depicting biblical scenes, with the donating family's name etched in the glass.

Kimberlee stepped toward the left side of the chapel toward a row of faded photographs on the wall. Each, the face of a young lad who would never grow old. Names and dates beneath the photographs confirmed her suspicion, identifying them as victims of WWI and WWII.

Her heart skipped as she peered into the face of a young, blond, soldier. Hans Kreuger, 1912-1954. That was long after the war ended but coincided with the PBS program and the date of Hans's last letter to Dewey. Perhaps his family wanted his service to be equally honored among his peers.

She moved down the side aisle, past the photographs and approached the altar. She passed a stunning statue of the Christ Child. Could this be the babe from the poem? Her heartbeat quickened. *Touch the feet of the babe...* She ran her hands over the statue—His face, His body and His feet. Nothing. What did she expect? Gold coins to fall from his feet, like quarters from a casino slot machine? Her face warmed. Hadn't she already determined this was a fool's errand? All her thoughts were in turmoil, the rings, the babes in the graveyard, the bells. None of it made any sense. What she should do is forget all this nonsense, find Dorian, and go back to that linen shop and buy the crocheted valance for her kitchen window. But, considering what the young woman in the pastry shop told her about the storm clouds and the bells, the thought that it pertained to Hans's poem was too strong to allow her to stop now.

She moved past the altar, planning to walk down the left aisle and leave through the front door. Passing several pews, she stopped and stared in amazement at a full-sized glass coffin with a slanted top lying atop an ornate base with carved legs. Inside, lay a mummified figure wearing a crown and holding a sword, fully dressed in shining satin garments trimmed with gold threads.

Above the mummy hung a gilded plaque inscribed—*Christlich martyrer.*

Kimberlee pulled out her German-English dictionary. *Christlich.* Christian. *Martyrer*—martyr. A Christian martyr. With his crown and raiment, he could be described as a king. Carved on each table leg holding the glass coffin was the figure of a baby the size of a child's doll, depicting an angel or…the Christ Child. The words from the poem raced through her head again. *Touch the feet of the babe who lies beneath the king. In the place where the storm clouds are frightened away by the ring.*

Kimberlee gasped. "It all fits. It must be the babe Hans described in his message." She ran her hand over the Christ Child's leg on the left corner of the table. As her fingers moved over the infant's carved toes, a tiny drawer popped open in the panel below, a secret hiding place designed for some unknown reason. Inside the compartment lay a tarnished brass key attached to a faded piece of paper. Her hand shook as she plucked it from the drawer and read: *Vontobel Bank—Zurich, Switzerland - 37193.* A safe deposit box key! The key in Hans's poem?

She had taken the words, *the key to the treasure*, to be symbolic, when, instead, Hans told Dewey exactly where to find the hidden key. There was no doubt the treasure in the poem referred to the stolen gold coins. Was it possible the coins were still in the safety deposit box? She forced her breathing to slow and her hand to stop trembling. She had to find Dorian. She would know what to do…

"So, my dear, I was right to follow you, after all. You've found the key, haven't you?"

Kimberlee whipped around, *Who…?*

Before she could react, the old man grabbed her arm and tried to wrest the key from her hand. The reek of his sweat turned her stomach.

Kimberlee tried to free her arm from his vice-like grip. Wedging her back against the coffin, he cupped his hand over her mouth, making it difficult to breathe. The biblical characters in the stained glass window swayed.

With his other hand, he pried open her fingers. "I'll take that key, thank you very much."

Chapter Thirty-Two

Are we at the pound? I'm not a stray. - Black Cat

ern Lake Country Road - Police cars and an ambulance arrived at the scene of the accident within twenty minutes of the truck driver's call, though it seemed like hours to an anxious cat concerned for his mate. The man gave a quick account of the situation, and then left Grandma in the hands of the EMT's. On the drive back to town, as much as Black Cat tried to stay awake, the swaying of the truck and the driver's soothing voice lulled him to sleep. He awoke being lifted from the seat and placed into a cat carrier. *No! Wait. I can't leave Angel.*

He watched through the front wires as a woman gently lifted Angel, cradled her in her arms, and whisked her away through a clinic side door. *Where are you taking her?* His carrier bounced down the sidewalk and into a building where the scent of disinfectant and animals assailed his senses.

The faint cry of dogs and cats filled the room. *I'm not a stray. I have a home.* Why hadn't Kimberlee given him a collar with her phone number on it? The technician set the carrier onto a table and went out the door. Black Cat's head throbbed in rhythm with his pounding heart. A few minutes later, a man came in and pulled Black Cat from the cage. "Well, hello, pretty boy. Let's see what's going on with you."

After a thorough examination of Black Cat's eyes, ears, mouth and a most embarrassing and uncomfortable examination of his *nether parts*, the man washed the cut on Black Cat's head and applied a soothing ointment. "Considering what you've been through, I think you'll be fine. We'll keep you safe until we find where you belong. Your owner is in the hospital, and in no time, we'll have you together again."

"Meow." I don't belong to that lady. She stole us. Where is Angel? Is she all right?

"There, there, now. You've got so much to say. Don't worry. You're fine." The doctor placed him back in the carrier, snapped the latch and picked up the phone. "Ed? Come to exam room three and take the black and white cat to the recovery area. Put a hold on him until tomorrow night. If he's not claimed by then, contact the Humane Society to come pick him up… Yes…from the accident site this morning. Thanks." The doctor hung up the phone and walked out without another word.

What about Angel?

Black Cat crouched in the corner of the carrier. Things didn't look promising and time wasn't on his side; stuck in a cage and scheduled to be sent away tomorrow. The doctor hadn't said a word about Angel. *Does that mean…? No. I won't even consider that. They think we belong to Grandma, but what if she didn't survive the accident?* How could they get back to Kimberlee?

Within minutes, a technician carried Black Cat's carrier to another room and placed him in a cage. The room smelled of other cats, litter pans, and medicines. An overhead fan and air fresheners failed to mask the smells or neutralize the truth. This was a place where cats fought for their lives following injury or surgery, and many failed. His stomach churned at the scent of the sick and dying.

In the cage beside him, a grey tabby with tubes extending from his mouth and bandages around his torso, lost his fight with death and crossed the Rainbow Bridge. The faint aura of his spirit still hovered overhead. The cats in nearby cages grew still to honor the sacred moment. Perhaps they sensed the instant that the tabby peeked beyond the Bridge, and seeing a place of health, happiness and bliss beyond, willingly stepped over.

Safe journey, my friend.

With a heavy heart, Black Cat put his head on his front paws. The door opened and a young woman entered. Black Cat closed his eyes. He didn't want to watch as she removed the tabby cat's body from the cage and placed him into a cardboard box. Black Cat closed his ears. He didn't want to hear the sound of the litter pan scraping across the metal cage floor as the young woman pulled it from the cage. He refused to listen to the *squish squish* of the disinfectant spray bottle, as she wiped the cage clean of the tabby's scent and readied it for its next inhabitant.

If Angel returned from the secret room where doctors labored and cats struggled between life and death, would she be the next occupant in the disinfected cage? It was good that he would be on the other side of the wire where he could add his healing thoughts and prayers when she awoke. Or was that empty cage the inevitable gateway to the Bridge, and the wire wall would keep him from reaching her or kissing her good-bye as she crossed over? He meowed and clawed the wire. He had to get out and find her.

How many times had he scorned the inferior humans in his life, laughed at their inability to forgive or work out their differences without violence? How often had he assured Angel of the superiority of cats and rejoiced in the fact that he was not human. But, at this moment, he would have given up eight of his nine lives to have opposable thumbs that could undo the latch and the ability to search the hospital rooms for Angel. What he would have given for the ability of two human feet and two arms to carry her away.

Black Cat lay quietly in his cage, his eyes closed. Had Angel survived her injuries? Would he ever see her again? With the future uncertain, he was helpless to affect an outcome. He squeezed his eyes tighter. *Concentrate on the now.* That's what cats do. He would accept the inevitable, whatever the future held, and dismiss the pain from his memory. He sniffed the scents and assessed the sounds in the room.

Furry toes scratched kitty litter, sending up the scent of urine and feces... The click and whish of a machine administering oxygen to a seriously ill cat... The occasional whine of pain or fear...

What terrifying incidents brought his brothers and sisters to this gathering of sick and injured souls? Did each of them have a doting master, hoping and praying for their recovery, anxiously awaiting their return? How would Brett ever find him and Angel?

The door creaked. Black Cat opened his eyes. *Angel!* The young technician entered, unlatched the cage next to Black Cat where the tabby cat had been, and laid Angel on a clean towel. She rearranged Angel's legs and straightened a blue plaster cast on her front leg. With a stroke on her golden head and a gentle pat on her haunch, the woman said, "There you go, little one. Have a nice nap. You'll feel better when you wake up."

Black Cat clawed at the wire. *Meow! Angel! I'm here. I'm right beside you.*

What did he expect? That she would waken from a sedated state, sit up and say hello?

The technician opened Black Cat's cage and examined the wound on the top of his head. "That's looking good. I brought your friend, old fellow. She'll be okay in time."

"*Meow.*"

She pushed Black Cat away from the door. "You stay there. Hopefully we'll have you both out of here pretty soon. We're trying to find your people."

The young technician walked around the room, opened cage doors, exchanged encouraging remarks to each cat, checked gauges on equipment, scooped a litter pan and filled a few water bowls. With a final glance around the room, apparently satisfied she had done all she could to make the cats as comfortable as possible, she turned down the volume on a CD machine playing soft music, left the room and eased the door shut behind her.

Black Cat picked at the wire separating him from Angel. "Wake up, Angel. Tell me you're all right. Don't worry. I won't leave you. We'll get out of here somehow, I promise."

Angel didn't move, the anesthesia keeping her in a painless place of darkness and peace.

Who knew what lay ahead, but Angel had survived surgery, and they were together. Wasn't that the most important thing in times of extreme adversity? Being with the one you love? The future would take care of itself.

Chapter Thirty-Three

I'm not moving an inch until I know what's
going on here. - Kimberlee

uttural laughter sent shudders through Kimberlee's chest. Her heart raced as the man's hand tightened over her mouth. Where was Dorian? She'd followed the old man out of town. How had he evaded her and circled back? How had he found her in the church? The hand over Kimberlee's mouth stifled her cries. She tried to break free, but he twisted her arm behind her back until she ceased to struggle. He had wrested the key from her hand. What might he do now? She could identify him. Blood rushed through her body in a flight or fight mode.

Thoughts of Brett and Amanda flashed through her mind. Would she ever see them again? *Think, Kimberlee.* What had she learned from the Women's Self-Defense classes? Remembering the instructions of the buxom blonde beauty in the tight pink jumpsuit, Kimberlee stomped her foot down on the man's ankle.

He howled and released his hold on her face and arm. The key clattered to the floor. He moaned and reached down to rub his wounded ankle. Kimberlee knelt, grabbed the key and raced down the aisle toward the altar. Nearly blinded by panic, she bumped straight into an elderly priest, who gripped her arms. "Hold up. What's going on here?"

Off to her left, a woman rushed down the side aisle toward the raging old man.

Kimberlee struggled against the priest for a moment. Her gaze swept toward the figures of the Virgin Mary and the Christ Child, and then to the kindly face of the elderly priest. She ceased to struggle and leaned into his chest. The candles and lights overhead dimmed and the sound of the old man's howls grew faint. Giving in to the desire to escape the fright of her experience, her legs buckled. A warm and peaceful blanket of darkness flowed over her. Feeling safe in the arms of the priest, she could let go.

"Wake up, Kimberlee."

A wet cloth soothed her eyes as the words pierced through a dark veil. She pushed away the cloth. "The old man... The key… He tried to take the key."

"I know. I know. Everything's okay now. Don't worry."

Dorian? How did she find me? Dorian helped Kimberlee rise to a sitting position. She opened her clenched hand to reveal the key on her palm. Dorian took it from her. "What's this?" She turned over the paper attached to the key and read the inscription. "Vontobel Swiss Bank?"

Kimberlee wiped her hand across her forehead. "I found it right where the poem said. The old man tried to take it from me." She gazed around the church. Her gaze stopped at the glass coffin and the carved Christ Child on the table leg. "Is he still here?"

"No. He's gone. He ran away when he saw the priest. Now, tell me where you found the key."

"You drove away and left me. And, then the storm came and... don't you see? The bells were driving away the storm clouds, just like the lady at the tea shop said, so I came in here and found Hans's picture over there, and the key was right where the poem told me to look. But then the old man—"

Dorian shook her head. "Honey, you're not making any sense."

She glanced toward the priest, standing nearby. "Is there somewhere we can take her? Maybe get her a cup of coffee or a cold drink?"

The priest and Dorian helped Kimberlee to her feet. "The young lady can rest in my office. Coffee is always available. Father Kurt has contacted the authorities. He's waiting for them outside. They'll want to talk to her."

Dorian dropped the key in her pocket and took Kimberlee's arm. "The young lady is Kimberlee Clarke and I'm Dorian Dilman. I'm a police detective from Fern Lake, California." She removed her police shield from her purse, replaced it, and put out her hand. "Nice to meet you, even under these less than ideal circumstances."

The priest shook Dorian's hand and nodded toward Kimberlee. "Ms. Dilman. I'm Father Kreuger."

"Kreuger?" Dorian and Kimberlee exchanged glances.

With Dorian and Father Kreuger on each side, they led Kimberlee into his office and settled her in a comfortable chair. The priest stepped to the door. "If you'll excuse me, I'll be right back with some coffee."

Kimberlee turned to Dorian. "Why did you leave me stranded without a word? I had no idea where you went. Maybe the old man wouldn't have attacked if you'd been with me."

Dorian pulled a chair closer and sat. "I'm sorry. I was watching his car when you went to the phone, and he drove away. I didn't have time to pick you up. As it happened, I lost him about a mile or so out of town. I drove around the countryside for a while and then returned to town."

"Then, how did you find me? You must have come in right after he attacked me. I wasn't *out* for very long." Kimberlee rubbed her arm where the old man had twisted it. She'd have a black and blue bruise the size of New Jersey tomorrow, for sure.

"I drove up and down the street looking for you and saw the beige car parked across the street. The young priest was outside. I gave him your description and he said you might be in the church. So I came in, and saw Father Kreuger holding you. That must be when you fainted."

Dorian's eyes misted. "If only I'd come in five minutes sooner. I should have been here. I'm really sorry, Kimberlee. I let you down."

"Don't be silly. You're there for me all the time. Just yesterday, as I recall, you loaned me money and bought my dinner." She took Dorian's hand and squeezed.

Father Kreuger returned with a tray of coffee and a small plate of cookies. "Here you go. Help yourself and tell me what this is all about."

Over the next ten minutes, Kimberlee showed Father Kreuger Dewey's diary, told him her thoughts about the poem, the storm, and the woman in the sweet shop's explanation that brought her back to the church. She concluded her tale with how the old man had been following them and their confrontation in the chapel.

Dorian took the key from her pocket and laid it on the desk. "Do you have any idea who he is or why he attacked Kimberlee? Or, for that matter, what's in the lockbox this key fits?"

Father Kreuger frowned. "I'm afraid I do. The man's name is Joseph. He helps around the church." He shook his head. "Now that you've told me about Dewey's journal, I understand why he tried to take the key. However, it's a long and complicated story. If you don't mind, I'd rather not have to tell it twice. I'd like to wait until the authorities arrive."

Dorian raised her eyebrows. "In that case, I'll take Kimberlee back to the Lindenberger Pension where we're staying. You can call us when you're ready to tell your story. I can't wait to hear all the details."

Kimberlee set her coffee cup on the table. "No. I'm fine, Dorian. We've come too far. I'm not moving an inch until I hear what the priest has to say."

Father Kreuger stood and smoothed the wrinkles in his gown. "Then, if you will excuse me, I'll go about my duties until the police arrive. You can wait here or in the chapel, as you choose." His robes rustled as he left the room.

Kimberlee laid her head back on the chair and closed her eyes, thinking about the circumstances that brought them to this place. It started at the bookstore when Black Cat knocked Dewey's diary to the floor, almost as if he wanted her to read it. What a fanciful idea to even think such a thing. Black Cat had no idea what was written inside.

"A penny for your thoughts. Does your head hurt?" Dorian touched Kimberlee's forehead. "Give me that cup. You're about to fall asleep and drop it."

Kimberlee opened her eyes and leaned forward. "What? I'm not asleep. I was thinking about how the smallest thing can set up a certain chain of events. Reading about a missing treasure in a diary led us to the key in Hopfgarten. The old man must think it's important or he wouldn't be so anxious to get hold of it."

Dorian shrugged. "We were coming to the convention anyway. It was just a coincidence that before we came, you read about a hidden treasure near our destination."

"Was it just a coincidence? I wouldn't have bothered reading the diary and learned about a hidden treasure if the cats hadn't made me take a second look. I nearly tossed out the diary."

"Oh, so now you think your cats are responsible for sending you on a treasure hunt to the other side of the world? I know you think your cats are special, but, isn't that a bit far-fetched?"

Kimberlee giggled. "That's not what I meant. They had no idea what was in the diary. I meant that when he pawed at the book, I took a second look, and that was the catalyst that set everything in motion. I'm not saying that the cat knew what Dewey wrote in the diary."

"I hear sirens. It's probably the police. Maybe we'll have some answers soon."

"Can't be soon enough. We know Hans hid the key and sent the message to Dewey. How Joseph became involved is a mystery, or for that matter, whether the key I found is to a lockbox full of gold coins."

Dorian shrugged. "I guess we'll soon find out." Hearing voices outside the door, Dorian stood and moved toward the bookcase.

Father Kreuger and a uniformed policeman entered. "Ladies. This is Constable Goble." The priest gestured toward the women. "This is Ms. Dilman and Ms. Clarke."

"Pleasure, I'm sure. If you'll have a seat, Father, we can get straight to the situation at hand."

Kimberlee leaned forward. "Did you catch Joseph? Did you find out why he attacked me? And, it's Mrs. Clarke."

"All in good time, Mrs. Clarke." The officer opened a briefcase and pulled out a notebook and pen. "Let me get a bit of information first. What were you doing when Joseph approached you?"

Interesting. Why had he used the word *approached* and not *attacked?* Was he trying to minimize Joseph's behavior? Even Father Kreuger seemed reluctant to condemn him. Maybe she needed more information before she filed charges against the old man.

Kimberlee put her hand to her forehead and sank down into the chair. "I…I…really don't feel very well, officer. Would you mind terribly if we postponed our interview for a few hours? I really need to lie down." She shot a glance toward Dorian, ducked her head slightly and cast a glance toward the door. *Help me here, Dorian.* Would she understand the silent request?

Dorian stepped forward. "*Umm.* Kimberlee has had a terrible shock. I was right. She needs to rest before we go into this. If you'll give me your card, I'll take her back to the pension and give you a call later this afternoon when she feels better."

The officer wrinkled his brow. "Well, I don't know. This is a police matter, after all. A charge has been made against one of our local citizens."

Dorian shook her head. "No official charge has been made. My friend fainted following an encounter with a local man. Listen, I'm a police detective from California. My friend and I are here on vacation. Let me take her back to the pension. We'll call you in a couple hours." She smiled and showed the officer her Fern Lake Police Department shield. All the while, Kimberlee sat wilted in the chair, calling on her college drama training to appear as fragile as a Kleenex in the rain.

The officer hesitated. "Well… I guess it's okay. But, I expect you to come to the police department this afternoon, or before 10:00 A.M. tomorrow morning, at the latest." He stood, left the office and shut the door behind him. Father Kreuger sat behind his desk, his eyebrows raised in question.

"Okay. You're not sick. What's going on, girl?" Dorian glared at Kimberlee.

Kimberlee sat up straight in the chair, all affectation of illness gone. She folded her hands. "There's more to this than meets the eye." She turned to Father Kreuger. "I want you to tell me about Joseph and the key before I involve the authorities. You said you wanted to tell your story one time, but before I bring assault charges against an old man, I need to understand why he attacked me. Please. Why was he so determined to get the key?"

Father Kreuger sighed. "Joseph and I have been friends for many years. At his age, I don't think he would survive going back to jail."

"Going *back* to jail? He's been in jail?" Dorian slid into the chair beside Kimberlee.

Father Kreuger stood and moved to his library shelf. "Let me start at the beginning. As you know, Hans fought for Germany during WWII, where he and Dewey met on the battlefield."

Time seemed to stand still as Kimberlee and Dorian sucked in their breath and leaned forward. Finally, all their questions would be answered.

The priest continued his tale. "Hans and I were cousins on my father's side. We grew up like brothers, and played football together in high school. We got drunk on more than a few Saturday nights. After graduation, the war broke out. I chose the priesthood, and Hans went into the army. We learned Hans was captured at Normandy and sent to an American prison camp, where he remained until fall of 1945."

"Yes. We know all this from Dewey's diary." Kimberlee said. *Tell me something I don't know.*

The priest nodded. "After they released Hans from the prison camp, he wrote to me at Divinity College where I was studying. He told me how Dewey saved his life. Hans married and worked at a security company in Munich. When I finished my studies and was ordained, to my surprise, the church sent me back to Hopfgarten."

Kimberlee's heart thumped against her chest. She nodded and circled her hand in the air. *Get on with it.* Her head throbbed and her ears buzzed as her interest waned and his words flowed together. Apparently, her feigned lightheadedness was more real than she thought.

"…letters…deliveries…baby…sick wife…lost his home…armored car, gold…paper securities…"

Why is it so hot in here? Kimberlee squirmed in the chair, dabbed her forehead with her handkerchief and reached for her coffee. She rolled her head as pain shot through her neck and into the back of her head. She turned back to the priest. *Pay attention, Kimberlee. He's bound to say something enlightening pretty soon.*

"…shocked to learn that Hans and his partner stole an armored car with a consignment of gold coins from a local Munich bank. The truck was found at the airport, but the contents, Hans, and the other driver had disappeared."

"Hans stole the gold." Dorian's eyebrows flew up. Her head whipped toward Kimberlee.

With her eyes wide, Kimberlee gasped. "It's hard to believe…" That wasn't quite true. She had thought it was true ever since she watched the documentary and read Dewey's diary. Now the details raced through her mind. This must be the key to a deposit box where Hans stashed the gold in the Vontobel Swiss bank. But, were the stolen coins still inside?

"So, they never recovered the gold shipment?" Dorian asked.

Before Father Kreuger could answer, there was a knock at the door. "Come in?"

Father Kurt opened the door and popped his head inside. "Sorry to disturb you, Father, but old Mrs. Klingmeyer is here. Her sister has died and she's distraught. I offered to pray with her, but she insists she must talk to you. Can you spare her a few minutes?"

Father Kreuger stood and spread his hands. "I'm sorry ladies, duty calls. I must go. Do you want to wait, or come back later?" He checked his watch. "I have a late mass at 5:00 P.M. but I'll be available by…say 7:00 P.M., or tomorrow morning at 9:00 A.M."

Kimberlee turned toward Dorian. "My head is killing me. Why don't we come back in the morning before we go to the police station? I'd like to get to bed early. What do you say?"

Dorian peered at Kimberlee's pale face. She stood. "That's fine. Run on, Father. We can see ourselves out." The priest hurried out the door.

"Well, that's that." Kimberlee said. "Guess we've waited this long. We can wait until tomorrow morning for the last bit of the story." She stood, picked up the key from the desk, and dropped it into her purse. "Let's go."

"Are you all right? You look as weak as a kitten. I'm taking you straight back to the pension and putting you to bed. I'll drive back into town later and get us something to eat." She took Kimberlee's arm, walked her out of the church, and down the street toward her car.

At the bottom of the stairs, Kimberlee glanced to the left, stopped short and clutched Dorian's arm. "Wait. Is that Joseph? I thought the police caught him."

"Where?"

Partially hidden behind a pillar, but with the shoulder of his red jacket protruding, Joseph jerked back and then dashed around the corner of the church. "Over there. He just ran around the corner. Something tells me we haven't seen the last of him."

"Then, we'd best be on the lookout until we're sure he's in custody."

Chapter Thirty-Four

Sleep, my pet, for in sleep nothing can hurt you. - Black Cat

Waking from a light sleep, Black Cat heard the bell around Angel's neck jingle. *Angel?* He jumped to his feet and picked at the hospital's cage wire with his sharp claws. His darling lifted her head and though shaky, did her best to gaze around the room. "Black Cat? Where are we? What happened?" Her meows were raspy as a result of the breathing tube during surgery.

"We're at the vet hospital. Remember? Grandmother's car crashed. You went up to the road to get help, and a bread truck hit you. The driver brought us here."

"I remember." Struggling to sit upright, her body wobbled, but the cast on her leg prevented her from standing. "What? I can't… What is this thing?" She tumbled back onto the towel.

"It's okay. You have a broken leg. The doctor fixed it and put it in a cast. You'll learn to walk on it when you get stronger. Try to relax. You're still wobbly from surgery."

"What's going to happen to us? Is Grandmother all right? Did she die?" Angel gurgled. "My throat hurts."

Black Cat turned his head away. "I don't know. The vet spoke as if she was alive. He thinks we belong to her. I guess she's in the people hospital. I'm not sure what…" He sighed. "Let's not talk about it. Brett will find us." *Though I have no idea how.* "Are you in pain, my sweet?"

"Not really. I am a bit dizzy and sleepy, and a little hungry. Do you suppose they serve vegetarian Kitty Crunchies here?"

Black Cat's whiskers twitched. "If that's the worst thing you're worried about, I think you'll be okay. Why don't you go back to sleep for a while? When you wake up, you'll feel better. I wouldn't be surprised if the doctor brings vegetarian Kitty Crunchies for dinner."

Angel laid her head back on the towel and within minutes, Black Cat could hear a soft wheeze on the other side of the wire. *Sleep, my pet, for in sleep nothing can hurt you.* He didn't think he'd ever sleep again as long as they were caged prisoners. How would Brett find them? But, within minutes, his eyes felt heavy, and he laid his head on the towel.

Voices in the hall woke him. *Who's out there? That voice sounds like…like…*

The door opened and the lady technician came in with a tall, blond man. Black Cat meowed and picked at the wire. Never in his life had he been so glad to see Brett. How on earth had he found them? *Angel. Angel. Wake up. Brett is here.*

Angel lifted her head. "Meow?" *Oh, Brett. I'm so glad to see you. Grandmother stole us and we made the car crash and—*

"Are these your pets, Mr. Clarke? They were found on the road near the crash. We thought they belonged to the lady in the car. They sure are excited to see you."

Brett handed the technician a paper. "Yep, they're mine. Black Cat and Angel. This is a copy of the police report I filed yesterday after Mrs. Lassiter stole the cats from my front yard. You can see it clearly describes them."

The technician read the paper. "*Uh-huh.* I'm satisfied. I'll let the doctor know you're here. He'll need to sign off before we release the cats. Did you bring a carrier?"

Brett nodded. "It's in my car. I can get it in a jiffy. I wanted to be sure…"

"Dr. Kneedler will instruct you on aftercare for…" The technician nodded toward Angel's cage.

"We call her Angel." Brett glanced into the cage. "Is she going to be okay?"

"She'll need to come back a few times over the next couple of weeks."

"We can handle that. I'm so glad to find them. Did Angel break her leg in the accident?"

The technician shrugged. "Hard to say, but I don't think so. The driver who brought them in said she was sitting in the middle of the road and he couldn't avoid hitting her. It's a miracle she wasn't killed. That's when he found the car over the embankment and called 911. In a way, I guess that's what saved the lady's life—the cat stopping the truck like that. Otherwise, he would have driven right on." The technician stepped toward the door. "You can wait in the waiting room. We'll call you in a few minutes. The doctor will probably send Angel home with some pain meds. Go ahead and schedule another appointment with the receptionist."

"Sounds good." Brett poked his finger through the wire and touched Black Cat's nose. "Hey, big guy. See you in a few." He followed the technician into the lobby.

"Angel. Did you hear? We're saved. We're going home." Black Cat snapped at the cage wires with his claws, until the wires pinged like a harp.

Angel lifted her head and sighed. "I suppose we'll be gone before the vet serves dinner. I'm not convinced that the Kitty Crunchies Brett brought home this week were vegetarian."

"Oh, Angel, I can't believe …"

"Just sayin'…"

Back home again, Brett laid Angel on a blanket beside the fireplace with her head resting on her paw, her casted leg stretched out in front of her. Whether Brett served vegetarian Kitty Crunchies or not, the half-empty dish beside Angel suggested she ate them anyway. A bowl of water sat within easy reach next to her blanket. Black Cat sprawled across the sofa, napping with one eye open, not only to be a present comfort but to guard against any threat, human or otherwise, that might interfere with Angel's rest.

No wonder Angel was depressed and anxious, despite his efforts to make her feel at home. He sucked in a breath, remembering her selfless act to help Grandma. Angel seemed to have a knack for putting herself in danger to save those she loved.

Bing-Bong

Black Cat jumped to his feet with a growl deep in his throat, and the hairs on the back of his neck on end. *Who's there this time?*

Brett hurried to the door. "Jack. Come in. Coffee's on. I just got home with the cats a little while ago." He turned to Angel. "She's a bit worse for wear, but at least they're home." He leaned down and patted Angel's back. She lifted her head, yawned, and managed a little purr to show her appreciation before lowering her head back onto her paw.

Jack leaned down and patted Angel's head. "How ya doin,' girl? I came by ta check on ya.'" He straightened up and sat on the sofa beside Black Cat. "You too, old fellow," he said, gently touching the top of Black Cat's head. "You got a whack too, didn't ya?"

"Can I get you a cup of coffee?" Brett asked.

"I'll get it myself in a bit." Jack pulled a sofa pillow off the couch, gave it a fluff and tucked it behind his back.

"Thanks for the head's up last night about Grandmother Lassiter."

"*Yeah*. The police called when they went through her purse and found the lodge key. They thought she might have family with her at the lodge."

"Thank goodness, they connected two cats found near her Honda and my report of Grandmother's Honda and the stolen cats. The police called the veterinarian hospital with the information and they called me."

"Must be a *God-thing* that you found them. They coulda' been sent to the Humane Society." Jack scratched Black Cat's ear, being careful to avoid the cut on his head.

"I left their descriptions with them, too. Maybe I should keep them inside the house. They could get into more trouble outside."

Black Cat hopped off the couch and ran to the door. *Meow. Don't keep us inside. I want to sit on the porch swing in the mornings.*

Brett went to the door and opened it. "You'd think he understood what I said, wouldn't you?"

Black Cat stood in the doorway, half in and half out, claiming the prerogative to change his mind as quickly as the impulse struck. In this case, having proven his ability to make Brett open the door, he no longer needed to go out.

"Make up your mind, Black Cat," Brett said, wiggling the door handle, "in or out."

Black Cat turned and raced back to the sofa. *I didn't want to go out. I just needed options.*

Brett closed the door and sat back down in the sofa chair.

Jack headed for the kitchen and brought back a cup of coffee. "Have you heard from the hospital? How is Kimberlee's grandma?"

"I called this morning before I picked up the cats. Her insurance provider wants to fly her back to their hospital in Texas as soon as possible. She has a few broken ribs and a broken collarbone. They said she's conscious, but pretty much out of it. I don't think I should go to the hospital. What's done is done. The cats are back. Mr. Ollingham says she won't get very far with a lawsuit about the house, and I doubt she wants to discuss a vet bill or her catnapping escapade."

"Are you going to call Kimberlee and tell her what her grandmother did?"

Brett shrugged. "Are you kidding? I don't think so. She'll have a cat-fit when she hears. Best that Grandmother dearest will already be back in Texas before Kimberlee gets home."

"If you say so..." Jack raised an eyebrow. "I don't want ta be in your shoes when she finds out all the stuff you haven't told her this week." A smile crinkled his cheeks. "She's gonna have your bum for breakfast."

"You're probably right. Hopefully, she'll understand it was for her own good. There's nothing she could do about any of this over there. Why ruin her trip? She's having fun. No need to make things worse than they are."

"True, that."

Black Cat jumped onto the arm of the sofa chair, rammed his head under Brett's hand and took delight in his ability to receive a demanded stroke. *Persons are so easy to train and Brett is coming along nicely, if I do say so myself.* Black Cat hopped off the sofa chair and flopped down on Angel's blanket where he proceeded to lick the top of her head. *Do you need anything, my pet?* He gave Angel's ears another slurp.

Yeah. You could make these guys shut up so I could get some shut-eye, Other than that...nothing.

Black Cat's whiskers twitched. *She must be feeling better— complaining, as usual.*

Brett chuckled. "The cats are chattering like magpies. They must be happy to be home."

"After what they've been through, it's no wonder." Jack stood. "I gotta go. Chance has a grooming appointment later and I gotta check the stock at the bait shop."

Brett walked him to the door. "Thanks for stopping by."

"Sure. Just wanted ta make sure my little buddies were okay." He grinned and went out.

Brett glanced down at the cats, "I intend to keep my family safe," he whispered, "if it takes the last breath in my body."

Chapter Thirty-Five

I guess I've battled the devil all my life. - Joseph

id-afternoon, following their discussion with the priest, Dorian and Kimberlee were back at their pension. Kimberlee declined a nap and opted for a seat on the patio. After tucking a blanket over her lap, Dorian drove back into town. She returned a half hour later with two sausage sandwiches wrapped in waxed paper and two sodas.

For the next several hours, they watched the sun move toward the horizon and discussed the key found in the church and what it meant. It seemed certain that the 1954 armored-car gold was the treasure Hans wrote about in Dewey's diary. Joseph believed the gold was still in the Vontobel deposit box, else why go to such lengths to get the key? If he was Hans's partner in crime, could a person guilty of theft claim a reward for returning the self-same stolen gold fifty years later? Perhaps he was just an innocent citizen who had heard the stories and thought he might collect a reward for the return of the gold coins…if there was a reward. And, who was the rightful owner of the coins? What a good crime scenario for a law school to put to its students.

Before long, the sun dropped behind the hills and dusk settled over the valley. The lights twinkled in the town below, and the twin towers of the church jutted into the reddish twilight.

"It's all still a big mystery," Dorian said.

Kimberlee shrugged and drained the last drops from her can of soda. "I guess we'll find out in the morning when we talk to Father

Kreuger. I don't suppose you have any Tylenol? My head still hurts."

Dorian stood. "I'll see if they have any in the office. If not, I'll drive back into town and find a drugstore. Why don't you go inside and lie down while I'm gone? I won't be long."

"Thanks, Dorian." Kimberlee ran her hand over her forehead. "I think I'll do that."

Kimberlee lay on the bed and pulled the down comforter over her. *I'll rest my eyes until Dorian gets back. Did I lock the patio door?*

Images of the patio and the sunset swam in her mind's eye. Odd, that Black Cat should be out there, perched on the stone wall overlooking the valley, his body clearly outlined against the setting sun. Odder still that Angel sat on the slate floor, looking up at him.

Angel stood, muscles tensed, as if prepared to jump onto the wall. She hesitated. Something was wrong. She seemed to favor her front leg. Black Cat meowed and arched his back. He was telling her not to jump! That she was too weak to make it safely to the top. Kimberlee's heartbeat quickened. She flung out her hand. "Don't jump, Angel. You'll fall."

Angel crouched and leaped. She scrabbled at the top of the wall, kicked her back feet for balance, and regained her stability. With an effort, she heaved her body to the top, teetered, and plunged over the back side of the wall.

"No. No. Angel!" Kimberlee moaned and twisted on the bed. Her body jerked, half awake and disoriented. She twisted away from the pressure on her nose and mouth. *Why can't I breathe?*

"*Shh.* Calm down. You're okay." The gruff voice intruded into her dream. Had someone come to rescue Angel? Weren't Black Cat and Angel alone on the patio? As she struggled, the feeling of something covering her mouth moved from dream to reality. She opened her eyes and stared into Joseph's shadowy face leaning over her, his hand over her nose and mouth, just as he had done in the church. Was this a nightmare?

"Don't scream. I won't hurt you," he whispered.

Not a dream. Kimberlee's chest heaved as she tried to breathe. He must have come through the patio door. Joseph moved his hand slightly away from her face. "Promise you won't scream, and I'll let you up. I only want to talk."

Kimberlee nodded. He released her mouth, and she scooted up against the headboard, her hands damp, and her head throbbing. *He's come back for the key. Where is it?* She tried to remember if she dropped it into her purse or into Dorian's. "What are you doing here?" She gasped, putting her hand to her mouth. Her gaze swept the room. Why didn't Dorian come back? She must still be at the manager's office, or perhaps she took the car back into town. "How did you get in?"

Joseph spread his hands in a helpless gesture. "You left the door open. Thought I'd talk to you, private like."

"Why should I? You about strangled me in the church. I should have you arrested, that's what I *should* do."

"What good would that do? I'm an old man, not about to change my ways at this late date."

"So, you think that's how it works? It's okay to steal because you're old? Why don't we all just rob a bank?"

Joseph threw back his head and guffawed. He wrapped his arms around his belly, doubled over and laughed until tears filled his eyes. Finally, getting control of his emotions, he said, "Lady! I already done that, and spent ten years in jail for it. Didn't teach me a thing. Why do you think I want that key you got stashed somewhere?" His gaze swept the room and stopped at her purse. "Is it in there?" He moved toward the table.

"Wait. You said you wanted to talk. Let's talk. Tell me about the key." Maybe if she kept him talking long enough, Dorian would return.

Joseph paused, halfway across the room and turned. "That key is rightfully mine." He pulled out a chair at the table and sat.

"How so? Apparently it's been hidden in the church for over fifty years. How does that make it rightfully yours, so much that you nearly broke my neck trying to take it from me?"

Joseph lowered his head. "I'm sorry about that. I didn't mean to hurt you. I got carried away when I saw you pull it out of that drawer. I've been searching for so long." He leaned forward and wrung his hands, then ran his fingers through his thinning hair. "I'm really sorry if I hurt you."

The door flung open and Dorian stood with a bag in her hand. "What's going on in here? Who…? Wait. You must be…" She dropped the bag, rushed forward and grabbed Joseph's arm. "Don't move a muscle. I'm making a citizen's arrest…*um*…*er*…if there is such a thing in Austria… I'm making one." Dorian pulled him to his feet and twisted his arm behind his back. "Hold still."

He squirmed and squealed. "*Ow!* You're hurting me."

Kimberlee sat up straighter. "Let him go, Dorian. He says he wants to explain his behavior, though so far, he hasn't done a very good job." Kimberlee slid her legs off the bed and stood.

"I can't help it," Joseph said. "I've been fighting temptation all my life. I try to change my actions, and then something happens and I screw it up. I can't tell you how many times Father Kreuger and I have discussed my weaknesses. I guess I've battled the devil all my life."

"How so? Are you a drug addict? An alcoholic?" Dorian said.

"Nothing like that. I'm a born thief, pure and simple. It started when I was a teenager. Even after the war, I worked as an armored car driver, and—"

Kimberlee and Dorian exchanged glances. "We suspected as much. You and Hans stole the gold, didn't you?" Dorian said.

Joseph's face looked drawn and pale. "I'm ashamed to say, we did. We used to joke about how easy it would be. With the high cost of living after the war, it was all we could do to make ends meet. We both had families we could barely support. That particular day, we were carrying a load of cash and gold coins. It all belonged to rich people who didn't need it."

Dorian scoffed. "I doubt the rich people would have seen it quite the same way."

"Indeed. We looked at each other, and I said, 'Let's do it.' We ditched the truck and took off for Switzerland where Hans opened a numbered account with the cash and put the coins in a lockbox. The cash account would automatically pay for the lockbox over the years, so we didn't have to do a thing. We swore we wouldn't go near it until the statute of limitations ran out. Then, we planned to come back and retrieve the coins."

Kimberlee crossed the room to the patio door and peered out. "Go on."

"We called the Munich police station a couple days later and made up a story about how we'd been ambushed, kidnapped, and managed to escape. They pretended to believe us, but they weren't fooled for a minute. They let us go, figuring we'd lead them to the stash. We split up like we planned. A few days later, I was arrested again, but Hans got away. He had the lockbox key."

"He thought he could escape, even after they arrested you?" Dorian popped the top off a bottle of soda she's brought back from town. "How did he figure that?"

Joseph shrugged. "Apparently, due to the foolishness of youth. Hans planned to hide out in Hopfgarten, where he had relatives, but the police tracked him to the church. He refused to surrender and was killed trying to escape." Joseph pinched the bridge of his nose, as if the memory brought him grief, even fifty years later.

"He had time to hide the key, but I have to wonder how the note with the clue to the location got mailed to Dewey," Kimberlee said.

"Dewey? The American guy he met at Normandy?" Joseph lifted his shoulders. A smile curved his lips. "That's what I thought. Hans wrote and told his American friend where he hid the key." His gaze moved to the journal lying on Kimberlee's nightstand. "That's why you came to Hopfgarten. You knew right where to look." He stood and edged closer to the bed, his eyes shifting from Kimberlee to the journal.

Kimberlee shook her head. "It wasn't like that at all. Hans didn't exactly say where he hid the key. He wrote more of a word puzzle in his letter to Dewey. It was almost an accident that I found the key under the coffin. You followed me into the church. You thought I knew where to find the key."

Joseph shrugged. "You have to understand. I spent ten years in prison for the robbery. I came back to Hopfgarten because I figured Hans hid the key somewhere in the church before he died. He didn't have it on him after… I've volunteered there for fifty years. Father Kreuger changed my life. Even though I never stopped searching for the key, eventually I repented and was absolved of my sins. After that, I hoped to find the key so I could return the gold and redeem myself." Joseph hung his head. His jaw quivered.

Kimberlee glanced at Dorian. *He wants to return the gold? He looks truly repentant.* She almost wished he had found the key. What was the right thing to do? A legal dilemma crossed her mind.

Fact One. Surely after fifty-plus years, the statute of limitations had run out for the theft of the gold.

Fact Two. Joseph paid his debt to society and spent ten years in jail for his part in the robbery.

Question. If the gold was still in the lock box and Joseph returned it, could he collect a reward for its return? Not in the USA, apparently, as criminals cannot profit from their crime, even fifty years later, but what about in Austria?

Kimberlee reached her hand toward Joseph. "I can imagine how you felt when you saw me with the key. Your life's goal snatched away, and now to make matters worse, you're in trouble for what happened in the church." She opened her purse. Yes, that's where she'd dropped the key. She held it up. "Well, don't worry. After hearing your story, I'm convinced that you're trying to make amends for your crime. I won't press charges against you." She glanced at Dorian and smiled. *It's the right thing to do.*

Dorian shook her head. "I think we should turn over the key to the bank and let them decide what's best."

Before she could react, Joseph snatched the key from Kimberlee's hand and raced out the patio door. Kimberlee and Dorian stood frozen, staring, as Joseph hopped over the stone wall, headed toward the parking lot and disappeared between the parked cars. For an old guy, he sure was spry. Dorian followed him, but returned a few minutes later, shaking her head. "I lost him in the parking lot."

"He grabbed it…before I could…" Kimberlee's mouth quivered. Tears pricked her eyes. "I believed him. I was going to give it to him." She turned and dropped onto the bed, her head buried in the pillows. "Now, what have I done? I can't do anything right these days."

Dorian hurried to the bed. "He didn't know what you were thinking. He thought you intended to bring charges. I'll run down to the manager's office and call the police. He can't possibly get away." She gave Kimberlee's arm a pat. "Don't cry. It's not your fault. I felt sorry for him, too." Dorian left through the patio door, leaving it open.

Kimberlee dried her eyes with a tissue. Now what could she tell the police? She agreed to go to the station in the morning and file charges for the attack in the church. How could she deny it? The bruises on her neck spoke for themselves, and the priest witnessed the attack. She promised Joseph she wouldn't press charges, but then he stole the key right out of her hand. Did that release her from her promise?

Questions spun in Kimberlee's head. How had this wonderful vacation in this beautiful country gone so awry? Perhaps it would have been better if the key had remained hidden. She put her head on the pillow and closed her eyes. *I miss my family and I want to go home.*

Outside, the church bells began to ring. The sound bounced off the surrounding hills and echoed back, and the clanging went on and on, the double knell and its echo coming almost on top of one another.

Occasionally, between the bells, another sound—the faint tinkle of the cow's bells on the nearby hillside.

Kimberlee lifted her head. The brisk breeze blew in a cool mist of rain and the scent of flowers from the garden. She rose from the bed, walked to the door and looked out.

Overhead, a streak of clouds drifted past the full moon. Rain began to fall, plopping onto the patio tiles, leaving a pattern of dark dots that quickly spread into a solid mass of wetness.

She breathed in the fresh scent of rain. A sense of *rightness* filled her chest. Whatever happened tomorrow…would be okay. She would report Joseph's attack in the church. Now that he stole the key, she no longer needed to protect him from prosecution.

Once he was caught, the police could take the key to the Swiss bank. If, indeed, the lockbox still contained the gold, the proper authorities would determine its legal owner. And frankly, she didn't care one way or the other. She wouldn't be in Austria long enough to find out.

With that settled in her mind, she breathed a sigh of relief. God was in his Heaven and things would be as they should be. She turned, slid the screen closed on the patio door and went back to her bed. With the scent of the rain still drifting in, she checked her watch. It must be very early in the morning at Fern Lake. Maybe Brett wouldn't mind waking up to talk to her. She picked up the phone and rang the manager's office. The mistress of the pension helped her put through the long distance call. On the third ring, she heard a very sleepy, "Hello?"

"Brett? Honey? It's me. It's so good to hear your voice. I miss you so much. I have so much to tell you when I get home."

Chapter Thirty-Six

Kimberlee snatched Angel and hugged her
until she squeaked. - Black Cat

illed with anticipation for Kimberlee's imminent return, Black Cat stood on the back of the sofa, peering through the curtains. He glanced down at Angel, lying on her blanket on the hearth, grooming her front paw. "It won't be long now and she'll be here. I wonder if she'll bring us presents."

Angel moved her leg cast and groomed her shoulder. "What could she possibly bring you from Germany that you'd want? A cuckoo clock? A hunk of Swiss cheese? I'm glad she's coming home. Our litter box needs changing. Brett isn't the most fastidious housekeeper."

Indeed, Brett had let the housekeeping chores completely lapse during Kimberlee's absence. When she found the house in such a mess, there would be grim retribution.

The household routine currently in chaos, Brett was pushing a vacuum, picking up Amanda's toys, and scrubbing three days of dirty pots and pans he hadn't bothered to clean. Amanda's sheets were piled in a heap in front of the washer. A stack of unsorted mail lay on the coffee table, and Brett hadn't paid bills since Kimberlee left town. Even the waste basket in the corner of the kitchen overflowed with pizza boxes, Chinese food containers, and soda cans.

Brett glanced at the clock on the mantle. "*Yikes!* She'll be here any minute." He grabbed the phone and dialed. "Jack. I'm in big trouble. You're my last hope." He paused. "Can you come help me clean up the house? Kimberlee is due home and I've sort of…*um*…well, I guess I haven't exactly kept things as well as I should. She's gonna kill me when she sees this mess. Please, buddy? I'll owe you big time."

Another pause… "Gee, thanks. Okay, hurry." Brett slammed the phone and yelled down the hall. "Amanda? Are you picking up your toys?" Apparently, Amanda was on as much of a neatness vacation as Brett with the rest of the housework.

Black Cat's whiskers twitched. Kimberlee always kept the household running efficiently. Brett could spin a good yarn that paid the bills and kept them in Kitty Crunchies, but a single parent and full-time housekeeper were not his strengths.

Jack opened the front door, gazed at the living room, and whistled. "What have ya been doing? Looks like a war zone. No wonder ya need help." He opened the door wider for Chance, and glanced at his watch. "When did ya say they're due back?" He picked up one of Amanda's coloring books and laid it on the coffee table. Crayons lay scattered across the carpet.

"I know. I know." Brett's hand circled his unshaved face. "I never claimed to be a good housekeeper. It's just…" He spread his hands and shrugged.

"Okay. Where do ya want me to start?"

Chance turned in a circle and lay down on the rug near Angel. Brett pointed to the laundry room. "There's a load of clothes on the floor in there. Could you start the washer? Amanda's bed needs changing. Sheets are in the hall closet. While you're in there, make her help clean up her room. She's been as careless as I have."

"Gotcha. Amanda?" Jack hollered down the hall. "You better be cleanin' your room. I'm coming in there in a minute. I'm gonna throw away any toys on the floor." Jack grinned as he headed through the kitchen toward the laundry room.

If you ask me… Angel hopped off the hearth, hissed half-heartedly at Chance, and stumbled toward the kitchen where dry cat food lay sprinkled across the floor tiles. *Cleanliness is important, but humans place entirely too much emphasis on neatness. There's nothing wrong with a "lived-in" look.*

Black Cat pulled his head from between the living room curtains and called, *Doubt Kimberlee would see it that way.*

Within the hour, tidiness reigned triumphant in the living room.

I see the car. Black Cat hopped off the sofa and streaked for the kitchen.

Brett shoved the last clean pot into the cupboard. A quick glance around the kitchen and he dried his hands, replaced the towel on the towel rack and went to the front door. He hurried down the sidewalk and opened Kimberlee's car door. "Welcome home, sweetheart." He gathered her in his arms and nuzzled her hair. "We really missed you. I'm so glad you're home."

Wasn't that the understatement of the year? Black Cat stopped on the porch and hopped onto the lawn swing. Wait until Kimberlee heard about everything that happened while she was gone. Brett might wish she had stayed away longer.

Jack came through the front door holding Amanda's hand. She pulled loose, raced down the sidewalk, and threw herself into Kimberlee's arms. Kimberlee picked her up and swung her around. "Hi, sweetheart, how's my baby? Did you miss mama?"

Dorian lifted Kimberlee's suitcase from the trunk, set it on the ground, and headed around to the driver's seat. "I'm going to take off, guys. I'm eager to see Virgil." She started the engine and waved.

"Thanks for everything," Kimberlee called as Dorian drove away. She followed Brett up the sidewalk and entered the front door, just as Angel stumbled from the kitchen, her gait hampered by the cast on her front leg.

Angel stopped; her gaze locked on Kimberlee's face. *Yeah, ask Brett. He'll give you all the gory details...Maybe.*

"What on earth?" Kimberlee hurried over and knelt beside Angel.

"How did this happen? Something tells me you forgot to mention a few things on the phone this week." Considering Kimberlee's frown, she must have known it was only the first of many things Brett *forgot* to mention. *Uh-oh.*

"Now, honey, you're right," Brett said. "Honestly, I didn't want to spoil your trip. What could you have done halfway around the world? I have everything under control now, and Angel will be fine in a few weeks. Come over here and sit down. You must be exhausted after that long flight. I'll get you a cold drink and we can talk later."

Kimberlee turned to Amanda. "Honey, bring me that little bag over by the door. Mama brought you a present." Amanda retrieved the bag. Kimberlee unzipped it, pulled out a musical teddy bear, and handed it to Amanda. "Isn't he sweet? He came all the way from Germany to live with you." She wound the key on his back and he began a lively tune.

"*Ooh!* He's so cute." Amanda hugged the bear to her chest. "Is he a German bear? What's his name?"

"Well, I don't know. Why don't you take him into your room and think of a good one? I'll come in a couple of minutes and we'll have a long talk. You can tell me what you named your bear and all about what you and Daddy Brett did while Mama was gone." She gave Amanda a little nudge toward her room.

Double *uh-oh.* Brett was on the hot seat now. If she intended to talk to Amanda, no way could he put off telling Kimberlee about Grandma kidnapping the cats, the car crash, and Angel's injury. Then, there were the things Amanda didn't know about, such as the vandalism at the bookstore, the attempted bait shop burglary, Ted's settlement offer for the lodge, or Grandmother's threatened lawsuit about the house…

Kimberlee received the news of Ted's settlement offer well and agreed it was a better alternative than contesting the will in a court fight. Chalk up one on the scoreboard for Brett. She also received the news of the bait shop break-in well, and agreed with Brett that Ted was not likely responsible, since it sounded more like the work of teenagers.

Score one more point.

A more troubling reaction came when she learned about the vandalism at the Book Nook, but was reassured that insurance claims were already in process. The artists would receive full payment for their damaged items, the window had already been replaced, and with Mrs. Wilson's help, the store was up and running as if nothing happened. Score half a point…

But, oh my! The tears and screaming when she learned how Grandmother cat-napped Angel and Black Cat, the accident, Grandmother's hospitalization and subsequent return to Texas, and Angel's narrow escape beneath the wheels of the bread truck. Kimberlee vowed to fly to Texas that very night and strangle the old woman in her hospital bed. She snatched Angel from the hearth, hugged her until she squeaked, and soaked her cast with tears.

Brett was hard-pressed to sooth Kimberlee's rage, and convinced her Angel's leg would not heal any faster with a red-eye flight to Texas and Grandma's murder. He asserted that he didn't expect evil Grandma to ever return to Fern Lake. Minus two-and-a-half points. In the end, it appeared the scoreboard on Brett's confessions had reached a final zero.

Brett neglected to mention Grandma's threat to file a lawsuit to take their restored Victorian house and charge Kimberlee with interstate fraud. Assured by Mr. Ollingham that any such legal challenge would be thrown out of court if Grandma ever found an attorney foolish enough to file it, perhaps Brett thought it best not to bring it up on the heels of so many other distressing subjects. Hopefully, if it never became a reality, he could store it under the Secrets Best Left Untold file. Despite the questions, tears, frustration, excuses, anger, and more tears, Kimberlee finally agreed. "I'm not saying you were right to keep all this from me, but I understand why you did. I would have been worried, and I had quite enough drama on my own, particularly the last couple of days."

"I can't wait to hear all about it." Brett raised her hand to his lips and kissed her fingers.

"I'm sure you must have had some fun. It's so beautiful over there. I hope you took lots of pictures."

Kimberlee blew her nose, dabbed her eyes, and glanced toward the hallway. "I'm going to spend some time with Amanda. Why don't you run downtown and bring back some hamburgers and fries. I'm starving. We'll talk more after we eat." Kimberlee drained the last of her iced tea, stood, and started down the hall toward Amanda's room.

"Good idea. I'll do that." Brett grabbed his jacket. "By the way, there's a letter for you on the buffet. It came a week or so ago." He reached the front door, paused and looked back. "You want to come with me, Black Cat?"

Black Cat bounced off the sofa, stretched, and followed Brett out the front door. How fortunate that Brett survived Kimberlee's wrath in learning about the Fern Lake troubles during her absence. He looked almost cheerful, striding down the sidewalk toward the car. Or was it relief to get away from Kimberlee, while she was in such a fragile mood?

Brett whistled a jaunty tune as he climbed into the SUV and headed to the nearest fast food outlet for hamburgers and French fries.

Black Cat stood on the seat with his front feet on the dash, peering out the window. Oh, the joys of the fresh air on a beautiful fall day, and a distraught and tearful woman left at home…even if only for a few minutes.

If Brett's luck held, exhaustion, a good cry, a visit with Amanda, and a bacon cheeseburger would drive Kimberlee to her bed. With more luck, she would awake refreshed and ready to face the challenges with a more positive outlook.

Chapter Thirty-Seven

Fine housekeeper Brett turned out to be. - Kimberlee

uddling with Amanda on her bed, Kimberlee told her about the Austrian cows and sheep that wore bells around their necks. When the phone rang in the living room, she left Amanda's room and hurried down the hall. "Hello?"

The recorded voice on the phone stated, "I'm returning your call inquiring about indwelling catheters. Midwestern Medical's indwelling catheters are the—"

"We never called about…" Kimberlee slammed down the phone. "Good grief. I hate robo-sales calls." Her gaze fell onto the stack of mail on the buffet. Brett mentioned a letter that needed her attention. She sifted through the envelopes, tossed the circulars and political requests into the wastebasket, and stacked the bills into a pile. She paused at the dirty envelope with torn edges addressed to the Book Nook. Glaring stamped images on the envelope stated, *Lost in Transit*, and *Received Damaged*.

The envelope had stains on the back that resembled tire tracks. It must have gone through a damaged envelope process at the post office and was finally delivered several weeks later. She ripped open the envelope and removed a typed letter...

Book Nook—To whom it may concern:

A box of books from my grandfather's attic, including his WWII diary, was inadvertently sold to a local book distributor. They informed us that your bookstore purchased the diary.

Grandpa Dewey Brooker's handwritten journal included not only his war experiences but twenty years of our family history—a precious family heirloom we hoped to pass down to his grandchildren. If you still possess Grandpa Brooker's diary, please give us the opportunity to re-purchase it. If the diary has been sold, can you put us in touch with the buyer?

We hope to hear from you within the next few days.

Sincerely, John Dewey Brooker, Jr.

Kimberlee re-read the letter. "Dewey's diary?" She checked the postmark date. Over three weeks ago? After all this time, with no response to his heartfelt request for the return of the diary, what must Mr. Brooker think of her?

She thought back to the garbled message on the bookstore answering machine before she left for Germany… Didn't the caller say something about giving back something that didn't belong to her? She tried to remember the message. 'You have no right to keep what isn't yours.' If John Brooker's call referred to Dewey's diary, no wonder he was upset.

Making matters worse, Brett hadn't opened the letter… She glanced at the stack of unpaid bills. In fact, he hadn't opened or paid any bills. Fine housekeeper he turned out to be. It would be a cold day in You-No-Where-City before she left him home alone again.

She penned a quick note apologizing and explaining the delay, wrapped the diary in the paper from a brown grocery bag, and addressed it to John Brooker. She would stop at the post office on the way to the bookstore tomorrow, insure the package and send it Special Delivery. She dialed Dorian's number. "Hello? It's me. I know you just got home, but I wanted to tell you what I found in the mail. Got a minute?"

"Oh, hi. Virgil's here. He's making coffee. What's up? Everything okay at home?"

"Yeah, if you don't count everything that's hit the fan since we left. I have a lot to tell you."

"Now you've got me curious. I've got something to tell you, too. If you're not too tired, how about Virgil and I come over later tonight and we can compare notes?"

"Good idea. We should have a war council." Kimberlee giggled. "I'll invite Jack, since he's involved too. I'll make pie. Let's say about 7:00 P.M.?"

"Sounds good. See you later." Dorian hung up the phone.

Kimberlee dialed Brett's cell phone. "Dorian and Virgil are coming over tonight after dinner. I'll call Jack. On the way home, can you stop at the grocery store and pick up a frozen pie?"

Chapter Thirty-Eight

May the fleas of a 1000 camels infest her arm pits. - Kimberlee

ou can read for a while, sweetheart. I'll have Dorian and Jack come and kiss you good-night." Kimberlee tucked the covers around Amanda and gave her a storybook. Angel stumbled in and stretched her good leg onto the bed. Kimberlee lifted her and set her alongside Amanda's hip. "There you go. Keep Amanda company until she falls asleep."

Amanda threw her arms around Kimberlee's neck and kissed her cheek. "I missed you so much, Mommy. I'm so glad you're home."

"Me too, sweetheart. I'll be in later to tuck you in." She kissed Amanda, patted the covers in place, and stroked Angel's back. "Now, take good care of Angel. Don't let her hop around too much. She needs to rest her hurt leg."

"I'll read to her. She likes that." Amanda caressed Angel's head. "This is my kitten's book. See?" She opened the picture book and showed Angel the pictures. "Three little kittens lost their mittens…"

Kimberlee pulled the door closed and left enough room for Angel to slip through if she needed to visit the back porch litter box. She returned to the kitchen and checked the peach pie bubbling in the oven, and peeked into the living room where Brett had laid kindling in the fireplace. As the weather cooled, a fire snapping in the fireplace and easy-listening music from his vintage record collection always created a serene mood conducive to snuggling. Tonight, it would be the background for discussing the serious events that occurred while she and Dorian were in Austria and the drama that kept Jack and Brett hopping in Fern Lake.

Brett and Jack were amenable to accepting Ted Herman's settlement offer. As much as she hated borrowing $150,000 against the lodge, it was a better solution than going to court.

Brett had no information regarding any progress the Fern Lake Police Department might have made regarding the bookstore vandalism. And, wait until Dorian heard about Grandmother Lassiter kidnapping the cats. Dorian would be outraged. She loved Black Cat and Angel as much as the rest of the family. And, then there was—

Bing-Bong

Kimberlee hurried to open the door. "Hi, come on in." She squeezed Dorian's hand and glanced at Virgil's face. "What's wrong? You look like you've been sucking lemons."

"I have a lot on my mind." Virgil's scowl deepened into his brow.

Kimberlee took their jackets and hung them on the coat rack. "Have a seat. I'll just be a minute. I have to check the pie. Can I get you guys some coffee?"

"I'll come and help." Dorian followed Kimberlee into the kitchen.

Kimberlee opened the oven and peered inside. "What's up with Virgil? Did you guys have a quarrel?" She touched the top of the pie with her fingertip.

Dorian shrugged. "Virgil says they're close to making an arrest regarding Mrs. Herman's death. I guess they've settled on murder as the cause of death, after all. I'm not working the case, so he won't discuss it with me. Yeah, I guess you could say it's been sort of a quarrel." Dorian pulled five cups from the cupboard and filled them with coffee. She added a splash of creamer to one and stirred. "I mean, we work together, so why shouldn't he talk—"

"An arrest, you say?" Kimberlee took the pie from the oven and set it on the counter. "I thought the coroner determined her death accidental. Or, at least indeterminate. What happened to make them reconsider?"

"No thanks to Virgil, but they're looking closer at a gold bracelet that was found in Mrs. Herman's house. There was a date inscribed on the back. Actually, it looked a lot like the one..." She glanced at Kimberlee's face. "Why, what's wrong? You're as pale as whipped cream." She pulled a chair from under the table. "Here, sit down. What's the matter?"

"A...a...bracelet?" Kimberlee clenched her hands to keep them from trembling and glanced toward the living room where Brett stood by the fireplace, talking to Virgil.

Why should she be worried? Thousands of people own bracelets with dates inscribed on the back. Should she mention that she couldn't find her gold bracelet? "Oh, I guess I'm still jet-lagged. I got a little bit dizzy, but I'm fine. Here," she stood and opened the cupboard where she kept her Depression glass dessert plates. "Let's cut the pie. Can you get the ice cream?" She turned away from Dorian. Surely, the bracelet found at Mrs. Herman's house wasn't the one her aunt gave her inscribed on the back with her graduation date.

Dorian took the ice cream from the freezer. "Where's your scoop?" She opened the utensil drawer. "Here it is. Let me do that. You still don't look like you feel very well."

"I'm fine. Take the plates into the guys."

Jack and his dog, Chance, had arrived by the time Kimberlee and Dorian returned to the living room. Kimberlee carried the tray containing the coffee cups, cream, and sugar bowl. "Hi, Jack. Chance." Kimberlee greeted them with a smile. "There's more ice cream in the kitchen if anyone wants seconds."

"This is fine," Virgil said, taking a dessert plate from Dorian. "You should know that there's been a break in the..." The tray rattled as Kimberlee set it on the coffee table and dropped onto the sofa next to Brett. "...a break in the bookstore vandalism," Virgil said. "I know this will upset you, Kimberlee, but we've arrested Bernard, the delivery boy from the Fern Lake Bakery."

"Bernard? I can't believe… Why?"

Virgil picked up a coffee cup from the tray. "When we found his fingerprints on a couple of the broken pots, we brought him in for questioning. He broke down and confessed everything. Seems it was pure jealousy and spite. His dad's Cloverdale bookstore went bankrupt last year. According to Bernard's messed up sense of justice, he didn't think you *deserved* to be successful when his family had to give up their store."

"He said something like that to me a couple weeks ago. He asked me what I did to deserve such a nice store. I never thought much of it at the time."

Brett took a bite of pie. "Sad. He seemed like a good kid, working part time, going to school. Sounds like a typical teenage lapse in judgment, maybe influenced by a couple Budweiser's. It was probably a spur-of-the-moment thing."

Kimberlee wrung her hands to keep them from trembling. It's not as if she hadn't ever done anything stupid and regretted it later. Understandably, kids screwed up, considering the pressures they were under and dealing with uncontrollable raging hormones. "I always thought he liked me. We talked about Harry Potter and several other books I've ordered for him. What can I do? Would it help if I didn't press charges?"

"I'm afraid it's gone beyond that," Virgil said. "He's already been charged with breaking and entering and vandalism. His sentencing date is next month. I suppose you could appear at his hearing as a character witness, and ask for leniency. His dad hired Attorney Ollingham to defend him. Why don't you talk to him? It's the kid's first offense. Your recommendation might go a long way to get him counseling and community service instead of jail time."

"If they give him community service, I could use some extra

help at the lodge," Jack suggested. "I could put him to work scrubbin' the dock. He wouldn't be thinkin' about vandalism again, when I get through with him."

Angel wandered into the living room, her leg cast making it difficult to navigate. She flopped down on the rug by Dorian's feet. She reached down and stroked Angel's back. "Oh, you poor baby." She looked up at Kimberlee. "Virgil told me all about Grandmother Lassiter's escapade. What's the latest on her?"

"Brett says her health insurance provider flew her back to Texas yesterday." *May the fleas of a 1000 camels infest her arm pits.* "I suppose someone should be concerned and give her a call, but it won't be me. Maybe you'd like to volunteer for the task?"

Dorian's face flushed. "Considering her recent behavior, I'll pass on that for now. Suppose I send her a get-well card instead?"

"You do that," Kimberlee said. "Let's change the subject. Guess what?" She frowned at Brett. "I read the letter today from John Brooker."

Brett looked confused.

"He's the grandson of the soldier who wrote the diary we took with us to Hopfgarten. He wants to buy back the diary. Apparently, someone sold it by mistake to a book agent and I bought it from him on line. I'm mailing it back to him tomorrow. It's time it went back to its rightful owner."

Dorian chuckled. "You can say that again. I doubt we'll ever forget its effect on our lives." She pulled her camera from her purse. "I brought my camera. Do you want to see my pictures?" For the next hour, they shared highlights of their trip and displayed souvenirs and brochures from various Germany and Austrian sites. Dorian clicked through the pictures on her camera. Kimberlee answered all the questions about finding the key under the glass coffin and then losing it to Joseph again at the pension.

As Dorian continued to regale the men, reminiscing about the sights and sounds of Germany, Kimberlee picked up cups and dessert plates and carried them to the kitchen. How good to be home again. The holidays were going to be grand. She expected the blown glass items from Munich to be a big hit for Christmas sales at the bookstore.

The clock over the fireplace chimed 10:00 P.M. "Well, look at the time." Jack stood and snapped his fingers. "Come on, Chance, we should go. Thanks for asking me over, Kimberlee. The pie was great." He nodded to Dorian and took his jacket off the coat rack. "I'll see ya tomorrow, Brett."

Virgil glanced at the clock. "It is getting late. I have to be at work at 5:30 in the morning." He stood and turned to Kimberlee. "Thanks for everything, Kimberlee." He put his hand on her shoulder. "You're a good friend." His face flushed and his eyes glistened with tears. "Let's go, Dorian." He grabbed Dorian's hand and rushed her out the door.

Brett stood in the doorway as Virgil pulled Dorian down the sidewalk. "That was weird. What do you suppose got into him? He looked like he was about ready to cry."

Kimberlee walked toward the front door. "I don't have a clue." She shook her head. "Dorian said they'd been quarreling. Maybe he's upset about that. He left in such a hurry, he forgot his coat. Something's troubling him, for sure."

Chapter Thirty-Nine

Why doesn't Dorian speak up for me? - Kimberlee

Visiting with friends and sharing holiday adventures the previous night kept Kimberlee from thoroughly checking the state of Brett's housekeeping duties. Early the next morning, while Brett fixed Amanda's breakfast, Kimberlee ran a dust cloth over the top of the mantle. It was apparent he hadn't dusted the entire time she was away. She picked up a ceramic bell and wiped it clean. She wondered how long before she received the first shipment from the Franz Mayer Glass Factory in Germany. Perhaps she would advertise in the Fern Lake Gazette and announce a sale on the new blown-glass items. Mrs. Wilson, her full-time employee at the store, could help with a special event—maybe an open house to introduce the new products. With the holidays' right around the corner, and most of the problems solved that had cropped up while she was gone, it promised to be an enjoyable holiday season.

Bing Bong

"I'll get it." Kimberlee called. She opened the front door. Her smile froze when she saw Virgil standing beside a policewoman, his head down and shoulders slumped. He lifted his head. "Kimberlee?"

"Virgil? What… What's wrong?" Had Virgil come in person to break some terrible news? Kimberlee glanced from one to the other. Wild thoughts raced through her head as she turned toward the kitchen. Brett and Amanda were safe. Had something happened at the bookstore again? She gazed toward the police vehicle parked beside the garden gate. *Dorian?* Her heart skipped a beat. "Has something happened to Dorian?"

The female officer stepped inside. "Kimberlee Clarke. We'd like you to come downtown with us for questioning regarding Mrs. Beverly Herman's murder."

Kimberlee's eyes opened wide. *Mrs. Herman? Murder?* "Brett! Brett!" Thoughts jumbled in her head. The officer's face looked fuzzy where everything else appeared frozen in place. The woman took Kimberlee's arm. She balked against the pressure of the officer's hand. "Wait. I don't understand. Let me call my husband. Virgil! What's going on?"

Virgil's cheeks paled and his mouth clenched in a hard line. "I'm sorry…" He wouldn't meet her gaze. How could he believe her capable of murder? In less than ten seconds, her contented life full of holiday plans and promises for the future crashed around her ears.

Brett hurried into the living room, Black Cat at his heels. "Virgil! What are you doing?" He reached out to touch Kimberlee. The officer pulled her out the door, led her off the porch and down the steps. Kimberlee's hair swung across her face as she lowered her head.

Virgil put his hand on Brett's chest to prevent him from following. "I'm sorry, Brett. We need to take Kimberlee to the station. She's to be questioned about Mrs. Herman's death."

Brett glared at him. "You knew this last night, didn't you? Why didn't you give us fair warning? I could have called an attorney. How can you treat a friend this way?"

Virgil shook his head. "I didn't know for sure. The Chief discussed it yesterday, but hadn't made a decision. He only decided early this morning and asked us to bring her in. Dorian doesn't even know. I'll do what I can for her until your attorney gets there. Tell him to hurry." He turned and followed his partner and Kimberlee. The officer thrust her into the back seat of Virgil's police car and climbed in beside her. Virgil slid behind the wheel and pulled away from the curb.

Kimberlee snuffled, tears coursing down her cheeks. Her heart ached with humiliation. How did this happen? They were treating her like a common criminal.

"Officer Parker, give her a handkerchief," Virgil said. The officer pulled a tissue from her bag.

Kimberlee leaned forward. "You don't really think I'm guilty, do you, Virgil? I told you I quarreled with Mrs. Herman that day, but I didn't—"

"Honey, please stop talking." Virgil kept his gaze straight ahead. His shoulders hunched. Clearly, his body language spoke volumes that he was not happy taking her to headquarters. "Don't say anything now. We'll have to report anything you say. I hate being in the middle like this. Just be quiet until your attorney comes. No one will question you until he gets there."

The tone of his voice sent a chill through her chest. She sat back and closed her eyes. She wiped her face and blew her nose. How she yearned to be back in Amanda's bedroom, cuddling with her, Angel curled at her hip, and the sounds of Brett's keyboard clicking in the background.

At the station, a police officer accompanied her into an interrogation room where she heeded Virgil's warning and sat without saying a word, though her heart cried out to defend herself. *Where is Dorian? Why doesn't she speak up for me?* The officer stood just inside the door. Before long, the comforting scent of Attorney Ollingham's Old Spice aftershave followed him into the room. "Kimberlee? Are you okay? Can I get you anything?" He tossed his briefcase on the table.

She shook her head. "Nothing, thanks. I'm so glad you're here."

"Okay, officer," he said to the policewoman. "Please leave so I can speak to my client." His glare sent the detective scurrying for the door. Mr. Ollingham slid into a chair across from Kimberlee. "Now, tell me what's going on." He pushed the box of tissue across the table. "I gather they've decided Mrs. Herman was murdered, after all. What brought about the notion you know something about her death?" He pulled out a pen and opened a notebook.

She shrugged and dabbed her eyes with the tissue. "The last I heard, they hadn't determined the cause of death. I have no idea what's changed their mind."

"I understand, but why do they think you had something to do with it?" He shook his head. "It couldn't be about inheriting her estate. That wouldn't make sense. Neither you nor Jack knew anything about the inheritance until after we read the will."

Kimberlee lowered her head and picked at her fingernail. Mr. Ollingham tapped his pen on the table. "So, answer my question. What has changed since a week ago? Why are you here?" His eyebrows raised in a question. "Take your time and start from the beginning."

Kimberlee shrugged. "They know I went to her house that afternoon and we had a pretty nasty argument." Her cheeks warmed. "But, I stayed home with Amanda that night, so I didn't have an alibi. Dorian questioned Jack and me about it. He didn't have an alibi that night, either. He was at Mrs. Herman's house that day, too, though I guess they didn't quarrel."

Mr. Ollingham scribbled on his notebook. "There must be something more. You had a quarrel, and no alibi. That's pretty thin, but it is means, motive and opportunity. That's hardly a recipe for a murder charge, but it makes sense to bring you in for formal questioning if they've determined it was murder." He frowned and made another note on his tablet. "Now, Kimberlee... You're sure there's nothing more? You're sure you didn't return to Mrs. Herman's house for any reason after your argument that afternoon?"

A shiver raced up the back of her neck. Even Mr. Ollingham questioned her innocence. "No, sir, I did not. I never left my house. I spent the entire evening alone reading Dewey's diary. Amanda was there, of course, but she was asleep. Brett went to a meeting in Fort Bragg."

"That's good enough for me. We'll answer their questions to the best of our ability. Try not to worry." He patted Kimberlee's arm and opened the door. Virgil stood out in the hallway. Mr. Ollingham nodded. "We're ready to talk to you now."

Virgil sat at the table. "I'm so sorry to put you through this, Kimberlee. It's my job. You know I have no choice…"

"It's okay, Virgil. Believe me, I'm not enjoying this either. Is Dorian here? I didn't see her."

Virgil shook his head. "Chief Yates has forbidden her to see you until after questioning. She can't be involved with the case at all now, due to your friendship. In fact, I'm surprised they asked me to do your interview. She knows you're here, and she sends her love." He picked up a pen and straightened the notebook on the table. "So, let's begin," he said with a quake in his voice and a determined expression that implied he wished he could be anywhere but here.

Chapter Forty

It's my bracelet! I don't know when I lost it. - Kimberlee

uestioned about Mrs. Herman's murder—how could this happen? Kimberlee folded her hands on the interrogation table. Despite all the previous problems at Fern Lake, her father's murder, the trouble with Mrs. Herman last year, and their recent argument, she never dreamed she would ever be accused of murder. Was Mrs. Herman's hatred still exacting revenge from beyond the grave?

Virgil bounced the tip of his pen on the table, and then glanced between Kimberlee and Mr. Ollingham. "Considering your complicated relationship with Mrs. Herman, don't you find it odd that she made you and Jack the sole beneficiaries of Fern Lake Lodge?"

Kimberlee leaned back in her chair. "My husband and Jack think it's possible Mrs. Herman wrote her will years ago. She and my parents were best friends when I was a baby. Jack worked at the lodge since high school. He was like a son to her."

Mr. Ollingham spoke up. "If you assume that inheriting the lodge is a motive for murder, Kimberlee knew nothing about the inheritance until *after* Mrs. Herman's death. In addition, since you seem to think Mrs. Herman's will is a factor in her death, Ted Herman has demanded his rights as the joint tenant. He will get 50% of the lodge, and Jack and Kimberlee each only receive 25%. Therefore, according to your suggested theory, Ted is a more likely suspect than Kimberlee. You'll have to do better than that, Virgil, if you're looking for a cause of action against her."

Virgil's cheeks flushed. "Point well-taken." He scribbled on his notepad. "So, let's move on." Virgil pulled a copy of a letter from his folder. "Mrs. Herman wrote a letter the very night she died, basically stating that if she died under odd circumstances, she thought Kimberlee might be responsible." He held a hand-written note.

Chill bumps dotted Kimberlee's arms. "Why would she write something like that? I don't understand."

"I'm not aware of such a letter," Mr. Ollingham huffed. "May I see it?"

Virgil handed him the letter. "Why don't you read it aloud, so we can all hear it?"

Mr. Ollingham put on his glasses and read… *To Whom It May Concern. Being of sound mind, on this day, I set my hand to swear that only two people hate me enough to cause my death. Ted Herman and Kimberlee Clarke. We assumed Ted died in the Cayman Islands. I blame Kimberlee for my husband's desertion and his betrayal. Now, he has returned and is threatening my livelihood and my life.*

"That's enough," Mr. Ollingham said, "I get the gist. Kimberlee, do you have any idea why Mrs. Herman thinks you're responsible for her husband's disappearance? What does she mean?"

Kimberlee's face warmed. "Since I was about two year's old when Mr. Herman left town, how could I know what irrational notions she has about his disappearance?"

"Well then, Virgil. I assume you've verified Mrs. Herman's handwriting? And I wonder if you've questioned Mr. Herman about all this? So far, the evidence you've presented implicates him as much or more than it does Kimberlee."

Virgil scowled. "Are you questioning how I run my investigations? Yes, we verified the handwriting. At the moment, my questions are for Kimberlee, not Ted, but for the sake of our friendship, I'll answer. We questioned Mr. Herman already. He admitted being at Mrs. Herman's house earlier in the evening, but according to her time of death, Ted provided an alibi. The coroner's report states she died between 10:00 P.M. and 2:00 A.M. Ted provided witnesses that place him at a local pool hall from 8:30 P.M. until closing."

Mr. Ollingham stood. "This is all very interesting, Virgil, but I'm sure we all have better things to do, so if all you have is a half-baked motive about an inheritance which has been logically disputed, and the victim's letter making wild and unfounded accusations against a two-year-old, we'll be leaving."

Virgil raised his hand. "Sit down, please. I'll let you know when you can leave. I'm not through with my questions. Let's talk about whether Kimberlee has an alibi for that evening."

Kimberlee's face warmed. "I've already told you that I don't. Brett was out, and didn't come home until about midnight."

Virgil glanced at his notes. "Yes. Dorian made a note of that the day after the murder...*er*...Mrs. Herman's death." His face flushed, and he twisted his shoulders. "According to your account, you went to Mrs. Herman's house that afternoon and a bitter quarrel ensued… The nurse's interview confirmed that, as well. And, you state you never went back to Mrs. Herman's house?"

Kimberlee sucked in her breath. "That's right. I admit we quarreled on her doorstep that afternoon, but I've told you a hundred times, I never left the house that evening."

Virgil reached into his briefcase and pulled out a plastic bag containing a gold bracelet. "Then, how do you explain this gold bracelet we found on Mrs. Herman's living room floor?" He laid the bag with the bracelet on the table and spread the plastic flat with his fingers. "Dorian identified it as your bracelet. She says the inscription on the back is the date you graduated from high school. If you never went back, how did it get into Mrs. Herman's house the night she died? She was hospitalized for over a year and only returned home the day before she died."

Kimberlee swallowed a lump in her throat. "It's my bracelet. I lost it, but I don't know when or where." She put her hands over her eyes and lowered her head. *Hold your head up, Kimberlee. Crying makes you look guilty.* She dabbed her eyes, lifted her head, and thrust back her shoulders.

"So, Kimberlee," Virgil said, "maybe you misspoke regarding your whereabouts that night. Perhaps you went back to her house after Amanda fell asleep. Maybe you wanted to apologize for the disagreement that afternoon. Perhaps you and Mrs. Herman argued again and things got out of hand?"

"No! No! I didn't," Kimberlee wiped tears from her cheeks.

Virgil reached across the table and placed his hand atop Kimberlee's hand. "Maybe during the quarrel, she accidentally slipped and fell. She could have hit her head on the metal door stop. You got scared, and ran away. We'd all understand if that's what happened. You didn't go there intending to hurt her. It was just a terrible accident, right?"

Even with the terrifying accusations, he must be trying to give her a chance to confess to a lesser crime. Perhaps he didn't want to bring a murder charge against his friend. If she admitted to the situation he described, it might be considered involuntary manslaughter, or even accidental. Kimberlee covered her face with her hands, and shook her head.

Mr. Ollingham touched her shoulder and glared at Virgil. "That's about enough, Virgil. She's already said she didn't go back to Mrs. Herman's house that night, and she's denied any knowledge of where she lost her bracelet. What's going on here, anyway? We understood the coroner's office to state they were unable to determine whether Mrs. Herman's death was accidental or murder. Ted admitted being there earlier that evening. You can bet they had an unpleasant conversation. The poor woman probably wrote that letter accusing Ted or Kimberlee right after he left. In her agitated state and weakened condition, Mrs. Herman could easily have fallen and hit her head. It doesn't sound like you have any definitive evidence to bring a murder charge or any charge, for that matter." Mr. Ollingham stood. "In that event, Mrs. Herman's letter and finding Kimberlee's bracelet in the house is only circumstantial. Either charge my client with something right this minute, or we're leaving." He pulled Kimberlee up from her chair.

Knock. Knock.

"Don't go yet," Virgil said. "I'll be right back." He stepped into the hall and pulled the door closed behind him.

Mr. Ollingham and Kimberlee sat back down. She dried her tears and blew her nose. The attorney handed her another tissue. "Before he comes back, Kimberlee, tell me about that bracelet. How did it get in Mrs. Herman's house? This is the most troubling evidence so far."

Kimberlee shook her head. "I have no idea. I don't even know when I lost it. I remember looking for it the morning we left for Germany."

"*Humm.* Since it turned up inside Mrs. Herman's house, you must have lost it the afternoon you were fussing with her at the back door. Who else do you suppose visited her house that day?"

"Let me think." She tapped her finger on the table. "Mrs. Herman's nurse was there, of course. Jack said he stopped by with Chance that afternoon. I don't know who else might have stopped by. And, Ted, of course. Maybe some other friends came to welcome her home. I suppose it's possible I lost it in the yard, and someone found it and carried it into the house."

Mr. Ollingham grinned and slapped his fist into his other hand. "That must be it. Have you got your cell phone? You call Jack. I'll contact Mrs. Herman's nurse and see if she saw it. Then, we'll see about getting you out of here, one way or another." He stood and went into the hall.

Kimberlee's hand trembled as she punched in Jack's phone number. The phone buzzed.

"Hello? Fern Lake Lodge. This is Jack. How can I help ya?"

"Jack. It's Kimberlee. Oh, please, please, tell me that you found my bracelet in the yard when you visited Mrs. Herman the day she died." She held her breath and crossed her fingers. *Please Lord. Let it be so.*

"Say what? Your bracelet? No. I never saw a bracelet. Why? What's going on? Brett said they took ya in for questioning. He's on his way to the station. He should be there by now. Don't worry. Brett kept Amanda home from school. I've got her."

Kimberlee let out her breath. "Thanks for taking her. I so hoped you'd say… Well, it's a long story. Brett's coming? That's good. Mr. Ollingham is with me." She sighed. "Don't worry. Everything will be okay. It has to be."

Virgil entered and stood by the table. "Kimberlee, your attorney is making a couple calls in the hallway. I'll have to put you in a holding cell for a while. I'm not charging you with anything yet, but we have the right to hold you while we sort out some things." His gaze traveled the room as he looked everywhere except at Kimberlee's face. She stood. Virgil took her arm and led her down the hall to a holding cell. "I'm so sorry about all this…"

"It's okay, Virgil. It's not your fault. Is Dorian here? I'd like to see her."

Virgil shook his head and lowered his voice. "She's here. She doesn't believe a word of this. For that matter, I don't either." Virgil led Kimberlee into a cell and locked the door. "I'll bring Brett in as soon as I can. In the meantime, I'll sneak in a magazine from the break room."

"Thanks, Virgil. Tell Dorian for me…" Tears pricked her eyes. She swallowed a lump in her throat. "Tell her…I understand."

He nodded, hurried down the hall and through a closed door into the outer office.

Chapter Forty-One

*I'm as positive as little green apples and kittens
in the spring - Black Cat*

Never had it been so quiet in the house. On any other day, Kimberlee would be at the bookstore, Amanda might be at school, but Brett would be clicking away on his computer in the office. Today, Brett and Kimberlee were at the police station, and Amanda was *helping* Jack at the bait shop, though it was questionable whether her presence was a help or a hindrance. Black Cat searched the house for Angel and found her huddled under Amanda's bed. "What are you doing here? Come into the living room. The sun is shining through the front window. It's nice and warm in there." He noticed Angel's dilated eyes. "What's wrong? Does your leg hurt?" He slunk down, scooted under the bed, and crouched alongside her.

Angel lowered her head onto her front paw. "I'm fine. Leave me alone. You wouldn't understand."

"Of course I won't, if you don't tell me. You don't usually hide under the bed except when the garbage truck is coming. They're not due until tomorrow. So, what's going on?"

Angel lifted her head. "They've taken Kimberlee away. They think she murdered Mrs. Herman. Brett is crazy with worry. My life has been in an uproar ever since we left Texas. A couple days ago, Grandmother Lassiter came to take me home and instead, we nearly killed her and—"

"*Whoa! Whoa!* Hold up a minute. I was with you there for a

while, until you got to the killing Grandmother part. She's not exactly a candidate for Granny of the Year. Care to elaborate? Where is all this coming from?"

Angel laid her head on her leg cast and closed her eyes. "It's hard to explain…"

"Try. I'm listening." Black Cat licked her ear.

Angel closed her eyes. "The Texas ranch was my home, and Grandmother was my *person*. The cows and horses were my friends. The stable master fed me. Life was good. When you and Kimberlee and Brett came, you turned my life upside down. It's true, I wanted to come back to California with you because I love you, but I felt guilty sneaking away and leaving Grandmother the way we did."

Angel turned to gaze into Black Cat's eyes. "Then, on the way home from Texas, we got lost and John and Cindy took us in and cared for us at the emu farm." She closed her eyes. "Just when I started to love John and Cindy and the emus, Kimberlee came and took me away from our new *persons*. Now, here we are in Fern Lake, and I love Brett and Kimberlee and Amanda, but, don't you see the problem? Everything good comes to an end. First, Grandmother, then John and Cindy, and now Brett and Kimberlee. The police have taken Kimberlee away. Who knows what will happen to her? Every time I allow myself to love someone, I lose them. And, now we're going to lose Kimberlee."

Black Cat pulled his ears back. "Oh, Angel. I never realized that you felt this way. I'm sorry." His heart ached, hearing how he had disrupted her life, repeatedly taking her from the *persons* she loved. "What can I do to make it better?"

"Nothing. We're cats. We have no control over anything. We depend on our *persons* to provide the quality of our lives, whether good or bad. Our *persons* decide how we live, whether it's here or there or nowhere at all, like the feral cats downtown, eating scraps behind Rajinder's delicatessen. We're powerless. We live or die if a human decides we're inconvenient. I can't go on feeling so powerless day after day. It's more than I can bear." She closed her eyes and shoved her face between her paws.

A chill raced down Black Cat's spine. "This is much more serious. We're not talking about Grandmother Lassiter or Nevada City anymore, are we?"

"No, we're not. We're talking about our lives and our future."

"It's not so bad, is it? We have a lovely home and *persons* who love us."

Angel snorted. "For how long? They're holding Kimberlee at the police station. She had means, motive, and opportunity to kill Mrs. Herman. With Brett gone that night, she has no alibi. Even you were out half the night doing whatever tomcats do. Well, I stayed home, and I know she's innocent. She never left the house. Not even for a minute. There's no way she could have caused Mrs. Herman's death, either on purpose or by accident, but I'm helpless to help her. If she's convicted, she'll go to jail. Brett will sell the house and move into an apartment near Chowchilla Women's Prison. They probably won't allow pets, and we'll be on the street with the feral cats."

Black Cat's whiskers twitched. How Angel loved to embellish a sad story. Now, he understood what was troubling her ever since coming to Fern Lake. Kimberlee's current situation made things even worse. Now, he understood her bitchy attitude and her reluctance to accept or enjoy anything about their new home with Brett and Kimberlee. She was terrified that, yet again, if she allowed herself to love, she would lose another set of loved ones, and a life that brought her joy. However, her exaggerated cause and effect of the current situation was somewhat amusing. How could he assuage her fears without diminishing her feelings and concerns?

Black Cat pondered the right words to say. "I understand how you feel about Grandmother. Considering what she meant to you in Texas, it was the right thing, going onto the road after the accident to try and get her help, but I'm sorry you got hurt. I'm sorry that coming into your life has brought you sorrow. All I ever wanted was to make you happy, because I love you. But, consider this. Yes, your life changed when we met. I took you away from Texas, and leaving Grandmother made you sad.

"Then we left Nevada City and you miss John and Cindy and our kittens. But, if you hadn't left Texas and come with me, we never would have met John and Cindy, and our children might never have been born. Angel, don't you understand? A full life includes both happiness and sadness, and we must accept one to appreciate the other. Sometimes we experience loss and sorrow, but if we receive both joy and sadness with an open heart, it can become the pathway to new opportunities and unexpected joy. I wouldn't change a minute since we met, and I'm sorry if you don't feel the same."

Angel lifted her head. Her eyes opened wide. "I never thought about leaving Grandmother in Texas and meeting John and Cindy in Nevada City quite that way. Maybe you're onto something. New opportunities and new adventures…you're right."

"As for Kimberlee's future, I feel in my bones that everything will be okay." His whiskers twitched. "If Kimberlee is innocent, nothing bad will happen to her. I'm as positive as little green apples and kittens in the spring."

Angel nuzzled Black Cat's shoulder. "I love you, Black Cat. I don't know much about little green apples, but since you've brought up the subject, *kittens in the spring* is definitely something to think about…"

Chapter Forty-Two

...there was something important in that diary - Angel

nce again, peace reigned at Fern Lake Lodge and at the little house by the lake. Three weeks after Angel's injury, the vet removed the cast from her leg and she walked and ran around the yard as though the accident never happened. The leaves on the trees began to fall and Thanksgiving approached. A holiday mood took hold of Fern Lake. Once again, Angel joined Black Cat on his travels through town, visiting the various businesses. She marveled at the holiday decorations where displays of pumpkins and cornstalks lined the store windows, and flower baskets hanging on the light poles overflowed with fall flowers such as chrysanthemums and ivy.

Unusually warm days near the end of November confused the bushes and trees into thinking spring had come, and if one looked closely, tiny buds could be seen on the branches. Chilly nights turned into foggy mornings that burned off toward noon, leaving clear blue skies and mild afternoons.

On one such afternoon, Kimberlee sat on the front porch swing with a lap robe thrown over her legs. She turned the pages of a photo album filled with duplicates of Dorian's vacation pictures. Each picture reminded her of the beautiful Germany countryside, and helped push away all thoughts of Joseph's attack in the Austrian church or the unpleasant day she spent being questioned at the police station. Wasn't there an old saying, *All's well that ends well?*

Kimberlee recalled how she had sat in the jailhouse cell that afternoon, waiting for Brett to arrive. She had looked up when Virgil returned and unlocked the door. "I have good news," he said as he stepped into the cell. Kimberlee stood. Did she dare hope? "Mr. Ollingham called Nurse Burkett and Ted Herman to ask about the bracelet. Apparently Ted remembered finding it on the porch the night he visited Mrs. Herman. It must have fallen off your wrist when you quarreled with her that afternoon. He carried it into the house and dropped it on an end table. No one ever questioned him about it until today, and he never gave it a second thought."

"Oh!" Kimberlee's face warmed. "I'm so embarrassed. If I hadn't quarreled with Mrs. Herman and tossed my basket on the ground, none of this would have happened."

Virgil took her arm and walked her from the cell toward the lobby where they met Dorian in the hall. She pulled Kimberlee into a hug. "It's over, hon. The Chief is satisfied you're not involved with Mrs. Herman's death. He's instructed us to close the case. Once we learned how your bracelet got into Mrs. Herman's house, that's all we needed to release you. Brett's waiting in the lobby."

Kimberlee had sighed with relief. "Thank God that's over."

Dismissing the memory of the day at the police station, Kimberlee turned the page on the picture album and ran her hand over the picture of the Hopfgarten church. She gazed up when the garden gate squeaked and the mailman came up the sidewalk. "Morning, Mrs. Clarke. I have a registered letter for you," he said, as he pulled a brown envelope from his mail pouch.

Kimberlee stepped off the porch. "Oh, hi, Jake. Probably from Brett's publishing house."

"I don't think so. It's addressed to you. It's got foreign stamps on it." Jake handed her a clipboard. "If you'll sign right here?"

She signed the sheet. "Thanks. Have a lovely day." Jake hefted his mail bag and returned down the sidewalk.

Kimberlee returned to the porch swing and read the return address.

What on earth? Father Kreuger—Hopfgarten. She tore open the envelope and removed several sheets of thin paper. She could hardly concentrate on Father Kreuger's delicate and precise handwriting.

Dear Mrs. Clarke,

I hope this finds you and your family well. I know you are anxious to learn the results of the investigation surrounding the key you found in the church.

First, I'm so sorry for Joseph's unfortunate behavior, both in the church and later in your pension. I'm glad you were not hurt in either encounter.

Following your police report, Joseph was arrested and charged with assault and theft. Consequently, awaiting arraignment, he suffered a massive heart attack. I heard his confession before his death. He asked me to beg your forgiveness.

"Oh!" Kimberlee's eyes pricked with tears. All his years of searching for his stolen gold brought him nothing but disgrace and death.

The Vontobel lockbox contained the missing gold coins, as we expected. Who owned the gold? The Insurance Co. had compensated the original owners years ago. The armored car company had long since gone out of business. The Vontobel bank had no legitimate claim since the fee on the lockbox was paid each year by an automatic withdrawal from the existing bank account.

Kimberlee's hand shook as she concentrated on the words. Where was Brett? She yanked open the front door, nearly tripping over Angel, stretched out on the carpet in front of the door. "Brett! Get out here. Come quick!"

Brett rushed from his office. "What's wrong?" He gazed at the letter Kimberlee shook in his face. "Is it from Grandmother?" His face paled as he reached for the letter.

"Grandmother? Why should it be from her? Oh, never mind. It's from Father Kreuger in Hopfgarten. About the...the...key. They opened the lockbox, and found the gold coins. Here, let me finish." She continued reading aloud…

"Legal claims for the gold coins were filed by the insurance company, the bank, and even the church, since the key has been here for over fifty years. With all former claimants compensated by various means, the authorities thought the insurance company the most legitimate, but their claim lost ground when it was learned they had written off the loss years ago. Also, they failed to officially withdraw the reward offered for the return of the coins.

"Though it may be some time before the matter is settled in court, I suggest your attorney file an immediate legal claim. The prevailing claimant might receive the gold coins, or a reward for their return. Your chance of prevailing is as good as any other claimant since you found the lockbox key that ultimately located the gold. Love in Christ, Father Kreuger."

Kimberlee collapsed on the sofa. Her gaze circled the room and stopped at the fireplace hearth, where Angel now lay sprawled, licking her paw. For a long moment, Angel's gaze locked on Kimberlee. She could almost hear Angel say, *I told you there was something important in that diary. And, look how it turned out.* Then, with a toss of her head, the cat returned to her toilette.

Kimberlee's eyes widened as she turned back toward Brett. Why had Black Cat pushed the diary off the table that morning at the bookstore? Had he known the clues in the diary would lead her to a lost treasure? Kimberlee shook her head. Nonsense! What an idiotic idea. She threw her arms around Brett's neck. "We could be rich."

"We're already rich, sweetheart. As long as we have each other, we have the world by the tail." He pulled her into his embrace.

Black Cat ambled into the living room and lay down beside Angel. *What's all this twaddling from the folks about being rich?*

Angel rolled over, exposing her tummy, and her feet in the air. *Kimberlee got a letter from Father Kreuger. The key she found in the church opened a lockbox full of gold, and Father Kreuger says she might get a reward for finding it.*

Black Cat glanced at his two *persons*, hugging and kissing on the sofa like a couple of teenagers. *Well, I'll be. Isn't that nice?*

Angel turned over and licked her left shoulder. *If she gets a reward, she can thank me, you know. I made her read Dewey's diary. The clue inside led her to the lockbox key.*

Black Cat jumped to his feet. *What do you mean, you made her read it? I knocked the diary on the floor. That's what made her read it, not you.*

Did not!

Did so! Remember? You said, 'Make her read it, Black Cat.' Those were your very words. You always take the credit and say everything is your idea. You think you're more important than me.

Do not! Angel boxed Black Cat's ears.

Black Cat reared back and smacked his foot onto her head. *Do so!*

Do not! Angel jumped up and streaked down the hall.

Black Cat stalked into the kitchen. *Isn't that's just like my Angel? Always has to have the last word. But, I wouldn't have it any other way.* With a twitch of his whiskers, he jumped through the cat door, raced across the lawn and down to the dock where he found Jack helping a tourist clean and scale his morning's catch. Ever mindful of the possible rewards, seagulls circled overhead, white dots against a cloudless sky.

About the Author

Elaine Faber is a member of Sisters in Crime, Cat Writers Association, and Northern California Publishers and Authors. She lives in Northern California with her husband and two housecats. Elaine leads two writer's critique groups and enjoys working with other talented authors.

Winner of multiple awards for her short stories and novels, she pens a series of cozy cat mysteries and a series of humorous WWII mystery/adventures. She has published seven novels and an anthology of short stories highlighting the lives of cats. Fourteen additional anthologies include her humorous tales.

Black Cat Mysteries: With the aid of his ancestors' memories, Black Cat helps solve mysteries and crimes. The books are partially narrated by Black Cat, who relates some of the stories from his often humorous and poignant point of view.

Mrs. Odboddy Mystery/Adventures: Elderly, eccentric Mrs. Odboddy fights WWII from the home front. She definitely believes war-time conspiracies and spies abound in her home town. Follow her antics in these hysterical, historical novels as a self-appointed hometown warrior roots out and exposes malcontents, dissidents and Nazi spies…even when she's wrong.

Black Cat's Legacy ~ http://tinyurl.com/lrvevgm

Black Cat and the Lethal Lawyer ~ http://tinyurl.com/q3qrgyu

Black Cat and the Accidental Angel ~ http://tinyurl.com/y4eohe5n

Black Cat and the Secret in Dewey's Diary~

All Things Cat (short stories) ~ http://tinyurl.com/y9p9htak

Mrs. Odboddy – Hometown Patriot ~ http://tinyurl.com/hdbvzsv

Mrs. Odboddy – Undercover Courier ~ http://tinyurl.com/jn5bzwb

Mrs. Odboddy – …There Was a Tiger ~ http://tinyurl.com/y96qshuv

Elaine's Website ~ http://www.mindcandymysteries.com

Email your questions or comments to:

Elaine.Faber@mindcandymysteries.com.

Amazon reviews are welcomed and encouraged.

Also by Elaine

Black Cat's Legacy

Thumper, the resident Fern Lake black cat, knows where the bodies are buried and it's up to Kimberlee to decode the clues.

Kimberlee's arrival at the Fern Lake lodge triggers the Black Cat's Legacy. With the aid of his ancestors' memories, it's Thumper's duty to guide Kimberlee to clues that can help solve her father's cold case murder. She joins forces with a local homicide detective and an author, also researching the murder for his next thriller novel. As the investigation ensues, Kimberlee learns more than she wants to know about her father. The murder suspects multiply, some dead and some still very much alive, but someone at the lodge will stop at nothing to hide the Fern Lake mysteries.

Black Cat and the Lethal Lawyer

With the promise to name a beneficiary to her multi-million dollar horse ranch, Kimberlee's grandmother entices her and her family to Texas. But things are not as they appear and Thumper, the black cat with superior intellect, uncovers the appalling reason for the invitation. Kimberlee and Brett discover a fake Children's Benefit Program and the possible false identity of the stable master. To make matters worse, Thumper overhears a murder plot, and he and his newly found soul-mate, Noe-Noe, must do battle with a killer to save Grandmother's life.

The further Kimberlee and her family delve into things, the deeper they are thrust into a web of embezzlement, greed, vicious lies and murder. With the aid of his ancestors' memories, Thumper unravels some dark mysteries. Is it best to reveal the past or should some secrets never be told?

Cover photo *lawyer with cat* © CURAphotography,shutterstock.com image 19277278

Black Cat and the Accidental Angel

When the family SUV flips and Kimberlee is rushed to the hospital, Black Cat (Thumper) and his soulmate are left behind. Black Cat loses all memory of his former life and the identity of the lovely feline companion by his side. "Call me Angel. I'm here to take care of you." Her words set them on a long journey toward home, and life brings them face to face with episodes of joy and sorrow.

The two cats are taken in by John and his young daughter, Cindy, facing foreclosure of the family vineyard and emu farm. In addition, someone is playing increasingly dangerous pranks that threaten Cindy's safety. Angel makes it her mission to help their new family. She puts her life at risk to protect the child, and Black Cat learns there are more important things than knowing your real name.

Elaine Faber's e-books are available on Amazon for $3.99. Print books. $16.00.

Cover photo *Black and White Cat*: © vivienstock, http://us.fotolia.com/id/46333972 (halo added)

All Things Cat

"A story isn't a story if there isn't a cat in it." Elaine Faber

All Things Cat is a selection of Elaine Faber's short stories about cats. Their stories take place both past and present in diverse surroundings: Salem, Massachusetts; a pirate ship off the coast of Maine; a haunted hotel in the Sierra Mountains; Roswell, New Mexico; the oval office in Washington, D.C., to name but a few locations.

The felines interact with extraordinary and remarkable characters including witches, leprechauns, a sewer truck driver, a hen-pecked husband driven to plot murder, and animal characters present at the birth of the Christ Child.

Some stories are self-narrated by a cat sharing most unusual circumstances—abandoned by his master, as the prize in an Old West poker game, routing a burglar in a WWII meat market, overcoming self-doubts about his hunting/stalking abilities, and adopting the First Family in the White House.

All Things Cat will delight the reader and provide a sneak peek into the heart and mind of cats from all walks of life. Elaine has brought both wit and tenderness to this charming collection of short cat stories. Several stories are excerpts from Elaine's full length cozy Black Cat Mysteries series and WWII novel, Mrs. Odboddy - Hometown Patriot.

Cover photo *Truffie* © Elaine Faber

Mrs. Odboddy Series

Mrs. Odboddy: Hometown Patriot

A WWII tale of chicks and chicanery, suspicion and spies.

Since the onset of WWII, Agnes Agatha Odboddy, hometown patriot and self-appointed scourge of the underworld, suspects conspiracies around every corner…stolen ration books, German spies running amuck, and a possible Japanese invasion off the California coast. This seventy-year-old, model citizen would set the world aright if she could get Chief Waddlemucker to pay attention to the town's nefarious deeds on any given Meatless Monday.

Mrs. Odboddy vows to bring the villains, both foreign and domestic, to justice, all while keeping chickens in her bathroom, working at the Ration Stamp Office, and knitting argyles for the boys on the front lines.

Imagine the chaos when Agnes's long-lost WWI lover returns, hoping to find a million dollars in missing Hawaiian money and rekindle their ancient romance. In the thrilling conclusion, Agnes's predictions become all too real when Mrs. Roosevelt unexpectedly comes to town to attend a funeral and Agnes must prove that she is, indeed, a warrior on the home front.

Mrs. Odboddy: Undercover Courier

Asked to accompany Mrs. Roosevelt on her Pacific Island tour, Agnes and Katherine travel by train to Washington, D.C. Agnes carries a package for Colonel Farthingworth to President Roosevelt.

Convinced the package contains secret war documents, Agnes expects Nazi spies to try and derail her mission.

She meets Irving, whose wife mysteriously disappears from the train; Nanny, the unfeeling caregiver to little Madeline; two soldiers bound for training as Tuskegee airmen; and Charles, the shell-shocked veteran, who lends an unexpected helping hand. Who will Agnes trust? Who is the Nazi spy?

When enemy forces make a final attempt to steal the package in Washington, D.C., Agnes must accept her own vulnerability as a warrior on the home front.

Can Agnes overcome multiple obstacles, deliver the package to the President, and still meet Mrs. Roosevelt's plane before she leaves for the Pacific Islands?

Mrs. Odboddy: Undercover Courier is a hysterical frolic on a train across the United States during WWII, as Agnes embarks on this critical mission.

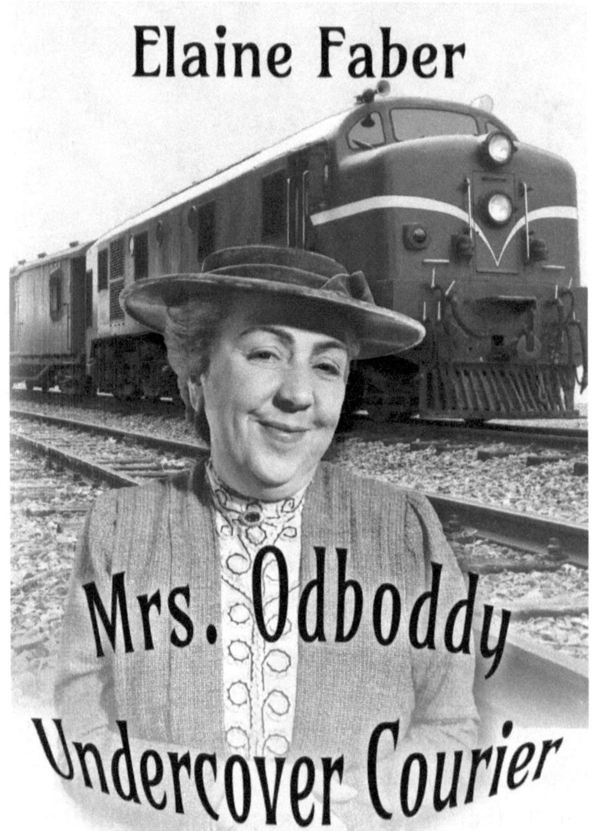

A WWII tale of mystery, mischief, and mishaps.

Mrs. Odboddy: And Then There Was a Tiger

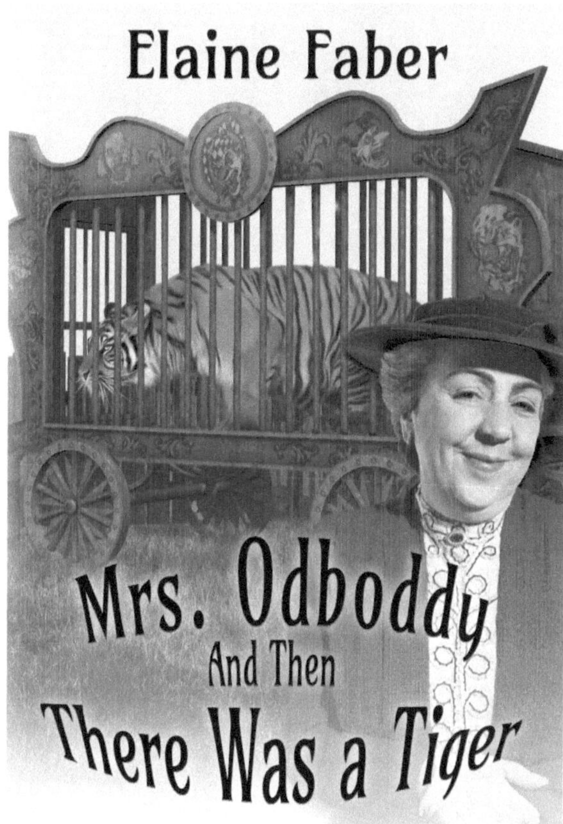

While the 'tiger of war' rages across the Pacific during WWII, eccentric, elderly Agnes Odboddy, 'fights the war from the home front'. Her patriotic duties are interrupted when she is accused of the Wilkey's Market burglary.

A traveling carnival with a live tiger joins the parishioner's harvest fair at The First Church of the Evening Star and Everlasting Light. Accused again when counterfeit bills are discovered at the carnival, and when the war bond money goes missing, Agnes sets out to restore her reputation and locate the money. Her attempts lead her into harm's way when she discovers a friend's betrayal and even more about carnival life than she bargained for.

Granddaughter Katherine's turbulent love triangle with a doctor and an FBI agent rivals Agnes's own on-again, off-again relationship with Godfrey.

In Faber's latest novel, your favorite quirky character, Mrs. Odboddy, prevails against injustice and faces unexpected challenges . . . and then There Was a Tiger!